FIRST
FLIGHT,
FINAL
FALL

FIRST FLIGHT, FINAL FALL

C.W. FARNSWORTH

Entangled Publishing, LLC
644 Shrewsbury Commons Ave., STE 181
Shrewsbury, PA 17361
rights@entangledpublishing.com

Amara is an imprint of Entangled Publishing, LLC.

Visit our website at www.entangledpublishing.com.

Edited by Tiffany Persaud
Cover illustration by LJ Anderson, Mayhem Cover Creations
Edge design by LJ Anderson, Mayhem Cover Creations
Stock art by photka/Gettyimages and Arkela/GettyImages
Interior design by Britt Marczak

ISBN 978-1-64937-834-7

Printed in China

First Edition April 2025
10 9 8 7 6 5 4 3 2 1

ALSO BY C.W. FARNSWORTH

For all the unapologetically strong women out there

Prologue

Find beauty in the broken pieces. That's what my mother used to tell me. My father would scoff and say life is about accomplishments, not beauty.

Given the fundamental difference in those two ideologies, it's not a massive surprise their marriage crashed spectacularly, but my five-year-old self was not expecting to leave for my first soccer game with two parents and come home to one.

Maybe I should have hated the sport after that; resented it for the loss that took place during the hour I kicked the black and white ball into the goal for the first time, clueless to the fact that my mother was speeding out of the town limits at that very moment.

I did the opposite.

I shut out everything *except* soccer.

After we became a family of three, my older sister Hallie retreated into normal things like friends, boys, and school.

My father withdrew into destructive things like alcohol, insane work hours, and a series of flings with women half his age.

I played soccer.

If my teachers had gotten ahold of my father, they probably would have passed on their concerns that my obsession with soccer was unhealthy. That I sketched passing drills on the sides of my worksheets and read biographies about legends in the sport during class.

If my coaches had been able to get ahold of my father, they probably would have informed him I had heaps of natural talent and a work ethic that put the Energizer Bunny to shame.

Instead, I shrugged at my teachers and informed my coaches of all the things I still needed to work on.

Before she left, my mother would say she named me Saylor because it sounded bold.

Fearless.

Brave.

It was the only thing she left me with that I took to heart.

To Hallie's credit, she tried to fill the gaping hole left by our mother's literal departure and our father's metaphorical one. Even so, we were never close, due to both our six-year age gap and our polar opposite personalities.

And it wasn't just Hallie. I didn't let anyone in. Not my many friends, not my soccer teammates, not any of the boys I kissed under the bleachers.

I never wanted to.

Until *him*.

Chapter 1

I tend not to think before I speak.

"Yellow is really not your color, Anne," I inform my redheaded housemate as she enters the kitchen through the opening to my right. "Red and yellow should only be combined on a hot dog."

Anne rolls her eyes as she grabs a hard seltzer from the fridge.

"Don't be a bitch, Saylor," Cressida chastises. She doesn't look up from the chocolate cake she's icing as she scolds me. Multitasking at its finest.

"Saylor can't help it. It's her default setting," my best friend and co-captain Emma Watkins contributes as she mixes whatever gross cocktail she's come up with tonight.

I flip Emma off. "I'm just being honest," I retort from my perch on the kitchen counter as I drum my bare feet against the cabinet below the butcher block. My body is thrumming with excess energy. The last time I missed my daily run was three months ago, thanks to the snowstorm that hit right before the start of winter break.

If only extreme weather were at fault today. Instead, there

was my father's unexpected phone call, followed by a half-hour lecture from my older sister Hallie to detail the many, many ways in which I did not respond appropriately to the news that our father is getting remarried sixteen years after our mother zoomed off solo into the metaphorical sunset.

Actually, lecture is probably the wrong word.

Hallie made it clear my lackluster "okay" wasn't what our father was hoping for, but most of our conversation was her going on about how wonderful it is that our dad is finally settling down with an age-appropriate, stable woman who's just as boring as he is. I added the last adjective—boring—in my mind while I painted my nails bubblegum pink and scrolled through social media on my laptop. I wouldn't have even indulged the conversation if not for the fact that Hallie's eight months pregnant. She's a worrier, and I didn't want sending her into an early labor on my conscience.

"Ignore her, Anne. She's having a bad day, and she's drunk," Cressida explains, smoothing things over like always—as she literally spreads chocolate icing.

I shrug because both are true. Doesn't mean I'm wrong about the *bright* yellow top, but I don't care enough to press the point. I've got other things to worry about, like which team captain to bring back here tonight. I've narrowed it down to lacrosse or hockey when Anne interrupts my inner debate.

"Bad day? I thought you were celebrating, Saylor?"

I shrug again. My interest in sharing what prompted my quick shift from euphoric morning to annoyed afternoon is nonexistent. Since I'm the only player on Lancaster University's women's soccer team who has never had a family member attend a game, I'm sure my teammates have all surmised my childhood was not the idyllic white-picket-fence-golden-retriever upbringing many of them took for granted. The best part of coming to Lancaster was finally leaving behind the sympathetic stares regarding my perennial lack of parenting. I'm in no mood to discuss my fractured family—even with my best friends. It will either lead to pitiful looks and awkward apologies, or more of the amateur-family-therapist lines Hallie spouts at me.

"It's not that big of a deal. I knew I'd get in." I down a third shot of gin. It's the only liquor I'll touch.

My brash words are a stretch. I was confident, sure, but Scholenberg is the most exclusive training camp in the world. I wasn't just competing for admission against the top college-aged players in the United States, but around the globe. An invitation is an honor, not a forgone conclusion—something Emma, Cressida, and Anne are all well aware of.

Emma scoffs as she measures out whiskey.

"Didn't they accept two Americans?" Anne asks, moving on. She's never been one to stoke animosity, and she, like everyone else who's ever met me, knows if I don't want to talk about something, I won't. Period.

"Yup," I respond, popping the P. "Ellie Anderson got in, too."

"That's a surprise," Cressida remarks. "I would have expected Cotes or Stevens."

"Ellie's got connections," I reply. "Her uncle's an assistant trainer for Kluvberg."

"That'll do it," Emma states, sticking the carton of pineapple juice back in the fridge. *With whiskey? Gross.* "I can't believe you'll be playing on their field."

"I know," I admit. The allure of attending Scholenberg isn't just the exclusivity or the prestige. The camp also provides an opportunity to play on the most famous field in the world: the home of FC Kluvberg.

"I literally have a poster of it on my wall," Emma continues.

"No, you have a poster of Adler Beck on your wall," I correct, leaning my head back against the upper cabinet so I can study the cracks in the plaster blemishing our kitchen ceiling.

"But I purposefully chose the photo of him *on* the field, not the shirtless one from the 'Sexiest Athletes' cover."

"Big of you."

Anne laughs at my comment, and Emma rolls her eyes as she downs her disgusting drink.

"Okay, let's go," Cressida announces, dropping the now-empty bowl and spatula into the sink. "The cake is done."

"It's cute how you think that will make it until tomorrow," I tell the ceiling.

"Saylor, I swear, if you..."

Emma laughs. "Cress, you need to hide that if you want there to be any left."

"All I need is for Saylor to—"

"Hey!" I'm the one who interrupts this time. "*I'm* not the one eating the stuff, okay?"

"But you are the one telling your overnight guests where the baked goods are," Cressida points out.

"Overnight guests?" Emma snorts. "They're her boy toys."

I ignore Emma. "I don't tell them where they are. They're hungry, and—"

"She uses the sweets to kick them out," Anne cuts in.

"Here's a cupcake for the three orgasms," Emma adds with a wicked smirk.

Three orgasms is overstating the talent of most guys on this campus, but I don't say so.

My gaze stays fixed on the jagged line that runs a couple of feet from the corner of the kitchen. *That probably shouldn't be there, right?* The four of us snagged this house sophomore year, so eager to escape dorm living we signed a lease for the first place we looked at, and then we were too lazy to explore other options for junior year. The Colonial-style structure serves its purpose: a place to crash between classes, practice, games, and parties.

I down one more shot and slide off the kitchen counter, adjusting my light blue dress so it covers some of my thighs. It's an outfit more appropriate for a beach barbecue in summer than a frat party in Connecticut's version of spring, which feels no different from winter. If Lancaster wasn't ranked as the top soccer program in the country, I definitely would have stayed in the South for my college years. *Dress for the weather you want* has become my wardrobe motto.

"Ready," I announce, tossing my blonde hair over one shoulder.

Emma pours a second batch of her whiskey and pineapple concoction into one of the travel mugs we use for transporting coffee to morning practice and claps a lid on top. "Me too."

"You better remember to wash that," I inform her, wrinkling my nose in response to the smell emanating from the cup.

"First thing I'll do when we return from this shindig," Emma replies, sending me a saccharine smile.

I roll my eyes. Emma's notorious for her inability to wash anything without leaving some form of residue behind. It's why she's perpetually assigned to trash duty while the rest of us alternate completing the other household chores.

It's a short walk to the frat house hosting tonight. I've never bothered to keep track of the various Greek letters and who belongs to which fraternity or sorority. I go to the parties I feel like going to, and I tend to be followed around by the rest of the soccer team. Being the top female recruit in the country gained me a celebrity following among the niche few who kept up with women's soccer before I even stepped foot on campus.

The past two-and-a-half years of on- and off-field antics have only added fodder to my notoriety.

So did winning Lancaster a national championship.

Drunk students are spilling out onto the lawn as we approach the frat house, many of them laughing and stumbling about. It's March—way too cold to be spending time outside voluntarily. No one has ever said drunk people make smart decisions, though. And when we step inside the house, I sort of understand the inclination to head outside. Every square inch of the floor is covered by feet or littered with discarded cups that skitter across the hardwood as people mill about. The scent of sweat and spilled beer hangs heavy in the air. Anne sighs at the scene, but I grin, feeding off the boisterous energy swirling around with sweet-smelling smoke.

I lead the way toward the kitchen, ignoring the shouts and suggestions being hurled my way. I got used to the attention guys paid me a long time ago—about the same time I figured out how to use it to my advantage.

Jason Williams' eyes light up as soon as the four of us step inside the kitchen already packed with tipsy college students. "Hell yes! The party has arrived!"

"And she's in fine form tonight," Emma responds. "You're... what? Four shots deep, Scott?"

"Drink your tropical sludge and stop counting my drinks, Watkins," I retort.

Jason sends Emma a questioning look.

Emma sighs. "She's in a mood."

"Hello, I'm right here!" I stalk over to the counter covered with an assortment of cheap liquor. People scatter out of my way. "Do you guys not have gin tonight? I said I wasn't coming back unless there was gin, Williams!" I call out as I survey the limited options.

Jason sighs and picks up one of the labeled glass bottles sitting directly in front of me, which is in fact gin. Probably a sign I shouldn't be imbibing its contents—a warning I don't heed. Emma's right; I am in a mood.

"Sorry, Saylor," he says. "I know how much you wanted it."

I splash a generous amount of gin into a plastic cup, adding some ginger ale I find in the fridge in a half-assed attempt at a cocktail. "What are you sorry about?"

"The German camp? You heard back today, right?"

"Right."

"You know it's the most competitive soccer—or football, whatever—program in the world. You should be honored you were even considered."

I snort. *Honored I was even considered?* "What are you talking about? Of course I got in. I'm ranked first nationally." Raising the full plastic cup, I shout, "To the fucking Germans!" Some fizzy liquid splashes over the rim and dribbles down my fingers, making a sticky mess I couldn't care less about. I'm not the only one who started drinking early, so my toast is met with hearty cheers. Satisfied by the resounding response, I take a large sip.

"Wait, you did? Then why..." Jason's voice trails off as I wander over to where Anne is standing a few feet away, leaving him with Emma and Cressida.

"Which one are you eyeing?" I ask Anne, giving her arm a soft nudge as I lean against the counter next to her. She glances over at me, abandoning her feeble attempt to look like she's texting someone, not checking out the baseball players who have set up a makeshift bowling alley on the kitchen table. I smirk as I watch one try to knock over an empty glass beer bottle with a ping-pong ball. Yeah, good luck with those physics, buddy.

Anne shoves her phone into the back pocket of her skinny jeans. "I'm not."

"Convincing." I take a sip of my drink. "If you just—"

"Hannah Mason."

"Come on! That's not—"

"Hannah Mason, Saylor!"

"I can't believe you're still bringing that up. It was three years ago!"

"And she *still* hasn't returned for a single alumni game," Anne replies.

"That is not my fault. She was interested in Trey, and I made it happen. Whatever went down after that is not on me."

"It's the 'made it happen' part I'm worried about," Anne remarks.

I roll my eyes. Freshman year, our team captain was obsessed with Trey Johnson, Lancaster's quarterback. I shared that information with him. Like most college hook-ups, their relationship burned hot, fast, and out. I got none of the credit for instigating their short-lived romance and all of the blame when Trey ended their fling by trying to hook up with me instead.

"Saylor!" Natalie, a sophomore on the soccer team, bounces over to me.

"What's up, Nat?" I ask, keeping an eye on Anne in my peripheral vision to see if I can figure out which guy she was looking at before.

"I heard you got into Scholenberg! That's amazing! I mean, everyone knew you would, but..."

I laugh a little as I tune out her excited babbling. My badass soccer skills and series of one-night stands with Lancaster's hottest male specimens have cemented a form of hero worship among my soccer teammates even running together until we puke hasn't tarnished. Mostly I find it entertaining, but there are moments when I wouldn't mind fewer starry eyes aimed my way.

"...Visit at the end."

"Wait, what?" I ask, fully aware that I sound like I wasn't paying attention. Mostly because I wasn't.

"I'm going to Amnerallons!"

Based on Anne's sigh beside me, it's not the first time I've been told that.

"That's awesome, Natalie. Congrats," I reply, finally giving her my full attention. Amnerallons isn't in the same league as Scholenberg, but no other program is. It's still a training camp most players would feel honored to attend.

"We're ending the second week by visiting Kluvberg. I checked the dates—you'll be just starting Scholenberg."

"Whoa, very cool," I respond, a bit more emotion in my voice. I'm imagining the competitive atmosphere at Scholenberg will be similar to entering an enemy army camp. A friendly face will definitely be welcome.

Natalie keeps chatting, continuing our mostly one-sided conversation. She only pauses for breath when some of our other teammates come up to congratulate me on Scholenberg as well. Lancaster isn't a small school by any stretch. But news—especially news involving me—spreads fast.

I lean against the counter and people watch, content to let others come to me. By now I'd usually be dancing or failing at bowling with the baseball boys. Tonight I'm drained. Emotionally, at least. My legs are still itching to run.

Plus, I'm drunk.

I'm not normally much of a drinker. In my experience, people tend to drink for fearlessness or to forget. I've never had the first issue. There is nothing I would do drunk that I haven't already done sober. The second motivation is why the corners of the kitchen look hazy right now. The last time the number of members in my immediate family changed was not a cause for celebration, and the past sixteen years haven't made me any less cynical about the general notion of romantic commitment, nor the specific institution that fails as often as it perseveres.

I take the final sip of my drink and drop the empty cup on the kitchen counter behind me. It's already littered with abandoned ones, some half-full, most empty. When I turn back around, it's to a welcome sight. A hot, hunky sight.

"Drew!"

The dark-haired captain of Lancaster's hockey team glances over from the doorway. He's being trailed by two girls who both give me death glares as he strolls over to me.

He smirks. "'Sup, Saylor?"

"Wanna get out of here?" I'm not the type to bother with pleasantries or false platitudes, but I usually throw out a "Hello" at least.

Drew doesn't seem to mind the lack of polite greeting. He immediately nods. "Hell yeah."

"Please be done by two," Anne requests from her spot next to me. "I have to be up at nine tomorrow."

I smirk. "Wear headphones."

Then I head for the door, with Drew right behind me.

Chapter 2

I'm here.

I'm finally, really, truly here.

The field is pristine. Green. Empty.

I take a tentative step out from the shade of the walkway and into the blazing German sun. The cheap nylon shirt I just pulled on chafes against my overheated skin, but the slight discomfort fades as I trace the steps of players I've admired for years out onto the firm turf. I pause, spinning in a circle to survey the thousands of empty seats.

Awe overtakes me, reminding me of the reason I resolved at age fourteen to one day stand here. I've played in front of large crowds before, but none of those stadiums possessed the gravitational presence I'm surrounded by now.

Reverence slowly dissipates, a litany of pitiful emotions pulsing through me as I study the immaculate grass I've dreamed of playing on for as long as I can remember. A sharp stab of pain—like the jab of a needle—races from my knee and along my nerve endings. A reminder that coming here was a questionable decision. Considering some of the ideas I've had, that's saying a lot.

There are moments you can achieve through hard work and perseverance. Others take place whether you fought for them or not.

This is a combination of the two, with a healthy helping of masochism.

I turn to leave but halt when I hear a rapid stream of harsh syllables spouted behind me. I look back to see a tall guy who looks to be about my age studying me curiously as he swipes a hand through his shaggy hair. The emblem on everything he's wearing identifies him as a member of the football club whose field I'm currently trespassing on.

Fan-fucking-tastic.

"Water cooler?" he asks, switching to heavily accented English. My expression must clearly convey I didn't understand a word of whatever he just said.

I glance down at the black polo I snagged that's embroidered with the stadium's logo and realize what he has surmised.

I flash him my most charming smile. "I don't actually work here," I admit, injecting my voice with a hint of the southern charm that has never failed to get me out of trouble or make males capitulate. "I just wanted to get a look at the stadium, but if I come across anyone who looks like they'd know where the water coolers are stored when I sneak back out, I'll make sure to pass that along."

There's a blank stare of surprise. He clearly was not expecting me to have snuck in, or to admit that I did.

Finally, he smiles. I relax, no longer having to feign a casual stance.

"You did not want to just take a tour?" he asks, still grinning.

"Nope," I respond lightly. Now that I'm reasonably certain he's not going to call security, I'm anxious to get the hell out of here.

Ellie told me FC Kluvberg was practicing at their training facility today. If there are other players at the stadium instead, I'm not eager to wait and see if they're as trusting of an American stranger.

"But don't worry, I'm headed out now." I turn to leave for a second time.

"Wait!" the guy calls, jogging closer toward me.

I spin back around to see his friendly expression has shifted to flirtatious and bite back a groan.

"I'm Otto," he shares, holding a pale hand out to shake. His fair complexion matches his light blond hair. Either he spends little time outside or is liberal with his sunscreen usage.

Since he's a professional soccer player, I'm assuming the latter. Even after the long, cold Connecticut winter, my skin has already accumulated enough melanin from spring training—what little of it my sprained knee allowed me to participate in—to tan several shades darker than his.

"Nice to meet you," I tell him, gripping his offered hand and then dropping it after a quick shake. A flash of disappointment crosses his boyish face, and I wonder if he was expecting me to act like more of a fangirl. Unfortunately for him, I'm not easily impressed. "I'm Saylor."

Belatedly, I wonder if I should have made up a name in case Otto mentions this to anyone later. No one at Lancaster will ever let me live it down if I get sent home from the most competitive soccer program in the world the day before it officially begins.

For trespassing, the most mundane of all the misdemeanors.

"Saylor," he repeats, drawing out the final syllable of my

name so it's lengthier than the first. "Would you like me to give you a tour of the stadium?" Otto grins, the insinuation obvious.

"Another time, maybe." Like never, most likely. My primary goal at Scholenberg is to minimize the time spent with my butt parked on a bench. "I have to head out. I'm meeting some friends." Temporary teammates who will likely become future opponents, actually, but that doesn't seem like the type of detail he needs to know to effectively end this encounter.

Otto opens his mouth to respond, but we're both distracted by the sound of pounding footfalls.

A figure emerges from the cement tunnel out onto the field, silhouetted by the blazing sunlight. I don't realize who it is until he stops about twenty feet from where I'm standing, blocking the brunt of the sun.

It's the poster on Emma's bedroom wall come to life.

Adler Beck.

Referred to only by his surname among his many, *many* adoring fans. The most famous soccer—fine, football—star in the world. Germany's chosen *Kaiser*. He led seasoned veterans to a nail-biting victory in the World Cup his first year of eligibility, making him a household name at sixteen. Now just twenty-two, he's already one of the most decorated players of all time. The offspring of two highly respected German players, his pedigree and raw talent would have opened any door even if he wasn't also insanely attractive. He's blessed in that department as well.

A triple threat.

Even though I've watched hours of footage of him playing, it doesn't prepare me for the sight of Adler Beck's signature stoicism in person. He's not one of the players you see laughing and joking on the sidelines or during warmups. He treats each game like the job that it is. One thing that we have in common,

I guess.

His dirty blond hair is ruffled and sweaty, his skin as sun-kissed as mine as he jogs toward us in his practice gear.

He's even better-looking in person, which in the age of Photoshop seems both highly improbable and supremely unfair.

There's a potent magnetism to his presence that makes me forget about the heat, the itchy shirt I'm wearing, and the eager guy drooling three feet from me.

Adler Beck barks out a rapid stream of German, and for the first time, I regret letting Brett Stephens do all my homework for me in our elementary German class. I even chose German as my foreign language elective in anticipation of this trip. I can't comprehend a single word Beck shouts, but the tone is clear.

Otto drops his easygoing manner immediately.

Drops me.

"Nice to meet you," he says, already backing away while pulling a pair of keeper gloves out of his back pocket. "I hope we'll meet again."

It's exactly what I was hoping for a moment ago, but I don't feel relief now. I feel miffed and irritated as I stare after Otto's retreating back. The feeling is exacerbated when I watch Adler Beck give me a cursory glance and then walk the couple of remaining feet to where a soccer ball sits, waiting.

As soon as Otto positions himself in the goal, Beck becomes a blur of practiced movements, sending a shot flying at a lethal trajectory. Otto reaches, but it sails past him effortlessly with over a foot to spare. It's a textbook penalty kick, with one exception. If not for the many hours spent analyzing Adler Beck's technique to complete this very motion, I never would have noticed it. Fueled by the annoyance and lingering self-pity I'm still experiencing, I decide to critique the man unanimously considered to be one of the most talented players to ever set foot on a soccer field.

"You dropped your shoulder too early," I call out.

Making certain my voice echoes across the pitch.

Ensuring he can't ignore my words.

A pair of piercing blue eyes pin me in place. "You're giving me pointers?" Unlike Otto, Adler Beck doesn't address me in German first. Either I look like a foreigner, or he knows an American accent when he hears one. His incredulous voice is less accented than Otto's, but the syllables sound as harsh as they did when he was shouting in German.

"Just stating a fact," I reply, holding my ground against the force of his gaze.

"By all means, show me your technique." Beck moves back from the ball he's trapped and gestures me forward. His tone is *almost* teasing, but it carries a hard undercurrent of derision.

I don't need a German dictionary to translate what that means.

I take a tentative step forward, the panic pressing down on me as oppressively as the summer heat. A large part of me wants to toss out a "just kidding" and flee, but the competitive spirit I squashed into being dormant for the past couple months flares and refuses to allow me to back down. Somehow, I don't think this is what Lancaster's physical therapist meant when she said to ease my knee back into full motion.

I walk forward as nonchalantly as I can, considering each stride brings me closer to the familiar shape I've barely touched in weeks. There's a chance—a very slim one, I hope—my knee is no longer capable of this. So, I don't give myself an opportunity to second-guess anything, sending the ball spinning through the air as soon as I reach it.

Otto lunges, but it arcs past him neatly to drop into the back left corner of the net. I shift my weight back to my good leg and bite my bottom lip to keep the smile from spreading across my face.

Otto glances back and forth between me and the now stationary ball a couple of times, a look of shocked disbelief frozen on his face.

I keep my expression neutral despite the swell of elation I'm experiencing. A quick glance to my left reveals a stone-faced Beck. Famous for his composure on the field, the only sign of irritation is a slight tic in the sharp jawline that looks like it's carved from granite, or some other equally infallible material.

Following an invisible command, Otto sends the ball back to Beck, who traps it neatly and then sends it flying effortlessly into the back of the net.

I watch his shoulders carefully and roll my eyes when I notice he makes a point *to* lower his right one early.

The rational thing to do right now would be to leave, so of course I take a step farther onto the field. Closer to Adler Beck.

He wants to show off? I'm really good at that game.

"Best out of five?" I suggest. I'm scalded by blue fire as Beck turns the full heat of his searing gaze on me. Evidently the last glare was just a warm-up.

Unfortunately for him, I'm flame retardant.

He takes a step back from the ball Otto has already returned to him, a silent acquiescence with an edge of challenge that's shown in his slight smirk. God, am I sick of people—of guys—underestimating me. I've earned a reputation at Lancaster, but none of my credentials followed me onto this field the way his have.

I take more time setting up, focusing on ensuring each part of my posture is perfect before I send the ball into the goal. The back of the net bulges against the velocity of my kick's momentum.

I allow myself a small grin as I flex the muscles in my calf. Otto looks both surprised and annoyed as he rolls the ball back to me. Penalty kicks are a challenge for any goalie, more of a test of the player's skill than their own, but if he was considered good enough for Germany's most elite club, then this is undoubtedly a blow to his ego.

FC Kluvberg only takes the best of the best. The athlete to my left is a prime example.

"Your turn, twenty-three," I say as I pass the ball.

If I thought I could get away with it, I'd pretend to have no idea who Beck is. Unfortunately, he's famous enough that I'd end up looking like the fool in that scenario, not him. Still, I refuse to feed his ego by using one of his worshipful nicknames, and since his number is prominently displayed on his practice jersey, I don't have to admit I know exactly who he is outright.

Beck stops the ball without comment and executes another perfect kick that finds the back of the net. When Otto returns it, he sends it in my direction with a quick flick of his ankle.

I score another goal.

Beck's expression remains carefully neutral, but Otto's face shifts away from annoyance to reveal glimmers of awe.

I allow the tiny piece of myself, the part that has spent the last two months terrified my soccer career could be over, a brief moment to absorb the bizarre notion that I'm currently tied in a shoot-out with the youngest player to be voted "Most Valuable" on a national team as Beck finds the back of the net again.

Forcing myself to focus, I stop the ball he sends my way and send my own kick back to Otto. His fingers come within millimeters of the spinning ball, but it still lands safely behind the goal line.

Otto passes the ball back to Beck. He shoots it back courtesy of a powerful kick, only this time Otto brushes against the side of the ball, sending it skittering to the left and past the post harmlessly. I don't say a word but glance over to see Beck's hands are clenched into tight fists. Otto looks nervous as he hastily collects the ball and kicks it back to me. I let out a long exhale, determined not to let my focus waver or allow myself to dwell on the fact that I could potentially beat *Adler Beck* in a shoot-out. Talk about a surreal moment.

"Saylor?"

I turn toward the sound of my name as it echoes across the mostly empty field. Franz Anderson, one of the assistant trainers for the team and the reason I'm kind of, sort of, possibly allowed to be in here, stands at the end of the same tunnel Beck emerged from earlier.

"What are you doing?" Franz continues, glancing in confusion at Otto and Beck. I told him I was going to take a quick glance at the field. I guess this probably looks a bit different from that.

"Hi, Franz," I reply. "I was just about to head out." Unable to resist, I turn back to the ball resting in front of me and strike, sending it into the white netting with a satisfying smack.

Without another word, I spin and jog over to Franz. "Thank you. Beautiful stadium."

Franz looks more confused than ever, but he nods. "Have a good night. Say hello to Ellie."

"I will. Thanks." I flash him a quick smile and then begin to walk back toward the gate I entered through earlier, resisting the urge to turn around and meet the blue eyes I can feel burning holes in my back.

As soon as I turn the corner, I strip off the itchy polyester polo, grateful for the extra breathability of the sweat-wicking tank top I'm wearing underneath. Not only was it uncomfortable, the polo didn't exactly have the incognito effect I was hoping it would.

I drop the sweaty top in the laundry hamper that sits next to the stack of clean shirts I borrowed it from. I still feel overheated, like I swallowed a lump of coal that's radiating relentless heat in every cell and cranny. Wish I could replicate this everlasting ember during Connecticut's chilly winters.

It's over ninety degrees today, but that's not entirely to blame for the inferno inside me. Neither is the thrilling realization that I might not be a retired athlete at the ripe old age of twenty-one. No, it's the thought of azure eyes and a chiseled jawline that's got flames flickering.

No idea why.

Okay, that's a lie.

But I've got bigger life goals than becoming another notch on the post of the king-sized bed Adler Beck probably sleeps in.

No matter how long any residual flush lasts.

Chapter 3

Animosity is an old friend by now. People, particularly girls, have often resented me. For my looks. For the attention boys give me. For my carefree attitude. For my unerring ability to ensure the soccer ball ends up in the back of the net. Sometimes, for how easily I ignore the hostility.

But girls who knew I'd previously hooked up with their now-boyfriends have given me warmer receptions than the majority of my fellow Scholenberg attendees.

I came in expecting it, to a certain extent. We're some of the best athletes in the world.

All competitive.

All used to being the best.

All perfectionists.

Put a group of people like that together, then add in the fact that we'll likely be competing against each other on the world stage wearing our home country's colors in the near future? Hardly a surprise; you would need a sharpened steak knife to cut through the thick tension in the small room. Maybe a machete.

My temporary teammates have trickled in over the past few days, but this is the first time we've all gathered in one tiny space.

I've passed some of the other girls in the hallway before or seen them preparing food in the kitchen. I even went out to dinner with a few last night. Ellie Anderson shoots me a small smile when I walk into the room, but the rest of the expressions are guarded.

There aren't any jokes or quips being tossed around. Sporadic, polite chatter in a smorgasbord of languages is the only sound echoing against cinderblock. Or it was. Silence descends when I enter, and I realize I wasn't imagining my reception around the shared house being frostier than everyone else's.

I know it's actually a compliment, in an underhanded way. There are a couple of familiar faces I recognize, but most I don't.

They all know who I am already.

We don't have to marinate in awkward silence for very long. I've barely taken a seat next to Ellie, my fellow American, when the door bangs open to reveal Christina Weber. Seeing her in person prompts that same surreal flash my encounter with Adler Beck did yesterday. I've watched her win championships, studied her playing style, and read countless articles about her all-around badassery. And now she's standing ten feet from me, talking through today's schedule in crisply accented English. As my coach. She provides an unnecessary introduction and then announces an endurance test is up first, which is hardly a surprise.

Although expected, the announcement still sends an icy chill through me that eradicates most of the thrill of being in Christina Weber's presence. Normally, I'd be chomping at the bit to show off my hard-fought-for fitness. Thanks to my damn knee, I know it means I'll be sitting most of the day's activities out.

Coach Weber ends her brisk instructions with, "Scott. A word." Everyone else takes it as a cue to leave, and in seconds I'm sitting in a sea of twenty-four empty chairs.

"Nice to meet you, Coach Weber," I state, standing and walking to the front of the room. Remaining in the empty row makes me feel like I'm back in high school, getting scolded in after-school detention for not paying attention during class.

"You too, Scott." The words are clipped, but genuine. "Your medical records arrived yesterday," Coach Weber continues. "You've got six more days of recommended rest."

"Yes, ma'am," I confirm. I couldn't definitively tell you what day of the week it is, but I'm completely certain there are six days until I'm cleared to resume normal play.

"We've got a full team scrimmage next week. You'll be starting."

I chew on the inside of my cheek to keep a broad grin from flashing. I sprained my knee nine weeks ago at a spring skills clinic. Needless to say, it scared the shit out of me. Despite my aggressive playing style, I'd never had a serious soccer injury before; certainly never one that threatened my future in the sport, that jeopardized my career.

Soccer has always been a constant in my life. The one thing I take seriously and prioritize. The fear of losing it, coupled with terrifying words like "possible permanent damage" and "surgery," has kept my normally reckless nature in check these past two months. I've followed every instruction to the letter: icing, compression, elevation. Except for my impromptu battle of the sexes with Adler Beck yesterday, I've also limited any movement to physical therapist-approved exercise.

"You'll have to sit out today. I've got one of Kluvberg's physical therapists waiting for you. She'll look at your knee and talk you through some additional exercises. Tomorrow's a film and weights day. We'll take it from there on what you can participate in."

"Okay," I respond. I came in expecting this, and after watching Lancaster's team practice without me for the past two months, I'm actually glad I won't have to watch everyone else run today. There's nothing worse than sitting on the sidelines.

"Head right down the hall. Last door on the left," Coach Weber instructs.

"Okay." I head toward the exit.

"Scott?"

"Yes?" I glance back.

"Looking forward to coaching you."

I smile. "Looking forward to being coached."

The hallway I walked through earlier has a cement floor with walls painted a cream color. I turn right this time, glancing over the massive glossy photographs lining the walls. They're mostly action shots of players running, lunging, or mid-kick. It's impossible to miss that one athlete is featured twice as frequently as anyone else.

I shake my head as I pass the tenth photo of Adler Beck.

No wonder his ego is larger than most countries.

The last door on the left reveals a room larger than I was expecting. We're on the lowest level of the stadium. The small room we met Coach Weber in was one that I'm guessing is ordinarily meant for storage. But despite its disparate location, this space contains a whole host of equipment I know must cost thousands of dollars. A brunette with a friendly smile is tidying a shelf of towels when I walk inside.

"You must be Saylor," she declares, in what I think is a French accent. "I'm Alizée."

"Yes, I am. Nice to meet you," I tell her.

"Take a seat up there, please." She nods toward the straight-line table, the kind I've become far too familiar with over the past two months. I climb up on it and stretch my legs out.

Alizée pokes and prods at the muscles in my right leg in a way I've also become too accustomed to. "Any pain?"

I shake my head as she continues to rub the ligaments and tendons. "None."

"Your knee feels good. Really good. Six more days until full activity?"

I let out a breath I didn't realize I was holding and nod.

Alizée rotates my knee for a little longer, then walks me through a few new exercises I can add to my current routine to ease my knee into full movement. She's demonstrating the last one when the door bangs open. I tense involuntarily, not realizing why until I register the new arrival has brown eyes, not blue. My body relaxes without me telling it to.

The man who just entered jabbers out what sounds like an apology. Alizée replies, and I hear Scholenberg mixed in with a series of unfamiliar words.

"You're all set, Saylor," Alizée says. "Keep doing those, and I'll see you next week. Should be able to give you the all-clear."

"Great, thanks." I hop off the table, passing the man I'm certain must be a Kluvberg player without a glance, even though I can feel his eyes on me.

I head back into the hallway, ducking into the first stairwell I come across. But when I exit the stairs, it's not into the industrial-looking lobby we entered this morning. Instead, I'm in a hallway covered with a lush carpet and lined with offices. I swear under my breath and turn to head back into the stairwell.

And almost collide with someone.

I glance up into gray eyes. This man is one I recognize. It's Stefan Herrmann, Kluvberg's current keeper. I'm guessing Otto's being groomed as his backup and eventual replacement.

Suddenly, I can't seem to go anywhere without bumping into famous, fit men. It sounds like a wonderful problem to have, but every Kluvberg player I encounter who's not Adler Beck increases my chances the next one will be. FC Kluvberg doesn't have any friendly matches scheduled until mid-July. Their season doesn't start until late August. According to Ellie, the club gives up the stadium for maintenance, tours, and Scholenberg this time of year. Either she has inaccurate information—which, given who her uncle is, seems unlikely—or I have questionable luck.

"Do you know how to get out of the stadium from here?" I ask, hoping Stefan speaks English.

"Two floors down and through the lobby," he replies.

"Thank you," I respond, flashing him a grateful smile before rushing into the stairwell.

His directions are accurate, and a few minutes later I'm outside, bathed in brilliant German sunshine. I wave at the security guard as I head out the gate reserved for players, coaches, and others with some form of special access to the stadium. For the duration of Scholenberg, that includes me.

Once outside the fence surrounding the stadium, I pause for a minute. I expected to have downtime during my first week here until my knee was cleared.

I didn't expect to have free time.

Coach Taylor, Lancaster's head coach, has a strict policy that requires all players to attend practice, even if injured. I was expecting something similar here.

Instead, I'm standing outside the most famous football stadium in the world with no idea where to go. Every person I know in Germany is inside that stadium, and it's not even ten in the morning—the middle of the night on the East Coast—so I can't call anyone back home to kill time.

The four-story dorm-style structure Scholenberg is housing us in is only a few blocks away, but returning to a twin bed and stack of unpacked suitcases doesn't sound very appealing. So, I just start walking.

Kluvberg's stadium is nestled amidst the oldest section of the city that shares its name. The location is a tribute to both the club's esteemed relevance and its entwined history.

I would have jumped on a plane to Antarctica if that was where the best women's training camp in the world was located. I didn't really give any thought to my destination beyond the ways it could advance my soccer skills.

Wandering along cobblestone streets that look straight out of a storybook, I appreciate the fact that I'll be spending the next two months living in one of the oldest cities in Europe for the first time.

A canal runs to my right, constrained by mossy banks and filled with stagnant, clear water that reflects the colorful exteriors of the buildings lining its shore. Pointed steeples tower in the distance. Wooden boxes line the street, overflowing with bright blossoms and wild greenery spreading toward the stone road.

Up ahead, the narrow path opens to a bustling square. There's a market open for business, rows of wooden booths displaying a staggering array of products for purchase. Striped umbrellas shade jam, cheese, honey, flowers, and cured meats, along with every variety of fruits and vegetables imaginable.

A church bell tolls out a booming, commanding sound. I trace the peals to my left, where one of the majestic cathedrals Europe is famous for casts a massive shadow. It's ten times the size of the small, white-washed chapel Hallie got married in two summers ago.

The building itself is an astounding work of art; the exterior so detailed and carefully crafted that cataloging the complicated texture of the dazzling architecture seems like an impossible task. The cathedral fits perfectly with its timeless surroundings while simultaneously completely overwhelming them.

I stare for a while, trying to reconcile how this stunning structure just *exists*. Standing here the same way it has for hundreds of years. It also serves as an amusing litmus test for distinguishing tourists from the locals. Those manning the booths barely glance up at the magnificent church, while many of the shoppers browsing are gaping upward or snapping pictures of the sight.

Eventually I move on, stopping to buy a soft pretzel and then continuing along the same street I was walking before. It veers left after a hundred yards, transitioning into an arch bridge that crosses the canal.

The building situated immediately on the opposite side reminds me of the cathedral I just passed. The exterior is comprised of the same dark gray stone, and it shares the same emanation of importance. But everywhere the cathedral was pointed steeples and sharply carved edges; this building is rounded. Circular windows, ornate arches, and a domed ceiling shape the curved silhouette.

There's a steady flow of foot traffic heading in and out of the stone structure, and I fall in line behind a couple speaking what I think is Spanish. I'd ask them where we're headed, but my Spanish is no better than my German. Plus, I receive an answer as soon as we walk into the cavernous lobby.

It's some sort of museum. There's a long counter that spans

one side of the room, covered with glossy pamphlets. Chattering tourists are grouped around signs displaying clock hands in various positions. I can't recall the last time I was inside any sort of museum—probably elementary school, if I had to guess—but that's not why I pause just inside the front doors. It's the stark contrast between the exterior and the interior that has me stalling to a stop.

The outside was a grimy gray, weathered by years of exposure to harsh winters and—as I can attest to personally—humid summers. The interior is white.

Blinding, pure, striking white. The total absence of color is jarring. I feel like I was just dropped into the center of a snow globe.

I continue walking, disregarding the tour groups and pamphlets.

The few museums I've been to before have had an admission cost, but no one stops me for payment as I pass through the winter wonderland into a gray hallway that matches the aged exterior. Priceless oil paintings hang on stone walls that look straight out of a medieval castle.

I veer left into the first gap in the wall, which turns out to be a small gallery.

There are about ten people in the tiny room, all appearing to be entirely absorbed in the artwork displayed. I don't think anyone who knows me would describe me as an art enthusiast. I took an art history class freshman year and was so bored, I barely passed. Everyone else in the seminar took it very seriously, which only exacerbated my own apathy.

I'm definitely not someone who would drop terms like brushwork or composition in casual conversation. But the room is absent of any of the know-it-all commentary similar to the soundtrack of that class, so I take the time to lean close to each painting and study the intricacies.

None of them are the abstract-style pieces where you look at one line of paint on an otherwise blank canvas with a placard explaining it's meant to portray the human experience as colorful and empty and think *I could have done this.*

Many of the paintings portray scenes like the ones I just saw outside: cobblestone streets, canals, and cathedrals. Others show countryside scenes of pastures dotted with the fluffy forms of sheep, streams, and distant mountains.

I move into the connected room. This one has more variety. There are a few vineyards, some sailboats, lots of portraits of people I don't recognize, and one painting I spend a long time staring at. It's simple: a field of wildflowers. Shades of green grass and purple flowers. The level of detail is masterful. I feel like I could reach out and touch the texture of blades and petals. The artistry is exquisite, but it has an intangible quality to it, as though the entire painting is a mirror or a mirage. There are smudges and smears you have to look closely to see, and they mar the scene, keeping it from being too perfect. The longer I look, the more I see.

It's a puddle.

Simply a reflection of a peaceful scene.

Once I realize that, I move on. I've just entered the next room when my phone rings, earning me dirty looks from everyone else already inside this gallery. I struggle to pull it out of the snug athletic shorts I'm wearing, and the sound is even more obnoxious when it's free from the spandex. It's my sister.

I end the call, only for it to ring again immediately.

The middle-aged woman standing closest to me mutters something in German that sounds decidedly unpleasant. Then again, I've yet to hear anything said in German sound pleasant. Any term of endearment might as well be a scolding.

I duck out into the hallway and answer my phone with a whispered "Hello?"

"Why are you talking so quietly?" Hallie shouts. And I mean *shouts*. Her voice is audible enough to catch the attention of the security guard strolling about, making certain none of the visitors attempt a heist. He shoots me a stern look and points to the door marked *Ausgang*.

I sigh and follow his silent command, pushing through the door that exits into a sculpture garden.

Immediately, I mourn the loss of air conditioning.

"Why are you screaming?" I ask. "You just got me kicked out of a museum. And it's sweltering out."

"Museum? You're at a museum?"

"Uh-huh," I reply, taking a seat on one of the cement benches and kicking at the pebbled path. Tree branches stretch overhead, blocking some of the sunshine. "I haven't been cleared to play." The words taste bitter on my tongue, even knowing the clearance is an inevitability according to Alizée. "Figured I might as well explore Kluvberg."

"That's awesome. Good for you."

I roll my eyes. I should have known that would be her response. Hallie's always been concerned about my focus on soccer. Me attending a training camp and instead expanding my cultural horizons walking around Europe is practically her dream come true.

"Are you settling in okay?" she asks, raising her voice to a bellow at the end.

I pull the phone away from my ear. "What the hell, Hallie? Why are you yelling again?"

"Sorry." Hallie speaks at a normal volume this time. "We're at the park. They're mowing one of the fields and I can barely hear when they pass by."

I remember those soccer fields, but I don't voice the memory. Instead, I ask, "Why are you calling me if you're at the park? Isn't it still super early there?"

"Yes." Hallie sighs. "Guess that's why they're mowing. Matthew wouldn't sleep and Matt has an important meeting this morning. I needed to get out of the house."

"Huh," I reply. Hallie's always been selfless, whereas I don't even remember what her husband Matt does for work. Something in finance? Investing, maybe?

"So, are you settled in?"

"Yes." If you count the suitcase I unzipped.

"We're going to Dad's for dinner tonight," Hallie says without preamble. There's no natural way to ease into a discussion of our father, and she knows I won't be the one to bring him up.

"Have fun." I trace the patterns carved into the bench's hard surface with my free hand.

The half-hearted sentiment earns me another heavy sigh from Hallie. "Last week he said he hadn't heard from you since March."

"Phones work both ways, Hallie," I point out.

It's a flimsy excuse, considering we both know I probably wouldn't have answered.

"He doesn't know what to say to you, Saylor. When he called about being engaged, all you said was 'Okay.'"

I could have said worse.

"I barely know the woman! What was I supposed to say? 'Glad she's closer to your age than mine. Big relief none of my old classmates are going to be my new mommy'?"

That earns me a third sigh. "None of them were *that* young," Hallie says in his defense.

"Jessica was twenty-six."

"She was?"

"Yup. She asked me if I thought she could pass for twenty-four because that was the age she told her modeling agent."

Hallie laughs. "You're making this up."

I wish. The state of my relationship with my father isn't something I'm proud of or amused by. And it's a direct product of the choices he made after my mom left.

"I'm not that creative." I tuck my phone between my cheek and shoulder so I can pull my hair off my neck. Not that it makes any difference. I can feel a bead of sweat trickling down my spine toward the small of my back.

There's a quiet snort, then Hallie settles back into her serious tone. "He asks about you all the time, Saylor. They've still got some stuff to sort out for the wedding. I'm sure he'd love to know your opinion."

Hard pass. Even if I were into event planning, which I'm not, I'd have no interest in this occasion.

"I don't have opinions."

"You're the most opinionated person I know."

I roll my eyes. "I'll show up to the wedding, okay? Doesn't make a difference to me if there's cupcakes or donuts at the reception."

"They already decided on a three-tier cake," Hallie informs me.

I exhale a laugh. "Of course they did."

"Have you booked your ticket?"

"It's still three months away, Hallie."

"Plane tickets only get more expensive."

"That's a myth," I counter. "They drop them closer to the date, then raise them again."

"Is it about the money?" Hallie asks. "Because you know Dad will pay…"

"It's not about the money. I'll book one tonight, okay?"

Damnit. Now I'll actually have to do that later.

"Okay." There's a pause. "Well, get back to the art. Love you, sis."

Hallie hangs up before I have a chance to say it back. She's not expecting me to.

Probably because I never do. I'd blame my parents, but Hallie turned out normal.

So I think it's just me.

Chapter 4

Natalie arrives in Kluvberg on Saturday with five other girls in tow. They all survey me with a hero worship I should probably be flattered by but mostly find to be annoying.

Except for one.

"Scott!" London Reynolds squeals as I walk into the café we agreed to meet at, giving me a quick hug.

In an attempt to spend as little time at home as possible, I've spent the past decade attending every soccer program I possibly could. I don't think London had the same motivation, but we've overlapped at more clinics and camps than I could count. Outside of my Lancaster teammates, she's the one person I've played with on a regular basis in recent years.

"I didn't know you were going to Amnerallons, Reynolds," I reply, hugging her back.

It's not on the same level as Scholenberg, but it's still worth bragging about.

"And of course you're at Scholenberg." London pulls back so I can see her roll her eyes. "I should have known you'd be here."

"I didn't have anything better to do for the next two months," I respond with a grin.

Natalie cuts in, introducing the rest of the girls she's with. Unlike Scholenberg, Amnerallons doesn't limit how many players it accepts from a country. They're all American; mostly from schools on the West Coast that Lancaster rarely plays.

"Where are we going first?" someone asks excitedly once introductions are over. I already forgot her name, but I'm more concerned by how everyone's suddenly looking at me.

"I barely know the city," I admit. "I've been here less than a week. I've gone to the stadium, a museum, and a couple of restaurants, and that's it."

"You've been to Kluvberg's stadium already?" Natalie asks eagerly. "How was it?"

"Yeah, we had a meeting there a couple days ago," I divulge, opting not to share my trespassing earlier in the week. "It was cool."

"I cannot believe you'll be playing on the same field as Adler Beck has."

Here it is, the perfect opening to share what happened the other day. The obvious opportunity to tell Natalie I met him. To share our electrifying, combative encounter; admit I'm probably on Adler Beck's shit list.

But something stops me.

I'm not sure what.

Normally, I revel in sharing stories. When Trey Johnson shifted his attention from Hannah Mason to me, he was so confident I'd be interested, he stripped in the girls' locker room when he knew I came in for extra practice. Athletes tend to be a cocky bunch, but he was significantly less sure of himself when I left with his clothes, forcing him to walk-of-shame through the athletic complex with nothing but a small towel covering the goods. That anecdote was heard so many times on campus it practically earned triple-platinum status.

Trey Johnson peaked during his years as Lancaster's quarterback, fading to irrelevance as soon as he crossed the stage.

Adler Beck's in an entirely different league. Natalie's new friends—even London—might be looking at me with admiration right now. The revelation that I met Beck would do more than earn me deity status. It would prompt questions—lots of questions I don't feel like answering.

So, I just shrug in response to Natalie's comment. "Let's go to a beer garden," I suggest. "I'll text Ellie and see if she has any recommendations."

"Ellie?" London questions.

"Ellie Anderson. She's the other American at Scholenberg with me."

"Oh, right. Her uncle's a trainer for Kluvberg, right?"

"Right," I confirm. I've uttered the same statement before, but having met Ellie, I feel a bit bad for concluding nepotism is the reason she received a spot in the program. Probably has something to do with the fact that she's the only person who hasn't acted like my presence is an insult. "And she's visited here before, so she'll probably know a good place."

Ellie recommends a beer garden on the opposite side of the city, resulting in my first encounter with public transportation. The tiny town in Georgia where I grew up didn't have any, and I have a car at Lancaster. From what I've heard from friends who grew up in larger cities, I wasn't missing much.

Thankfully, there's no sign of any of the horrors I've heard described when we find the correct entrance and head underground. No graffiti, no urine scent, no garbage. We buy our tickets from a machine that helpfully has an English selection and then hop on the first train that arrives; one that is hopefully heading to our destination.

The inside of the subway is just as clean as the station was, with spotless plastic chairs we settle in and a map of blinking dots that display where we are. With a soft *whoosh*, the doors close, and we speed off into darkness.

Two stops later, we emerge from the cool underground, back into the warm sunshine. This area of the city looks very similar to the section we came from, except it's much busier. Less residential and more commercial. Restaurants, gift shops, bookstores, coffee shops, and bars line the street, interspersed by tourist traps that boast windows filled with flouncy clothing and T-shirts bedazzled with snappy slogans.

Natalie drags us all into the third gift store we pass. It's small and narrow, but what it lacks in width, it more than makes up for in height. Soaring shelves cover each inch of available wall space, packed with every souvenir imaginable. There are cuckoo clocks, Hummel figurines, leather-bound books of Grimms' fairy tales, outfits with full skirts and suspenders, ornaments, bits of rubble claiming to be pieces of the Berlin Wall, beer steins, fedoras, mustard, and more gummy bears than I've ever seen in my life. The towering display is an explosion of culture and color.

We fan out to browse the store with the other shoppers looking around. I'm flipping through the postcard selection to find ones to send to Emma, Cressida, and Anne when Natalie bounces over to me holding up two T-shirts. "Which one for the Theta kegger?" she asks me.

I glance between the white option that reads *I'm Just Here for the Beer* and the pink *Life is Brewtiful* one.

"Pink," I decide.

"That's what I thought, too," Natalie replies. "But I think Gamma's colors are pink and white, and I don't want people thinking I'm part of that shitshow. Or is it Kappa that's pink?"

"I associate pink with Alpha Sigma I-don't-give-a-shit," I respond, grabbing three postcards. "Just get whatever shirt you like better."

Natalie deliberates for a minute. "I'll get both."

She heads for the cashier, and I walk deeper into the store. The back wall is entirely dedicated to clothing. I spot both the shirts Natalie found, along with a variety displaying the German flag; faded, as a heart, as a soccer ball. The last iteration is located next to the top displayed front and center.

An Adler Beck jersey.

I stare at it for longer than I should.

Thanks to his breakout performance on the world stage as soon as he was eligible to play, Beck was living the life of a professional athlete back when I was a freshman in high school, despite being just eighteen months older than me.

Ever since then, I've admired his athleticism—along with the rest of the world. He's a legend, larger than a person. Our interaction both exceeded my expectations and fell short. I want to relive it and also pretend it never happened.

"Are you going to get one?" London asks, appearing next to me. I startle. She nods to the jersey I'm staring at. Busted. "You could wear it to practice in Kluvberg's stadium."

The suggestion makes me cringe. My impression is Scholenberg does everything it can to separate its female attendees from FC Kluvberg players because: hello, distractions. It's part of the reason Kluvberg supposedly spends the summer months training elsewhere. Although, I have to say, my experience so far has suggested that's some pretty spectacular false advertising.

Professional athletes don't really have an offseason, as evidenced by Beck's presence at the field just the other day. Once you reach the top, you have to fight to stay there.

The thought of Adler Beck seeing me wearing his jersey is repellent. I've always been the type to push back just to show I can. Falling in line as an Adler Beck fangirl feels like capitulating, lessening my small victory against him.

"Nope, just grabbing this," I reply, snagging a baby onesie with a German flag on it off the shelf.

London eyes me speculatively. "Something you need to tell me?"

I roll my eyes as I head for the register. "It's for my sister. She just had a baby."

"Look at you being a doting aunt."

That adjective seems like a stretch considering I've never even met the kid, but I don't argue. "Are you getting anything?" I ask.

"No, I bought way too much in France already. Thank God there's only a week left, or I'd have to get a new suitcase, too."

"The program is that short?" I ask, surprised.

"Yeah, just the three weeks."

"What are you going to do for the rest of summer?"

"Lounge on the beach." London grins. "Hook up with a hot lifeguard. Eat ice cream. Drink margaritas. Who knows?"

I snort. "Sounds lovely."

"What are you doing after Scholenberg? It's what—six weeks?"

"Eight. I'll head back to Lancaster to start training for preseason as soon as it ends."

London shakes her head. "I don't know how you do it. My teammates think *my* training is crazy, and I'm taking most of the summer off."

I shrug as I plop the onesie and postcards on the checkout counter, then dig some euros out of my pocket. "If you're doing the same as everyone else, you're not going to be the best."

"That's a better T-shirt slogan than *Life is Brewtiful*," Natalie comments to my right. She's spinning the carousel of keychains next to the cash register.

I smirk. "I'll tell Nike when I sign my endorsement deal."

A few minutes later, we exit the store and continue down the street. The beer garden Ellie recommended is a couple of blocks farther, the first hint that we're drawing near the sudden change in our surroundings. Dense greenery appears on the right rather than more storefronts. There's a wrought iron archway halfway down the block. A wooden sign affixed to the center is carved with a few German words. The last one says *Biergarten*, which I take as an encouraging sign we've navigated the city correctly. Then again, I'm sure Kluvberg has more than just the one beer garden.

I lead the way down a stone pathway that cuts through the foliage. We emerge onto a wooden terrace. Verdure is draped over and twisting through it, sheltering the picnic tables below and dripping down the sides in tendrils of leaves. A wooden hut is nestled to the left, with a line of customers waiting to place their orders snaking around the side. Most of the tables are taken, people dipping pretzels in an array of mustards and drinking beer.

It takes me a moment to realize, but the beer garden also overlooks most of Kluvberg. We're in a newer part of the city, one that's on higher ground, evidently. I can see the canal in the distance. The steeples of the cathedral. And the outline of the stadium, of course.

"You guys grab a table. I'll get in line," I offer.

"I'll come with you," Natalie says. "Text me your orders, ladies."

Our group splits. Natalie and I join the end of the line, and thankfully, it's moving pretty fast. We're close enough to see the menu within minutes, and there's a lot more than just beer and pretzels being offered.

My relationship with German cuisine has been strained so far. The restaurant I went to earlier in the week with Ellie and a few other Scholenberg attendees was offering a wide variety of foods that did not sound appealing at all. But all the German dishes here have English descriptions written underneath, and bratwurst on a pretzel bun or fried pork doesn't sound terrible.

We reach the counter, and Natalie relays everyone else's orders to the young blonde woman behind it as I continue to survey the menu. I've always been indecisive when it comes to food. Some might call me a picky eater.

Finally, I settle on just a pretzel to go with my beer.

We move to the side to let the next group order and take up positions along the wrought-iron fence that circles the perimeter of the eating area to wait. I stare out at the city for a couple of minutes and then turn my gaze back to the terrace, just in time to watch a brown-haired guy saunter over. The cocky grin he's sporting tells me all I need to know about why he's approaching us. Or approaching me, rather. He ignores Natalie, focusing his attention exclusively my way.

"Hello." He addresses me in English, but there's a thick accent underlying the greeting. I say nothing, just raise an eyebrow. "I know you speak English—I heard you ordering," he adds.

"So?" I ask, raising both brows now.

"I was wondering if you'd like to sit with us." He jerks his head toward a table filled with a boisterous group I'm not the least bit surprised to learn are his friends.

"We already got a table," I inform him.

Predictably, his smile only grows. In my experience, men love the chase. And I'm a really fast runner. "That's not why I was inviting you."

I'd smile if I didn't think it would encourage him. "We're good."

"If you change your mind..." He nods toward the same table, as if I might have forgotten where he is sitting in the past ten seconds.

I nod once to acknowledge I do in fact recall the location he *just* shared with me.

Natalie turns to me as soon as he saunters off. "Damn, he was hot."

"He was?" I reply, genuinely surprised. I barely remember what he looked like.

Natalie gives me a weird look. "Yeah, he was."

I shrug. "Not my type, I guess."

She makes a small sound of incredulity. "You're hard to please, then."

Uninvited, blue eyes and chiseled cheekbones flash before my eyes. A face women everywhere lust after.

Not *that* hard to please.

Chapter 5

I definitely don't improve anyone's opinion of me when I lead six tipsy strangers into the Scholenberg house. Ellie's not around, so I don't have a single ally.

"Stay here," I instruct the group when we enter the living room. "I'm just going to change real quick."

I rush toward the stairs, passing Sydney, the fittingly named Australian who's scrolling through her phone on the couch.

Another girl blocks the first step. "Seriously?" Olivia asks. She's Norwegian. Maybe Swedish? We've yet to step on the field together, but she's preemptively taken an aggressive stance, glaring at me every chance she gets.

"We won't be here long," I assure her.

"Meaning you're going out."

"Yes."

She sniffs disdainfully. "Interesting training routine you have."

My temper flares at the absurdity of someone accusing me of not training hard *enough*. "Tomorrow is Sunday, also known as our day off. And we'll see what you have to say about my *training routine* next week." I brush past her, heading into my room. I change in record time, swap my cross-body bag for a clutch, and hurry back downstairs.

Natalie lets out a long wolf whistle when I appear.

"Damnit, we should have made you come in your T-shirt and shorts," London says from the couch, giggling as she surveys the dress and leather jacket I changed into. "How do you manage to just look like *that*?"

I roll my eyes. "Get up. Let's go."

Our next stop is the hotel they're all staying at. The exterior blends with the local architecture, but as soon as we enter, I feel as though I've stepped back into the States. There's the same generic carpeting and bland art as every hotel I've ever stayed in.

The girls have adjoining rooms with twin beds and cots set up. I don't ask who's getting stuck with the cots, but pity whoever the two are when I take a seat on one. They're just as uncomfortable as one would expect sitting on a canvas-and-wood construction to be. At least they're free of whatever questionable fluids are preserved in the comforters covering the beds.

Natalie and the rest of the girls packed like they're staying for a week instead of one night. I'm definitely guilty of traveling with twice the amount I need, but I lose patience after the fourth outfit Natalie parades around in, especially since it's the same short-skirt-silky-tank-top combo as the last three outfits.

Emma calls halfway through the fashion show.

"Hello?" I answer grumpily.

"Lovely to talk to you too, darling," she replies, laughing. "Did I wake you up or something? I thought it was only—"

"You didn't wake me up. You interrupted Natalie's fourth outfit option."

"Oh, I forgot Natalie was coming this weekend! Are you guys going out?" The sounds of seagulls and surf echo in the background. Emma's from New York City but spends every summer in the Hamptons.

"That was the plan," I respond. "We'll see if we ever leave the hotel."

Emma giggles. "Not everyone can throw on a dress and look like a runway model, Saylor."

I don't answer.

"So, how is it?" she asks eagerly.

Filling her in on an Adler Beck-less version of Scholenberg so far takes up the rest of the time the girls need to get ready. By the time we're hanging up, everyone's ready to go.

We traipse down to the lobby and out onto the street.

"So, where are we going?" London asks.

I prepare for everyone to turn to me. I'll have to text Ellie again.

But Natalie's the one who answers. "I know the perfect place."

I don't have a suggestion and she sounds confident, so I climb in a cab already waiting outside the hotel with everyone else. It's a sedan, definitely not designed to seat seven, but the driver doesn't seem to mind. He deposits us in an industrial neighborhood I wouldn't expect to contain a trendy club and cheerfully collects his fare.

"How did you hear about this place?" I ask Natalie after we've all tumbled out of the cab, critically studying the bland concrete exterior in front of us.

"*Extensive* research," she replies, grinning. "It was the most consistent hit for a Kluvberg player hangout. According to TravelAdvisor, there's always this long of a line for just that reason." She nods to the line curving around the exterior of the building. To her credit, they're all trendily dressed people about our age.

"You're joking," I say flatly. The last thing I want to do is to spend the night fending off a bunch of Adler Beck-wannabes.

"Nope, totally serious."

"Sounds like a rumor they might have started themselves," I mutter.

"Come on," London declares, striding toward the front of the line. Everyone else follows, me included. "Hi, we'd like to go in," she tells the beefy man clad in all black. Protests sound behind us, but a raised hand from the bouncer quiets them.

"Name?" he asks gruffly.

"Wh-what do you need a name for?" Natalie asks, losing a bit of her bravado.

"This is a private club, miss. No entry unless you're on the list," the man responds. None of the other girls speak. Natalie looks crestfallen. I may not want to be at this particular club, but I'm not great about being told I *can't* do something.

I step forward. "My name is on the list."

Natalie gapes at me, contributing nothing to the act.

"What is it?" the bouncer asks, tapping a pen against the clipboard impatiently.

"Well, here's the funny part," I start, giggling slightly. The guy glances up and falters a bit when he focuses on my face. I crank up the ditzy blonde act, twirling a strand of hair around my pointer finger as I sway in my heels. "See, there was this guy I met earlier at a restaurant, Lecker—I don't know if you've heard of it?" I toss out the name of the ritzy eatery Ellie told me she was meeting her family at hoping to add some credence to my story.

First rule of lying: add random details. It seems to work,

because the bouncer nods, his stoic expression softening.

"Anyhoo, he came up to me and was flirting. Then, he asks me to meet him here later. But he'd already asked for my name, and my friend Tiffany here"—I yank Natalie forward—"read some article about how you should never give a strange guy your actual name when you're traveling because then he could track you down later. I mean, you should hear some of the stories my sorority sisters have told us about the creeps out there. So, I didn't tell this guy my real name, but then he tells me he'll put my name on the list here. And I couldn't come clean then, right?"

The bouncer eyes me apprehensively. I have no idea if he believes me. If this place is really as popular as Natalie claims, I'm guessing he's heard it all.

"What name did you tell this guy?" he asks. Well, maybe not *all*.

"I forget," I respond, smiling sheepishly instead of triumphantly. "I panicked and just made one up. Lisa Linderhagen, maybe? Is that on the list?"

There's a quiet snort behind me, and I hope the bouncer didn't hear it. If one of these idiots ruins the compelling tale I just conjured, I will never let them forget it. The bouncer studies me for a minute, not even bothering to glance down at his list to check for my fake name.

"All right, you ladies can come through," he finally says, unclipping the ceremonial-looking rope barrier.

There are loud protests from those in line, but I don't wait around to listen to them or give the bouncer a chance to change his mind. I stride through the doorway into what, I have to admit, is a pretty cool atmosphere. If Kluvberg players do hang out here, they've got decent taste. It's not flashy or extravagant, but minimalistic and sleek.

"That. Was. Brilliant!" Natalie announces, bouncing in beside me.

"Seriously," London agrees. "I feel like I should be looking around for the poor guy who fell for the 'I'm Lisa Linderhagen' line."

I snort. "I'm going to grab a drink from the bar."

"I'll get a booth," London announces.

"Let's hit the dance floor." Natalie pulls the rest of our group along with her.

The interior of the club is structured in a U shape. The bar sits to the far right, while the dance floor and DJ booth take up the left side. The bottom curve is split by the doorway, with booths lining the brick walls.

I skirt through the crowd, ignoring the glances I'm garnering. I'm not in the mood for it right now, but it's impossible to tune out the people close to my own age, all dressed in sophisticated clothes that suggest designer labels. They all seem to be locals. Nothing but German punctuates the thumping bass pumping through the speakers.

Finally reaching the bar, I order a gin and tonic, then study the expensive bottles of liquor displayed behind the bar as I wait for my drink. There's a muted light shining behind them that adds to the alluring ambiance.

"You're not supposed to be in here," a deep, male voice says.

Why is it the last person you want to see is always the one you run into? There is *one* guy I didn't want to encounter in Germany—actually all of Europe.

A geographic region comprising millions of square miles.

Thousands of clubs.

One Adler Beck.

I turn to face him, which is a mistake. Adler Beck looked

gorgeous sweaty and pissed off. He looks even better leaning against the bar in jeans and a gray T-shirt that clings to a muscular torso I've seen splashed on more magazine covers than I care to admit. He still appears annoyed. Either it's his default setting, or I draw it out.

Or both.

"How do you know? Maybe I was personally invited by the owner," I respond, mirroring his pose and leaning against the bar. It's so unfair hot guys are often the assholes. Hair that blond and eyes that blue should not be genetically possible.

"You weren't," Beck states flatly. He's holding a bottle of beer, and the beverage choice surprises me. He looks more like the type to sip expensive liquor from a crystal tumbler. Then again, I'm just basing that off paparazzi photos of him with models exiting cars that cost more than four years of tuition at Lancaster.

Beck sets the glass cylinder down on the black bar top made of some sort of stone. Maybe marble? Can marble be black? I took geology, also known as "rocks for jocks" as my science requirement, but I remember about as much as I do from my art history course. The smooth, lustrous surface fits with the sultry vibe. Classy and chancy.

"How do you know?" I ask, before glancing over my shoulder to check on the bartender I ordered from. He's busy flirting with some girls farther down the bar, meaning my drink is not about to appear. Whelp, there goes his tip.

"Because I own this place." The words are matter of fact, no hint of boastfulness.

Thank God I didn't compliment the décor out loud. It would ruin my perfect record of not feeding his ego. "I don't believe you."

"Why not?" He grabs his beer from the maybe-marble surface and takes a sip.

"You don't really look like the nightclub-owning type. Show me some paperwork." That sounded a *lot* less lame in my head. I'm speaking like some sort of amateur mobster. I blame it on the fact that I never expected to see him again. And how he throws me off-balance by exerting no effort at all.

"What exactly does the nightclub-owning type look like?" Beck asks.

"Not you," is the best response I can come up with. I would love to leave this conversation where I can't come up with anything witty to say, but it's fairly obvious I'm standing here waiting for my drink, and there's no cocktail to be seen.

"Is that a compliment or an insult?" The barest hint of a smirk appears, which makes me think Beck might be aware of the fact that I'd very much like to walk away right now.

"No idea," I tell him honestly. Yup, there's definitely some amusement in his expression now. "Maybe you should spend less time managing your club and more time practicing penalty kicks."

I went *there*, and the flash of surprise on Beck's face makes it clear he didn't think I would.

I turn to look at him fully for the first time, enjoying watching him decide how to respond. Defend or ignore?

"Otto's young."

I smirk. Or blame the goalie. "He blocked one of yours," I'm quick to point out.

"You caught him a bit off guard."

"I can't think of a single game I've played in that went the way I expected it to."

"I meant that you're American."

"I wasn't talking all that much," I respond cheekily, finally finding some footing in the conversation. I've never fished for a compliment in my life, but for some reason I really want Adler Beck to acknowledge he means my appearance, not my nationality.

Eyes the exact color of the clear sky after a storm flit away from my face, down the dress I'm wearing, and back up. "Hard to ignore that accent," he remarks.

Fine. He's a worthy competitor off the field, too. Adler Beck doesn't just have confidence; he oozes charisma. It exudes from every invisible pore, clogging the surrounding air with cockiness.

"The only player in the club over ninety is me." Grudging, barely discernable respect is hardly noticeable in his tone, but I catch it.

Adler fucking Beck checked my conversion rate.

"You looked me up?"

"Mm-hmm." He takes another sip of beer.

I mastered the art of appearing indifferent a long time ago, but the knowledge that Adler Beck took the time to check my stats is surreal—not that I have any intention of telling him that, or saying I'm impressed he found my conversion rate based on nothing but my first name. My soccer stats aren't exactly splashed across the internet the way his are.

Thirty seconds of silence pass before Beck speaks again. I start counting, simply for something to do.

"You here alone?"

"No, with a teammate from home. She's at Amnerallons and came for a visit with new friends. I needed some... I came to grab a drink."

"What did you order?"

"Gin and tonic."

Beck turns and says something in German. I look behind me to see the bartenders are now rushing about. Maybe he really does own this place. Or maybe they're just responding to the presence of the world's most famous footballer. In seconds, a glass filled with bubbly, clear liquid and topped with a lime wedge appears before me.

"Tha—" Beck swipes the glass mid-word. "What are you doing?"

He doesn't reply, just starts walking to the left, clutching what I assume is my drink. Foolishly, I follow him. He takes an abrupt right and heads down a short hallway. Then pushes open a side door and gestures for me to enter first. I walk into what must be the stock room.

Glass bottles and brown boxes line shelf after shelf after shelf, the small space barely illuminated by the solitary lightbulb dangling from the ceiling. Beck grabs a blue bottle, opens it, and adds a generous splash of its contents into the glass he's holding.

Silently, he holds it out to me. I take the glass and sip some of its contents. Lime, botanicals, and pine hit my tongue, followed by the aftertaste of fizz.

"It's good," I inform him.

"Good."

Beck doesn't move. Neither do I.

I hold his gaze, suddenly very aware—excruciatingly aware, in fact—that the two of us are in a room alone. Together. There shouldn't be any familiarity between us, but I know what he's about to do before it happens.

One step.

Two.

Three.

I hold my ground as he comes closer, setting my glass down

on the nearest shelf once only inches remain. His body heat seeps through the thin satin I'm wearing.

"We should've played for something," he tells me.

I tilt my head back to maintain eye contact. "Even though I won?"

Beck makes a sound in the back of his throat. A dissatisfied vibration I think means he'll argue about the outcome. He shocks me by agreeing. "Even though you won."

My lips curve up automatically. "So, what's my prize?"

He presses me against a shelf, prompting loud clangs as the glass bottles shift in protest. And then he kisses me. I'm kissing Adler Beck. But it doesn't feel like I'm kissing a soccer superstar. There's no distance—literal or metaphorical—to view the body pressed against mine as belonging to a famous footballer.

I have two options right now, but I don't want to stop kissing him, so that brings me down to one.

Beck's domineering. Overwhelming. Clearly used to being the alpha. Just like during our shoot-out, I don't let him.

We're already careening down a decline at a thousand miles an hour, so I yank the brake stick and toss it out the figurative window. He tugs my hair; I slip my hands under his shirt to dig my nails into his back. He slides his hands up and under my dress; I struggle with the zipper of his pants. The entire time, our tongues duel for dominance.

Adler Beck may be German, but he's mastered the French kiss.

He's already hard, his cock straining against the boxer briefs he's wearing. Our brief, clothed interactions have never given me the impression Beck is compensating for anything. I receive visual confirmation of that when I yank down the fabric covering his dick. He's huge. I run my fingers along firm, hot skin, tracing the erection that's jutting up between us. Beck groans.

We're both breathing heavily, the only sound in the small room aside from the muffled activity on the other side of the door. I've done this many times before, and I'm sure Beck has too. But I wasn't expecting it to happen here, tonight, with him. I'm sober aside from the beer I had hours ago and the one sip of gin, completely aware of what's happening. *Too* aware. There's an unfamiliar flurry low in my stomach that has nothing to do with lust.

Yes, I'm attracted to him. Partly because of his appearance and partly because I admire him as an athlete. Those were known variables. But I wasn't expecting to feel nervous around him. To enjoy talking to him. To care what he thinks of me.

Fingertips brush against the wet spot in my lace thong, discovering I'm just as affected by him as he seems to be by me. The flimsy fabric gives way easily. I gasp, first in response to the unexpected sound—he *ripped* my underwear—and then as a reaction to the sudden invasion. I clench around his fingers, moaning when his palm hits my clit. It feels so good. So consuming, the burst of pleasure overwhelming all my other senses.

Beck groans again—this time deeper and throatier. Then he says something in German. Something I don't understand, and that's somehow hotter than any of the dirty talk I've heard in the past. It's the first time the harsh language has sounded erotic.

Whatever expression is on my lust-addled face makes his eyes even more heated. They blaze like twin flames, the same way they did when we faced off on the field.

"Turn around," he tells me, tugging a foil packet out of his pocket. I'm not the least bit surprised to learn he carries condoms around in his pocket.

I decided approximately two minutes ago I was going to fuck Adler Beck, and delaying that lost its appeal about ninety seconds ago. But I'm not going to make it that easy for him. I'm a competitor too.

I lounge back against the metal shelves, keeping my eyes on his face as he concentrates on ripping the wrapper and rolling the rubber over his erection.

"Maybe I'm a missionary girl."

One raised eyebrow is the only reaction I get at first. Then his gaze rises to meet mine, the split second when our eyes connect hitting like a jolt to my heart. I don't get starstruck easily and I'm hard to impress, so I can't figure out my own reaction to him just *looking* at me.

"You're at Scholenberg to learn new things."

I snort, not sure what to make of the fact he knows I'm here attending the camp. Lucky guess? Did he research more than my stats? "You're not going to *teach* me anything I haven't already— *fuck*."

I'm facing the shelves now, barely having time to register the blunt tip of his cock pressing against my pussy before he's pushing inside.

"*Fuck*," I repeat, as he bottoms out and then starts to thrust. It feels incredible, even better than his skilled fingers. I'm also stunned—a little impressed—that he managed to catch me off-guard. That he's taking control and I'm sort of letting him.

The pressure in my pelvis is already building at a dizzying pace, my muscles tensing and shaking as he manages to hit that elusive spot with every stroke. I have to grab on to the edge of the metal shelf to stay upright, scowling when I hear him chuckle. I grind back against him, meeting each rock of his hips, and that shuts him up fast.

His hands fall to my waist and his grip tightens, trying to regain control of the pace. Our bodies are weirdly in sync, adjusting in synchronized tandem. We've never done this before, but it feels like we have. Not in a tired, overdone way—in a best hook up of my life kind of way.

I don't normally think about who's fucking me when I'm having sex. It's much easier to let my mind go blank and focus purely on the pleasure. I thought that would be the case with Beck, especially once he told me to turn around. But I can't *not* think about it. It's too obvious that it's him behind me, him challenging me. Since I can't see him, it seems like feeling him has been heightened.

I'm close to losing control. The coil low in my stomach is pulling tighter and tighter. Shockwaves skitter across the surface of my skin. A warm flush spreads across my skin like a fever. Beck says something else in German, and I know he can feel the changes in my body. His syllables sound thicker when he's aroused, and the hard—pun intended—evidence of that is rapidly sending me toward a very happy ending.

My instinct is to fight the approaching orgasm, to push it further away. Which startles me, because I'm usually rushing toward release. The point of sex has always been to get there, then send the guy off with a baked good and head back to bed alone.

But his right hand leaves my hip to rub the swollen spot right above where he's filling me, and I tumble over the cliff immediately.

Pleasure floods my body, coating every centimeter of my skin and making each cell tingle. I free-fall through a stratosphere of delectation, barely aware of the thickening throb when he comes too.

Deep lungfuls of air help revive my shaky limbs. I tug my dress down hastily, hoping my thong isn't too damaged to stay up. I'll have to take a trip to the restroom as soon as I get out of here.

Beck looks smug as I spin to face him, tugging the condom off and tossing it in a trash bin that's probably there for exactly this purpose. I doubt I'm the first girl he's brought back here. Way easier than taking her back to his place, and with more privacy than a bathroom. He probably trains his staff to knock before entering.

We stare at each other as he tugs his zipper back up, the rasp of the metal teeth reuniting the only sound I focus on. I reach for the drink I set on the shelf, taking a long sip.

I'm at a loss for what to say right now. Odds are, I'll never see Beck again. None of my usual post-coital lines work in this situation, and I'm fresh out of cupcakes to hand him.

"Thanks for the drink," I state.

He nods but says nothing. I take that as the perfect opportunity to leave, striding toward the door.

"Saylor."

It's the first time he's said my name. If not for the fact he looked up my conversion rate for penalty kicks, I'd assume he'd forgotten it.

I glance back. "What?"

He hasn't moved, standing with the confidence of an emperor surveying his kingdom. "I get to pick the prize next time."

I shake my head. "I don't do rematches."

Then I turn around and leave before he can say anything else.

Chapter 6

"**Y**ou were out late last night," Ellie comments the following morning, appearing in the doorway of my room and flopping down on my unmade bed.

"Yeah, I guess so," I respond, not looking up from the course catalog I'm scrolling through on my laptop. I have to choose my fall classes this week. Attending class is one part of life at Lancaster I definitely won't miss. School has never been of much interest. I cycled through four majors before landing on public relations, and I already have regrets about my final choice because none of the requirements sound all that interesting. "Natalie turned it into a whole thing."

Ellie snorts. "You are aware I follow you on social media, right? If there was anyone instigating anything, I bet it was you."

I roll my eyes. "Whatever."

"Did you meet any German boys?" Her playful words dredge up the memories I've been trying to repress ever since I woke up hungover with a distinctive soreness between my thighs.

A calloused palm sliding across my skin. A hot tongue in

my mouth. A thick cock stretching me wide. Dragging Natalie, London, and the rest of the girls out of Beck's club shortly after I left that storage closet, claiming a guy at the bar told me about some hip new place around the corner. The club we ended up at was neither hip nor new, but they were all too drunk to notice.

"Nope." The lie comes out easily.

Natalie misses my glance at the heap of fabric that's my dress from last night. My ruined thong is in that pile too.

She sighs with disappointment. "Well, that's disappointing. I was relying on living vicariously through you this summer."

"What? Why?"

"Again, I follow you, Saylor. You're basically a hot-guy magnet."

"How was your day yesterday?" I ask, eager to change the subject.

"It was fine. Uncle Franz is all excited about some exhibition match the team has coming up."

"Huh." Switching topics to FC Kluvberg was not exactly what I had in mind.

I keep scrolling through descriptions of courses, and then the screen decides to freeze. I sigh, taking it as a sign I should stop.

Standing, I stretch and then grab my sneakers from their spot by the door.

"I'm going for a run. You want to come?"

"You're joking, right?" Ellie asks. "It's our day off!"

I shrug, then start lacing up my sneakers.

"What about your knee?"

"I'm cleared to jog. Not about to run a marathon."

"Have fun," Ellie calls after me as I head down the hallway. I hear springs squeak as she flops back down on my bed.

Several other girls are relaxing in the common area

slash living room when I walk down the stairs, all looking as comfortable as Ellie. They study me with judgy stares as I pass them in my athletic shorts and tank top, and I sigh internally. I didn't expect to leave here with lifelong friendships, but I've been here for over a week and there's no sign of anyone but Ellie liking me at all. I doubt me getting cleared to play will help.

The four-story house that hosts Scholenberg attendees is centrally located, and it's only a few blocks to a park I've passed before. The streets are busy, filled with chattering locals and tourists alike. The scenery of the city is still an adjustment. Aside from a spring break trip to Mexico and a soccer camp in Canada, this is my first time leaving the US.

The scarred cobblestones, ancient buildings, and colorful architecture look nothing like the sleepy southern town I grew up in, or the college town Lancaster is located in. The scent of street food and the chatter of foreign languages fill the air still damp from rain the sky shed earlier. Watery sunshine peeks through light gray clouds here and there, extending misty fingers that trickle down to the damp street.

The crowds last until the park that's my destination, milling about, unbothered by the overcast day. Even the park looks different from the ones back home. Wrought-iron gates mark the entrance that's surrounded by trimmed topiaries. Carved concrete balustrades and oak trees line the walkway that opens into a plush spread of grass. Past it, there's a massive marble fountain sending shifting sprays of water upward toward the cloudy sky.

I start jogging along the gravel path as soon as I pass through the open gates. Once I reach the fountain, I realize the park is much larger than I initially thought. It's a massive green oasis in the center of the city. There's a playground, dog park, snack bar, and some soccer fields. I stop at a bench to retie my left lace, which has become nothing more than a loose loop. I was in a hurry to get out of the house.

Once I've double-knotted, I straighten. Glance around, deciding on which direction to head first. Then…freeze.

Adler Beck is walking toward me, wearing sunglasses, a baseball cap, and an inscrutable expression. He's dressed in athletic attire, same as me, but none of them sport the emblem of his club. He looks like any ordinary guy—any ordinary *hot* guy—not a famous soccer superstar.

I curse out my bad luck in my head.

"Don't tell me," I drawl, as he pauses a couple of feet away. "You own this park too."

One corner of his mouth twitches with amusement before his expression smooths back to neutral. "No. I live across the street."

I glance in that direction, shading my eyes with one hand. "Do you own that building?"

"I'd have to ask my real estate agent."

I can't tell if he's kidding or not, which bothers me. I've been told I'm hard to read countless times, but I've never thought that about someone else before now.

Beck crosses his arms, surveying me superiorly; like I'm a peasant in his kingdom. "You're training?"

"Just going for a run." I woke up feeling restless, and it's partially his fault. He kept creeping into my head last night, long after I'd left him behind.

"It's your day off."

"It's yours too," I remind him as he continues studying me.

If I saw him again—which I didn't think would be the case—I assumed we'd ignore each other. I can't tell him I'm running late for class or have practice. I'm alone, not with a group of friends.

Once again, I'm at a weird loss for what to say to him. His gaze is too intense, easily permeating the thick shield I usually keep up. His eyes drop to my bare legs, the interest on his face obvious. We're standing feet apart, both fully dressed, and I somehow feel naked.

I study him back, the lighting outside better than it was in his nightclub last night. The chiseled cheekbones. The unforgiving jawline. The short blond hair peeking out the sides of his hat. The ropes of muscles flexing along his golden forearms. Looks that have landed him on the covers of dozens of magazines—most of which couldn't care less that he earned the mouth-watering physique and sun-kissed complexion on a soccer field.

"What are you doing here?" I finally ask, ending our silent staring contest.

"I like to play alone sometimes."

I stare at him, taken aback by the answer. Soccer is a team sport. Most of my Lancaster teammates have never visited the sports center solo. But I thrive practicing alone. I can work on exactly what I want at my own pace. Yeah, I'm a part of a team, but I'm the one controlling my part. I've never met another soccer player—another athlete—who shared the same mentality. And the fact it's *Adler Beck* is shocking. He proved himself a long time ago. He doesn't need to be training alone on his day off. He could be in bed getting a blowjob. Admiring his accomplishments wasn't supposed to turn into being impressed by his work ethic.

"Oh," is the best response I can come up with.

"Unless you have more pointers?"

I have to work to keep the shock off of my face. Unless I'm hallucinating, he's teasing me. More than teasing me, he's *inviting me to play with him*. He's a household name considered to be the best soccer player currently playing in the world, and he's asking me, a woman who's never participated in a professional match, to play with him.

I'm suspicious of the timing. Of the challenge in my parting words, telling him I don't do rematches. I'm not interested in being entertainment, the American with accurate aim who talks back to him. Or worse, a hot girl he's trying to indulge because he wants to fuck me again.

I cross my arms back at him. "You're open to criticism now that we had sex?"

"I'm open to criticism now that I've seen you play," he replies.

I frown, recalling our first meeting and realizing he's right that I mentioned his shoulder before touching the ball. "You haven't seen me *play*," I tell him. "Just shoot."

His sunglasses are blocking his eyes, but I'm positive his gaze is aimed straight at me. "I've seen enough to know you're good."

Good.

I'm used to more effusive praise. Incredible. Astounding. Unbelievable.

But I doubt Beck compliments other players very often, and it's impossible to miss the sincerity in his voice. So, somehow, Adler Beck telling me I'm *good* overshadows all the praise I've received from coaches and teammates and guys in the past.

"You're not terrible yourself."

That comment earns me a full-blown grin. Fuck, he's good-looking. The kind of gorgeous that hijacks thoughts and hormones.

"So?" He tilts his head toward the empty fields.

I should say no. We had sex last night, which makes this more complicated. And I'm supposed to get the all-clear on my knee tomorrow, but I haven't officially been approved to play yet. An easy jog is one thing, playing with an elite athlete is another.

Risking my health—my career—just to spend more time around a hot guy is not a stupid mistake I'd normally make.

But ever since my first game at age five—the match my mom left during—I've always been the best player on the field. I've known it, and they've known it. The chance to not be, to be challenged by a player I've watched dominate on television, is too alluring to resist. Truly a once-in-a-lifetime opportunity.

"Let's play," I decide.

His expression doesn't change, like that was the answer he was expecting all along.

Competitiveness flares in response. I'm determined to shatter that indifference.

Beck heads toward the farthest open field and I follow, tightening my ponytail as I walk. I feel his eyes on me a couple times, but I keep mine trained forward on our destination. He pauses to unzip the bag he's carrying, pulling a brand-new soccer ball out.

I take the opportunity to wipe my sweaty palms against my shorts. The last time I played with or against a guy was back in elementary school. And I know for a fact that none of those boys grew up to be players of Beck's caliber. I'm confident in my own skills. But he's better than me—not to mention stronger and faster—and that disparity will be much more obvious today than it was during penalty kicks.

Adler Beck is good at soccer. *Really* good. The kind of talent that comes around once in a generation—once a century. His parents were both successful, but Adler Beck is revered on a staggering scale. He's beloved. He was winning international championships when I was attending high school games where half the participants were stoned, and he's far from a washed-up has-been at twenty-two.

I stride farther onto the field, expecting him to follow me. He does, dribbling as though it's second nature to him.

Beck doesn't ask me if I'm ready to play or stop for a face-off. He continues dribbling, forcing me to back up or else let him pass. His expression is completely transformed from how he looked when he first approached me, his movements as animated as his expression. It's a look I recognize—from seeing photos of myself playing. He loves this, loves it like I do. That's rare.

Beck grins as I do my best to mirror his movements. I've watched enough footage of him playing to know a few of his signature moves, but he's not exactly pulling out all the stops right now. We're barely jogging. When he finally spins to get around me, I'm ready. I snake my foot between his, knocking the ball into my possession. There's a nod of acknowledgment that lets me know I passed some test. It also tells me that he's still underestimating me.

We weave up and down the field, neither of us allowing the other to score, but guarding each other loosely. It's...fun. I can't recall the last time I played soccer so casually. Normally, I'm showing off—for coaches or teammates, to preserve the reputation I've carefully constructed; to smash expectations. To push myself. For the first time, it occurs to me that Beck might feel the same. The spotlight on him is a thousand times brighter. The expectations a thousand times higher.

He blocks me from scoring again, and this time I don't back off. I press him, broaching the invisible boundary that's been between us. Beck responds with a speed and dexterity I would have been expecting if he hadn't spent the past half hour lulling me into a false sense of complacency. He steals the ball back immediately, literally pulling it directly out from under me. I barely have enough time to twist so I can protect my knee before

I collide with the firm ground.

The impact doesn't hurt, but it's unexpected. Breath whooshes from my lungs like a deflating balloon.

I sit up, wincing when my shoulder throbs. It took the brunt of the hit.

Beck is standing next to me, the ball neatly trapped under one foot. I ignore the hand he holds out, standing on my own and gingerly rolling my shoulder once I'm vertical again. It'll be sore for a couple of days, but I'm fine. I shake my arm, then straighten my shoulders so I'm prepared to play again.

"You protected your knee," Beck states.

I pretend like I didn't hear him, focusing on the fresh grass stain on my shorts. *Damnit.* I did laundry yesterday, and these are my favorite pair.

"*Saylor.*" He says my name like it's a command, the current of authority impossible to ignore. "You protected your knee."

I blow out a long breath. "Yeah, I heard you the first time."

"You're injured?"

Most girls would probably find the concern in his voice sweet. I find it annoying. "I'm fine."

"What happened?" His voice is a muddling mix of confusion and concern.

I exhale again. "I sprained it a couple of months ago."

"A *couple of months ago*?"

I bristle in response to the incredulity in the question. "That's what I just said."

"Why the fuck are you playing on it?"

"Because *I'm fine.*"

Beck shakes his head. "You haven't been cleared yet, have you?"

"Not for full play. Pick-up in the park doesn't count. And you asked me to play with you, remember?"

He rakes a hand through his hair, surprised edging into anger. "I didn't know you were hurt!"

"I'm *not*. Jesus. They're clearing me tomorrow, okay? I'm all healed."

"Getting cleared tomorrow is not the same thing as being cleared now. You shouldn't have even been out running. You're risking your career; do you get that?"

Now, I'm pissed. "*My career* is none of your fucking business, Beck."

This was such a mistake. And not for the reasons he's saying. If my knee started hurting or if Alizée had told me something different last week, I wouldn't have stepped foot on this field. But my knee is in the same shape today as it'll be tomorrow when I get cleared. This wasn't the risk he's making it sound like.

We're athletes. Injury is always a possibility. That doesn't mean you stop playing.

"It would've been my fucking business if you'd just fallen on your knee and reinjured it. You should have told me."

Fine. Maybe he has a small point. But I didn't want him to look at me differently, look at me the way he's staring right now. Like I'm fragile. Like I'm not an equal. And I'm too annoyed— and embarrassed—to admit that now.

"Well, I didn't. Enjoy the rest of your day off—alone."

I spin and stalk off, showing off just how uninjured my knee is with each stride.

And this time, when he calls out my name, I don't turn back around.

Chapter 7

Bright sunshine makes me squint as soon as I step outside. I fish my sunglasses out of my pocket and perch them on the bridge of my nose.

I got the all-clear on my knee yesterday, and tomorrow's the first day I'll be practicing in Kluvberg's stadium with the rest of the Scholenberg attendees. Today is our weekly film day. There's a bus that shuttles us the dozen blocks to the stadium, but I prefer walking. I've grown surprisingly attached to the scenery of Kluvberg, and it's a beautiful day.

Halfway into my walk to the stadium, I spot a tiny coffee shop I impulsively decide to duck into. Right as I join the line, my phone rings.

I sigh when I see my sister's name flashing on the screen. I thought being in a different time zone than Hallie would mean fewer phone calls. Less frequent guilt trips. Thanks to my nephew's erratic sleep schedule, they've only become more common. There have only been a couple days she hasn't called since I arrived in Germany.

"Hello?"

"Don't sound too excited, or I might call more often," Hallie replies dryly.

"More often? I'm not sure if that's possible. I thought you'd stop mothering me now that you have your own child to take care of."

"He hasn't learned to talk yet. You're a chatterbox in comparison."

I snort. "As long as you're not calling to pass on info about more wedding shit you know I don't care about." That's been the main topic of our past few conversations.

Hallie doesn't deny it. "There's not much new to report. Sandra doesn't want to make a fuss. All that's left to decide on is the flowers."

"Not make a fuss? But you only get married—oh, wait, this is her third wedding, right?"

"Saylor," Hallie chastises, a clear note of warning resonating in her tone.

"I'm right. I distinctly remember her mentioning her second husband at your wedding."

"You 'forgot' her name when Dad told us they were engaged, but you remember she was married twice before?"

"She only said her name once. The second husband came up multiple times."

Hallie lets out a long sigh, but I can hear the amusement hidden deep beneath the irritation. "She's going to call you this week to talk about the bridesmaid's dresses, okay? I gave her your number."

"Hold up—I'm supposed to be *in* the wedding? What happened to not making a fuss?"

"He's our dad, Saylor."

"Barely," I mutter. Harsh, but true. I've had more meaningful conversations with the man who owns the corner convenience store one block from campus than my father. I haven't seen him in person since Hallie's wedding—two years ago. Haven't talked to him since he called to say he was getting married—four months ago.

"He's happy. Happier than I've seen him since..." She doesn't utter the words, but she doesn't need to. Our mom fills every silence, emphasizing the gaping hole she left behind. "Just don't...complicate things."

"Don't complicate things? That's your advice? Poor Matthew Jr. These are the pep talks he has to look forward to?"

Hallie ignores my heavy sarcasm. "I'm glad you brought that up. Let me grab him. It's good for him to hear his family's voices."

"Wait, what? Are you kidding? He's a baby. He's—Hallie? Hallie!"

The line is silent. I huff an impatient breath as I study the coral color I painted my toenails last night. Against the navy of my flip-flops, the color seems too garish. I should have stuck with the light blue I was originally planning on.

"Okay, he's on," Hallie helpfully informs me. The line sounds no different than it did before. The other end of the phone call is silent, supposedly with my three-month-old nephew nearby.

"Hello, Matthew," I state, feeling ridiculous. I have many talents. Conversing with a baby that's a dozen weeks old is not one of them. "Your mother has lost it." Hopefully Hallie is listening. "I think your father has more sense, but to be honest, I've never really talked with him enough to tell. You're lucky you can just sleep through everything now. Enjoy that. It gets worse. Soon you'll have to—"

"Are you going to order?"

I freeze.

I know that voice. That superior, silken tone with the slightest whisper of a German accent. A timbre that can caress one syllable and then send the next one hurtling through the air like a sharpened blade.

You're risking your career, do you get that?

The haughtiness still stings. Like I'm a child he has to talk down to.

Encountering Adler Beck in this small coffee shop is an unpleasant surprise—it's a *city*, for fuck's sake, how do we keep running into each other—but I don't allow my face to betray the slightest hint of emotion as I slowly turn to face him.

Damn him, he looks as gorgeous as usual. Smarmy and arrogant and sexy.

Arms crossed.

Eyebrows raised.

He's right behind me, a line of three other impatient people snaking out the door.

I spin back around to order my iced coffee without saying a single word to him. Except they don't sell iced coffee in Europe, according to the barista.

It takes several minutes to haggle a latte and a cup of ice. Those minutes feel more like an hour thanks to the self-assured athlete standing right behind me. Personal space or manners seem to be foreign concepts to Beck. The former faux pas would be a lot easier to enforce if my own body didn't enjoy the proximity quite so much.

I step to the side so he can order his own drink, fiddling with the display of granola bars next to the register. There's the same pulsing sensation resonating inside me I experience when I haven't exercised; like a caged animal. Except, I already went for a run this morning.

As I study the list of ingredients on one bar and listen to Matthew Jr. gurgle, I eavesdrop on Beck's conversation with the barista—well, on the tone of it since I can't actually understand a word of the German they're speaking. I guess she didn't spot him hovering behind me before because she's a shocked, fumbling mess now.

It sounds like he has to repeat his order three times, during which she drops five cups. I think she's going to faint when he hands her his credit card and their fingers brush. And yes, I'm the weirdo studying their interaction *that* closely. It takes longer for Beck to order than it took me to explain the foreign concept of cold coffee when it's eighty degrees outside.

Hallie picks the phone back up a few minutes later. "Hello?"

"Yep, still here," I say. "Did he spit up at one point?"

She sighs. "Yes. I thought you were going to hang up after a few seconds."

"That was an option?" Truth is, I probably would have done exactly that if Beck hadn't shown up and distracted me.

"It's more like your trademark, Saylor."

I prove her right by hanging up. At least I mutter a goodbye and "Good luck cleaning" first.

Beck finishes ordering and moves to the side. To my side. He's standing much closer than is necessary, even in a coffee shop this size. He's near enough for the distracting scent of his body wash, cologne, or maybe just his laundry detergent to wash over me. My entire body reacts to his proximity. I really need caffeine. Or anything to distract myself from the aggressively arousing aroma. Why can't he smell like sweat and dirty clothes?

"Is this the only coffee shop in the city?" I ask Beck testily.

"No. But this is the one closest to the stadium that I always stop at," he tells me.

"You're on your way to the stadium?"

"Yeah, why?"

"Why do you think? I'm supposed to be there in…" I glance at the clock hanging behind the counter. "Crap. Fifteen minutes."

"It's not that far of a walk," Beck drawls. "As long as your knee holds up."

I shoot him a dirty glare for that comment. "I got cleared, not that it's any—"

"Any of my fucking business?" There's a smirk on his face that makes my heart rate speed up for absolutely no reason.

"I overreacted, okay? Is that what you want me to say?" Before he can respond, I say, "Pretty sure you don't let other players decide if you're in any shape to play."

"Other players? No. *Doctors*? Yeah, I usually take that advice."

"Here's your ice and latte," the barista announces, not taking her eyes off Beck as she sets both in front of me.

"Thank you," I tell her, hastily dumping the hot liquid over the ice. I'm down to ten minutes now.

I don't really account for basic scientific principles as I pour. The ice crackles and hisses as the steaming coffee hits the stack of cubes before they promptly dissolve, sending the now lukewarm coffee over the rim of the plastic cup. I curse under my breath, glancing around for some napkins.

Beck's the one who snags a stack and sticks them underneath the cup to soak up the excess liquid. The exasperated sigh he releases takes away from what would otherwise be a thoughtful gesture, but I still feel obligated to mutter a "Thanks."

By the time I've cleaned up the mess I made and successfully transferred the rest of my coffee atop what little remains of the ice, Beck's drink is being handed to him. I'm tempted to ask the barista for more ice, but she looks frazzled enough already. Tepid will have to do. And of course, I'm now stuck exiting the coffee shop with Beck right behind me. I was hoping I'd be able to put at least a block between us before he departed for our mutual destination. No such luck. My only option to gain any lead would be to sprint. Doing so would put my coffee in peril again, not to mention I'm wearing flip-flops to show off my vivid pedicure.

Side by side it is.

Beck slips on a pair of sunglasses as we walk along, which makes him look a little more like an insanely attractive guy and less like a world-renowned soccer superstar. Meaning there are stares, but no autograph requests or photos. Getting kicked out of Scholenberg for trespassing on Kluvberg's field would be nothing compared to anyone at Lancaster seeing a photo of me with Adler Beck.

"It sounded like you were talking to a baby," Beck states, seeming oblivious to the attention we're receiving. The attention *he* is receiving, rather. I look like the poster child for American tourists in my baseball cap and the Statue of Liberty T-shirt Emma bought me. Or maybe he's just really used to it.

I make a face as some coffee sloshes onto the back of my hand. "Yeah, I was. He belongs to my older sister."

"Are you two close?"

"Yes. No. Sort of," I blurt, caught completely off guard by his question. What does he care if I'm estranged from my sibling or calling her every twenty minutes? I'm not a sharer, and I never encourage sharing. Which makes my next couple words a surprise. To me. "Are you?"

"Close with your sister? No, but I'd love to meet her."

Wow. He does have a sense of humor.

"She's married and inherited the morals in the family," I tell him. "I meant yours, *obviously*."

I'm giving away more than I meant to. Yeah, I know exactly who he is. Know his accolades and the basics of his background. But I've mostly pretended like I know nothing about him, and it's a facade that's cracking more with each interaction.

"We get along fine." A vague answer to rival my own.

I don't press, turning my gaze ahead to watch the imposing shadow of Kluvberg's stadium appear in the distance.

"She's younger," he states.

"What?"

"My sister. She's younger than me."

"Okay...not sure if that's her fault."

His tone implies it is.

There's a ghost of a grin. "*Obviously*. But it means she gets all of the perks and none of the pressure."

"What do you mean?"

"She's never played football. Never had to deal with the expectations. I mean, do you have any idea what it's like to walk on the pitch and see your parents sitting there, expecting you not to fuck up their legacy?"

"No, I don't," I reply honestly. "My dad's idea of exercise was walking from the couch to the fridge for a beer. He couldn't win a gold medal for anything except 'Absentee Parent of the Year.'" Yeah, didn't mean to say that much. I never talk about my dad. Thankfully, Beck doesn't know me well enough to know that.

"Is your sister close with your dad?" he asks me.

Rather than *none of your fucking business*, what I *should* say, I reply, "Closer than me. Especially since she got married, had a kid."

"Maybe the same thing will happen to you."

I snort. "Doubt it."

"You don't want kids?"

"I don't want distractions."

"Plenty of successful athletes have families."

"Plenty of *male* ones, maybe. Your contribution to the whole making-a-human endeavor would be thirty seconds of fun. Not nine months of nausea and vomiting and swollen ankles and sore boobs and then pushing a watermelon out. Maybe, once I was retired, I'd consider it. But we women also have this fun thing called a biological clock, so I probably couldn't get pregnant by then."

He's just staring at me.

I smirk. "Glad you brought it up?"

"My mom made it work," he replies, startling me. "She took a season off after having me, then started playing again."

"For how many more seasons?"

"Three. She tore her ACL, had to have surgery. Chose to retire, then had my little sister Sophia."

"And how many seasons did your dad take off?" I ask.

"None."

"Exactly. Just admit it's different."

"I never said it wasn't different."

"You know, most guys are terrified about knocking someone up. Not asking girls if they plan on having kids."

"I'm not most guys."

"Does that mean you're planning to have a soccer teams' worth of kids?"

"A *football* team, you mean?" he responds. "I don't know. It would depend on what she wanted."

I open my mouth to respond but snap it shut when a security guard steps out of the booth to the right of the gate, interrupting the fence that surrounds Kluvberg's famous stadium. I was so focused on our conversation, that I didn't realize we were practically atop it. The whole reason I walked was to appreciate the scenery, and I missed most of it.

Beck lets out a rapid stream of German and then the man responds, giving him a friendly smile as he waves both of us through the gate. Every other time I've entered the stadium this way, the guard made me swipe my temporary badge. *And* go through the metal detector.

My phone rings right as we enter the stadium. "Fuck," I grumble, and Beck shoots me a curious glance. "Hi, Dad." What is *he* doing up at this hour? He doesn't have an infant to feed.

"Saylor. How are you?"

"I'm fine. Is something wrong?"

"No, everything is fine. I just—"

"I'm running late for practice. I'll call you later." I hang up, immediately creating a list of possible reasons for his call. We mostly communicate through Hallie. The wedding can't be off though, or she would have just told me.

Beck, grabbing my phone from my hand, snaps me out of speculating.

"What are you doing?"

He doesn't answer, just hands it back to me. When I glance down, I have a new contact.

"In case you reconsider the rematch," he tells me.

"What about my knee?"

He smirks. "You got cleared, remember?"

Beck's gone, turning to the right, before I can respond.

I head in the opposite direction, down the hallway toward the room we meet in for film. A dark-haired girl is approaching the stairwell from the opposite end of the hallway. Annie? Ali?

I'm terrible with names, and I can't recall hers. It's the second week, but I haven't been spending as much time with everyone else, thanks to my knee.

"Hi, Saylor," she says as we draw closer. Her voice is sweet and shy, with a distinctive British accent. And she knows my name, which makes it worse; especially since she's the first person aside from Ellie to acknowledge me here.

"Hey," I reply. "Ready for film?"

She lets out a little laugh. "Not looking forward to it, to be honest. I'd rather be out on the pitch. Though I'm guessing you get that more than anybody."

"Yeah," I agree.

"How's your knee?"

I slant a side glance her way as we enter the stairwell. It's an innocent question that could also be construed as fishing for weakness. Injuries are ordinarily kept under wraps for just this reason, but not participating in anything more strenuous than sit-ups was bound to raise some suspicion. Not to mention the knee brace I've been wearing around the house. "All clear."

"Glad to hear it," the girl replies. Her tone sounds genuine, but I don't fully drop my guard. "My cousin plays in the States. Said you're absolutely insane on the pitch."

I don't say anything at first, just keep walking down the stairs. False modesty has never been my forte. "You must not be terrible if you're here."

"Saylor!" We emerge from the stairs, and Ellie's waiting in the hallway. "Hey, Alexis."

I was right about the A, at least. "Hey," I reply.

"What happened to you this morning?" Ellie asks.

I shrug. "Went for a walk. Got a coffee." I hold up the mostly empty cup as evidence.

"All right. We'd better get in there." Ellie heads toward the door that leads to the same room we met Coach Weber in the first day.

The seat formation is the same, too. So is the silence when I enter with Ellie and Alexis behind me.

Coach Weber is already at the front, setting up the projector next to the whiteboard she's drawn out a play on. I feel her steely gaze on me as I make my way to one of the few free folding chairs. Ellie plops down on the one beside me. To my surprise, Alexis takes a seat on my other side.

It feels good to have another ally, especially since I doubt our scrimmage tomorrow will earn me many new friends. None who aren't on my assigned team, at least.

But I'm not appreciating Alexis's presence as Coach Weber starts the first video or listening to her point out strategy on the field.

I'm thinking about my conversation with Adler Beck.

Chapter 8

"**K**luvberg is going to be at the stadium today," Ellie informs me as she takes a seat opposite me at the table.

"What?" I glance up from my phone, where I'm texting Cressida.

She nods. "Uncle Franz said they have some sort of exhibition match for charity coming up, so they're changing up their practice schedule this week. The team wants to play on the field before the game or something."

"Huh."

Ellie rolls her eyes. "Of course you'd be this nonchalant about it. *Adler fucking Beck* is going to be on the same field as you, Saylor."

I don't tell her it won't be the first time. Or the second. "He's not the only player on the team, Ellie."

"Uh, he sort of is. I got to meet him at an event with my uncle last year, and he lives up to the hype."

I shovel another bite of yogurt and granola in my mouth to avoid responding.

"Ladies, let's go!" One of the Scholenberg organizers appears in the doorway, and we're hustled out of the house to the van idling at the curb.

I drop my bowl off in the bin for used dishes on the way.

A knot of trepidation tightens in my stomach as the van rolls to a stop in front of the massive stadium. I twist the hem of the sweat-wicking tank top I'm wearing, attempting to settle my nerves.

Ellie catches the movement from her seat beside me. "Your knee will be fine." She pats my thigh comfortingly.

I smile in acknowledgment of her assurance, although I'm acutely aware my old injury is not the reason I'm anxious about being here.

I should be excited. This is my first time practicing with the team in the stadium—my chance to show off what I can do.

And all I'm thinking about is what Beck might do if I see him.

I need to get my fucking head in the game. Focusing has always been effortless for me. Soccer has always been my primary focus. I've never had to prioritize it, because nothing else has ever trumped my interest. But Beck and the sport are intertwined; I haven't figured out how to untangle them.

"Saylor?" Ellie says. I look up to see all the rows before us have cleared. I'm blocking her in and holding the rest of the van up.

"Sorry," I mutter, standing and shuffling out of the cramped seat to walk down the aisle.

I need to pull it together. Immediately. I've never let a guy distract me before. I have no intention of starting to allow it now.

This is my first time not heading down two floors. Since the stadium isn't currently being used for professional play, we're in the visitor's locker room. I've played at plenty of wealthy universities, and Lancaster didn't spare any expense with its own facility, but I'm acutely aware that Kluvberg's stadium is on an entirely other level when I step inside the locker room.

My trips here before—both clandestine and invited—didn't involve any of the luxury tucked beneath the cement risers and metal seats. Every surface gleams.

"Hurry up, ladies." Coach Weber appears, looking like her usual stoic self. It puts an immediate end to any dawdling. One girl bangs her shin trying to pull her socks on faster.

Once I'm suited up, I follow Ellie out of the locker room and toward the main tunnel.

Each step teases more of the field until it's fully revealed, spread out in a pristine green carpet. Just like Ellie said, FC Kluvberg is huddled at the opposite end of the pitch. My gaze flies to one figure first.

I tear my eyes away from him when Coach Weber starts talking, splitting us up by our positions for warm-up drills. My insides feel fizzy; electrified. The thrill of being back out on the field is a potent rush, and it washes away the weird effect Beck's presence seems to have on me.

None of the exercises are anything I haven't done before, and I'm relieved my muscle memory is perfect. My feet follow the expected motions automatically, and I revel in the satisfaction of executing each drill perfectly.

Finally, Coach Weber blows her whistle. "Scrimmage time."

I'm the recipient of more than a few side glances. Everyone else has already played together...except me.

I shift from foot to foot, competitive fuel spreading through my warmed muscles as I pull on a yellow pinny to signify the group I'm assigned to.

We don't get a chance to strategize with our temporary teams before the scrimmage starts, but it doesn't matter. My teammates want to use me. To test me.

Alexis passes to me as soon as she receives the ball, and I'm ready.

I sprint full speed down the field. Kluvberg has cleared off the pitch, but a few players are still standing along the sidelines. Stretching, drinking water, talking with trainers. Maybe watching. Who cares? Not me. I'm focused on nothing except sending the sphere I'm dribbling down the field into white netting. I spin around a defender, feint left, and find an opening that leads directly to my goal—to *the* goal.

I'm cleared for full activity. No restrictions. No conditions. No limitations. I send the soccer ball flying with as much power as possible.

It soars, straight and direct.

Faster than any of the defenders. Faster than the goalie. I know it's a perfect shot as it separates from my foot, but it's no less gratifying to watch it smash into its destination.

I had something to prove today.

I just did.

Yellow pinnies mob me, today's assigned teams creating temporary truces amidst competition. I accept the praise with a grin. That goal meant a little extra. The women I just sprinted around and scored against? They're some of the top athletes in the world.

Not only can I still play, but I'm also still *good*.

Ellie's the last one to melt away, following a final squeeze. She's beaming, and I'm touched by her support, even knowing it's exacerbated because of my strange behavior earlier. She thinks this is a triumph over an injury that could have ended my career, and it is. But it's also a less noble victory.

I was showing off.

For everyone else who scored a coveted Scholenberg invitation.

For Coach Weber.

For Adler Beck, who's leaning against the advertisement-splashed divider that surrounds the perimeter of the field. Watching our game with an inscrutable expression and crossed arms.

Play resumes in our scrimmage. Time always passes differently when I'm playing soccer, rushing by in measures of kicks and sprints rather than seconds and minutes. I score two more goals before Coach Weber blows her whistle, signaling the end of this morning's session.

"Nice job, everyone. Get changed, then meet out front for the team lunch."

"Team lunch?" I whisper to Ellie as we head back toward the tunnel. All I want is a shower and maybe some ice cream. Pretty sure any goodwill with the yellow team has already faded. If anything, there's more animosity aimed my way now that I've proven I'm a threat.

"Forget about lunch," she says. "You kicked ass, girl!"

I smirk. "What did you expect?" I ask her, pulling my pinny over my head and tossing it in the hamper outside the locker room. "Adler Beck is not the only one who lives up to the hype."

"Um, speaking of which, I saw him staring at you," Ellie tells me as I stop at the water fountain.

There's a weird squeeze in my chest, and I immediately regret mentioning him.

"Spectators tend to watch the player with the ball," I reply as nonchalantly as I can.

"I'm just saying. You're totally his type."

"What type is that?"

"Gorgeous."

I shrug off her compliment. "I'm just here to play soccer." The words are assured. Based on Ellie's disappointed sigh, she believes me.

I wish I was as certain. I didn't need Ellie to tell me Beck was watching me; I noticed it myself. Concerning, considering that means my focus wasn't fully on the scrimmage the way it should have been.

Ellie continues into the locker room to change, while I finish filling my water bottle. I take a long sip, glance up, and then still.

Beck is standing at the opposite end of the hallway, his intense gaze aimed straight at me. My body instantly reacts, my stomach clenching and my heart rate accelerating. He nods to the left, then opens the doorway there and walks inside.

I glance around. The rest of the girls are already in the locker room, and I think Coach Weber and the rest of the staff are still out on the pitch cleaning up. There's no one around.

I suck in deep breaths as I walk down the hallway, second-guessing each step. I haven't texted Beck since he gave me his number, because I meant what I told Ellie: I'm here for soccer. Because I don't do distractions. Or I *didn't* do distractions, I guess I should say. Because I'm willingly walking toward one right now.

The space I step into is some sort of equipment room. It's tidy but tiny, the guy leaning against the wall immediately drawing all of my focus.

"Nice office."

He straightens as soon as I speak, taking a step toward me. The expression on his face scares me a little. It's the same animation and ferocity I noticed when we played together, except there's no soccer ball in sight. Worse than Beck's reaction is *mine.* The way my equilibrium shifts like the ground beneath me is suddenly unsteady. The way the throbbing ache between my thighs is making me wet.

"Enjoy the show?" I smirk, throwing some bluster up like a shield.

He says nothing, just takes another step closer. Another. And another. Until the ridges of my spine are pressed against the cold cinderblock wall.

Beck kisses me with no preamble. No flirting. No shots. He kisses me like this is just something we *do*, his hot, firm body covering mine and his talented tongue invading my mouth.

And I surrender, my muscles relaxing even as awareness hums. Even as the ache of arousal turns into a persistent, almost painful pulse.

His lips leave mine to trail down my neck, his tongue swiping across sensitive skin.

"I guess that's a yes," I manage to gasp.

His chuckle is low and throaty, raising goosebumps on my arms.

"Do you know what I was thinking about when I was watching you play?" he asks. His hands are flirting with the hem of my shirt, making it really hard to think straight.

"World peace and what you ate for breakfast?"

Now his palms are spanning the small of my back, touching the elastic waistband of my soccer shorts. I can feel the length of his dick pressed against the inside of my thigh, straining against his blue FC Kluvberg shorts. Rather than relief about his reaction, it makes me even more nervous. I don't want to know kissing me while I most likely stink turns him on. He's *Adler*

Beck. He knows more models than a fashion designer.

"No. Doing this," he says in a low, sexy rasp that further ignites the warmth spreading through my body.

I shiver when his hand slides to the front of my shorts. "I'm all sweaty."

"I don't give a fuck. So am I."

"I'm not shoving a hand down your shorts."

He grins. "I wouldn't complain if you did."

I snort. "I know you wouldn't."

His finger circles my clit through my cotton underwear. I bite my bottom lip to contain the moan that wants to escape, my hips jerking forward involuntarily.

"You're the sexiest fucking thing I've ever seen."

I taste the metal tang of blood, my teeth digging deeper than I realized. It's not a line. My bullshit detector is excellent. And he's not talking about how good I look leaning against a cinderblock wall. He's not turned off by my dedication to soccer, not incredulous or annoyed by it the way other guys have been. I'm pretty sure he's *attracted* to my commitment, not just that incessant training means I have a great ass.

It's unexpected. If I'd had to guess, I would have said he went for women who stroke his ego. Who are in awe of him. Who would happily pop out however many kids he wanted.

One finger pushes inside, then he stretches me with two. I exhale, instinctively rocking into his hand. My breathing quickens, desperate inhales matching the motion of my hips as I try to get even closer.

I didn't lock the door. I'm not even sure if it has a lock.

Anyone could walk in and see us like this. See me riding Beck's hand. If it was someone from Scholenberg—someone who knows who I am—then I know mutters of *slut* would join the murmurs of *bitch* that echo around the house. It would elevate him in everyone's mind. The guy who can get any girl he wants, even a heartless, motivated one like me. And they'd look down on me, the girl who let a pretty face distract her.

Even the risk of those repercussions isn't enough to douse the fire kindling inside of me. Beck has the type of presence you couldn't forget you're in if you tried. Being the sole recipient of his full attention is intoxicating. Beck's focused on my face, noticing every shift as he fucks me with his fingers.

"*Fuck*, you're wet," he says. His palm hits my clit, and this time I can't stifle the moan.

Pretty sure the narration of my fantasies is going to have a German accent from now on. I don't think I'm ever going to be able to unhear the sound of Adler Beck swearing as he touches me, each syllable wrapped in layers of lust.

I'm not even touching him. I *haven't* even touched him.

Heat is unfurling inside of me, spreading so quickly and thoroughly I couldn't douse it even if I wanted to. It's a natural, biological reaction, but I'm mentally focused the same way I was last time. I'm aware of—actively thinking about, actually—who is touching me. I'm not just enjoying the pleasure. I'm responding to *him*.

My thighs start quivering, the pressure building to a crest I know means explosion is imminent.

"Say my name."

I'm in a haze, my eyes slow to meet the blue ones bearing into me.

His fingers stop moving, holding me right on the precipice as fire simmers low in my stomach. "*Say my name*, Saylor."

I squirm, trying to force some friction. The hand that isn't between my thighs lands next to my head, erasing the distance that was already basically nonexistent.

"Beck." I spit his name out like I'm talking to a teammate.

He smirks. "You close?"

"I *was*."

His grin only grows in response to the obvious irritation in my tone. But his fingers start moving again, and that's quickly all I care about. I'm barely aware of the gibberish coming out of my mouth, but I know I'm saying his name a lot, and not in the annoyed way I did before. I come with a cry he covers with his mouth, kissing me as I squeeze the shit out of his fingers. My toes curl inside my sneakers as my entire body lights up.

I tell myself it's this good because I scored a hat trick during practice. That it has nothing to do with him.

But I think it's a lie.

The wall is supporting most of my weight as I enjoy the lax state my body is in. I'm still sweaty and disgusting, but I feel *good*. So, so good.

He's backed off a couple of inches. There's enough space between us for me to touch his chest. To drag my hand down his abs and then lower, until I'm palming the outline of his erection. Blowjobs are not my favorite—uncomfortable and unpleasant— but I'm weirdly unbothered by the prospect of getting on my knees for him. Another way to prove mine is, in fact, fine.

Before I can decide my next move, he takes another step back, forcing my hand to fall.

My eyebrows knit together. That's a first.

"I have a meeting with Wagner." The name sounds familiar. I'm pretty sure he's Kluvberg's head coach.

Then he's turning and walking away, obviously intending to leave.

"Wait, what? What the hell was this?"

"You're welcome," he calls over one shoulder.

The door slams shut behind him a few seconds later. I stay in place against the cinderblocks, trying to figure out what the heck just happened. He sought me out, made me come, and then kinda turned me down. Technically, I was the only one who got anything out of our encounter, but I feel like he gained the upper hand somehow.

I stare at the shut door, feeling unsettled instead of satisfied. I came, but our encounter feels…incomplete.

I think he did it on purpose.

And I have no idea what to make of that either.

Chapter 9

My phone buzzes with an incoming call from a Georgia number while I'm lying on my bed scrolling through social media. My stomach drops like I just missed a step.

It's Sandra, calling about the bridesmaid dresses. Or a telemarketer.

But I'm almost certain it's Sandra, thanks to Hallie's warning. And very tempted to not pick up, but I know it'll only prolong the inevitable. This wedding is happening.

I exhale, then answer. "Hello?"

"Saylor! Hi! It's Sandra. How are you? Is this an okay time to talk? I can call back later or tomorrow or—it's Sandra." She laughs awkwardly. "I already said that, didn't I?"

She's nervous.

I don't have any problem with Sandra, the person. I have a problem with Sandra, the woman my father is marrying. She's caught in the crossfire of our shitty relationship, and my solution has been to avoid her as much as possible. That won't be an option at their wedding.

"I'm not busy," I tell her. "And I'm fine wearing whatever, so no worries about the dresses. Just pick out what you like best."

"Oh. You, uh, know why I'm calling?"

"Yeah. Hallie mentioned it."

There's a pause. "Oh."

I guess I shouldn't have mentioned that Hallie called to prep and lecture me. But it's not like Sandra doesn't know my older sister is more of a mother to me than she ever will be. She tries to smooth over the tension between me and my dad, but I know she's not oblivious to it. What he's told Sandra about the aftermath of my mom leaving is his business. I'm not going to justify the state of our relationship to someone who's essentially a stranger.

"Well, I'd love if you picked out your own dress. I'm not the fashionista you girls are, and I want it to be something you're comfortable wearing. Hopefully something you can wear again, even."

I roll my eyes, wondering if she's recycling one of her old wedding dresses or if she bought a new one. Bridesmaid dresses aren't meant to be worn multiple times, but I'm not going to argue with Sandra about it. Even if it means I'm getting stuck with homework.

"Okay, fine. I'll order something."

Maybe Sandra expected me to argue, because there's a long pause before she says, "Great," like she was scrambling to come up with something.

I'm so uncomfortable it feels like ants are crawling across my skin, listening to the empty air.

"Well, I should—"

"How is the—"

We speak at the same time, then stop simultaneously.

"How is the program going?" Sandra forges ahead first.

"It's great."

"Oh, that's wonderful." Her voice is warm and relieved, and it makes me feel weird.

Sandra's nice, and I sort of hate that about her. This would be way easier if she wasn't sweet and pleasant.

Two adjectives that no one would use to describe me, so I decide to proactively end the conversation before I slip up and say something I shouldn't. "I need to get ready for practice, actually."

"Oh, of course." If Sandra suspects we have Sundays off, she doesn't let on. "Enjoy your practice. I'll, uh, I'll let your father know things are going well."

Or he could call and ask himself, I think, then remember he did call the other day, and I never called him back.

"Okay," I say. "Bye, Sandra."

"Bye, Saylor."

I hang up first, then stare at the screen. I should call my dad back, but I'm supposed to be getting ready for practice. Plus, I'd rather put off that conversation.

Instead, I pull up the number I'd decided not to use.

SAYLOR: Hey.

Lame opening. And Beck gave me his number, but he doesn't have mine. So I shoot off another text, because I'm sure he gets a lot of random messages from girls.

SAYLOR: It's Saylor.

I shake my head and toss my phone toward the bottom of the bed before lying back down to stare up at the ceiling. I'm a fool. What the fuck am I—

My phone buzzes, and I sit up like I was just electrocuted.

BECK: Hey.

He replied. Replied *instantly*. I gnaw on my bottom lip, deliberating. Warring with myself. Waffling between *no distractions* and *it's my day off.*

I can have some fun, I decide. Just because he affects me doesn't mean I'm losing focus.

SAYLOR: You busy?

BECK: About to go for a hike.

BECK: Want to come?

A dirty response comes to mind first. This was basically a booty text. But a hike sounds better than lying on my bed.

SAYLOR: I'll meet you outside the park in twenty minutes.

I don't want to risk anyone from Scholenberg seeing us together. They're all still oblivious to the fact Beck and I have even spoken, and I'd like it to stay that way.

BECK: Okay.

I climb off my bed and start sifting through my suitcase to try to find a cute outfit. My phone buzzes with a new text right after I've shrugged into a white T-shirt.

BECK: Wear a swimsuit.

I raise my eyebrows, intrigued. Then quickly change into the blue bikini I brought before pulling the same shirt back on with a pair of jean shorts. Since we're hiking, sneakers seem like the best option. I pull my hair up into a high ponytail, add a swipe of mascara, stick my phone in my back pocket, and then head out into the hallway.

Alexis is sprawled out on the couch in the living room when I walk downstairs, sucking on a popsicle. "You're headed out?"

"Yeah."

"Are you wearing a bikini?"

"Uh, yeah. Laundry day. See you later." I continue outside before she can ask any more questions.

Beck is already waiting at the front entrance of the park, leaning against a shiny black sports car parked along the curb.

I snort as I survey the sleek lines. "Of course this is the car you drive." It practically screams *I'm a sexy millionaire.*

"You don't like it?" Beck asks, feigning disappointment. At least, I think it's false.

"I didn't say that." I smirk when I catch him checking out my boobs. The bright color of my bikini is visible through the thin cotton, and I'd be lying if I said that wasn't a factor when I decided to wear it.

He says nothing else; just straightens and heads for the driver's seat. I climb into the passenger side.

Beck's car smells like him. Masculine and musky. With a rich undertone of expensive leather.

I study the spotless interior. My car is always littered with hair ties, empty water bottles, and spare shin guards. Beck's looks like it was driven off the dealership lot twenty minutes ago.

"Where are we hiking?" I ask.

"You'll see."

I snap the seatbelt into place, surveying the fancy dashboard. "Isn't it blasphemous to drive an Italian car when half the country considers you their *Kaiser*?"

"Wow. You learned *one* German word."

I roll my eyes. Admittedly, I'm not doing much to dispel the self-centered American stereotype. Every other Scholenberg attendee is bilingual. At least.

"And it's a lot more than half," he continues.

"I can't believe your ego fits in this little car."

One corner of his mouth curves up, and I experience a flash of victory at the sight.

"It's common knowledge that Germany produces the best soccer players and Italy builds the best cars," Beck tells me.

"So you didn't buy one of the most expensive cars in the

world just to show off how much money you make?" I don't know the exact number, but I'm positive it's a lot more than I—or any other female athlete—will ever make.

"I didn't buy this car."

"You stole it?"

He snorts. "I did an ad campaign for them. The car was part of the deal."

"Must have been one hell of an ad. Did you have to show your dick?"

"If I had, I could've gotten a lot more than this car."

I roll my eyes. "Your penis isn't *that* impressive."

"Impressive enough for you to text me about a *rematch* on your day off," Beck shoots back.

I'm not sure what to make of the fact that he knew I was texting him looking for sex and stuck with suggesting *hiking* instead. Based on the way he was just looking at my breasts, attraction isn't the issue.

"Whatever," I reply.

His lip curves higher.

Beck drives the same way he does everything else: aggressively and assuredly. Not that I'm complaining. We're outside the city limits in minutes, flying along mostly empty roads as civilization disappears behind us.

When he exits off the highway, we end up on another tree-lined road. Beck pulls the car over in a dirt parking lot ten minutes later and climbs out, stretching. I scramble out the passenger side to survey the surroundings. It's just a lot of greenery. Trees, shrubs, saplings, grass, weeds. We could be in the wilderness anywhere.

I'm underwhelmed, and I know it's obvious on my face. "Why a swimsuit? To *sunbathe*?"

He shakes his head. "There's a lake nearby."

"Nearby?"

The only blue in sight is the clear sky stretching overhead.

Beck points upward to a peak that looks *really* far away. "That way."

"You didn't mention this was an *expedition*."

"If you don't think you can handle it, then we can head back."

Adler Beck does not know me very well if he thinks I'm going to back down from a paltry challenge like scaling a mountain that looks an awful lot like Everest. Who even knew Germany had mountains that size? Not this American.

"We drove all this way." I have no idea how far, because Beck drives like he's taking part in a car chase, but the lack of anything but nature in sight suggests we're pretty far from the city.

Beck smirks. I narrow my eyes.

Forget him not knowing me well.

I totally just got played.

I follow Beck toward the base of the mountain. I would have forged ahead first, except there's no obvious entry into the wilderness, no clear path or signs. I grew up in a small southern town where the preferred outdoor activity was sipping sweet tea on the front porch. My experience with hiking is *very* limited.

As in, nonexistent.

The pavement turns into damp dirt covered with decaying leaves and spotted with fresh sprigs of growth. The scent of moss and sunshine flavors the warm air. With each step I advance deeper into the woods, my apprehension grows. I'm uncertain about following him, but I comfort myself with the thought that this is Adler Beck. He's beloved. Famous. Rich. Search parties will be sent out. If I stick with him, they'll rescue me as well.

The climb isn't terrible, the incline gradual. A leafy canopy above blocks the brunt of the sun. Birds chirp and chat.

Beck seems completely at ease amidst the trees.

"Don't you live in the city?" I finally ask.

"Right now, yeah."

"What do you mean, right now?"

"I'd like to get a place with land at some point, like my parents'. I didn't grow up in Kluvberg."

"Where did you grow up?"

"The town is called Altenhain. It's small, about an hour outside of the city. They had a place in the city too, but my dad prefers the quiet. He gardens."

Two homes. *He's* rich *rich*, I remind myself.

"I grew up in a small town too," I tell him.

"Yeah?"

"Yeah. I sorta hated it at the time. Sometimes I miss it now."

"Does your family still live there?" he asks.

"My dad and sister do, yeah."

"What about your mom?"

"She's gone."

That's the wording I've found to be most effective at shutting down this topic of conversation. Not *she left* or *she's dead*. She's *gone*. Simpler and cleaner.

But I'm not surprised when he asks, "Where?"

Or when I admit, "I don't know."

"I'm sorry."

I swallow. "Thanks."

The light ahead grows brighter and larger as we continue trekking through the forest, and then we're through the trees, overlooking the view we've come all this way to see.

"Whoa," I say, taking in the scene spread before me.

I used to think there was no nicer view than an expanse

of green only interrupted by stark white lines, but this is crazy impressive. A sight like I'm only used to seeing as the automatic screensaver my computer generates. The kind that makes your breath hitch and your eyes blink to ensure it's not a mirage.

"Not bad, huh?" Beck comments, clearly enjoying my reaction.

Translucent, viridian water pools in a hidden oasis guarded by craggy peaks. Tall and proud evergreens line the water's edge, dotting the landscape with darker dashes of green.

"What is this place?"

Beck rattles off a series of German words. He grins at my confused expression. "It's a national park."

He leads the way down closer to the shore. I follow closely behind, yanking off my sneakers and socks once we hit sand so I can dip my toes in the water. It's colder than I expected it to be. If not for the relentless sunshine beaming down on us, it would be unpleasant.

With one hand, Beck yanks his T-shirt over his head. It's the first time I've seen him shirtless. In person, at least. The carved torso I'm staring at has been photographed more times than the Mona Lisa. I bite the inside of my cheek as I watch his abs clench. He leans over to take his shoes off, the powerful muscles of his shoulders bunching and rippling.

I pull my top off too, enjoying the feel of his eyes on me. My nipples pebble beneath the spandex of my bikini top, and it has nothing to do with the cool water lapping at my ankles.

"We're swimming?"

"Up to you." He wades into the lake, not even flinching at the temperature. In a flash, he's dipping below the surface, emerging a few seconds later.

His muscles look even better with water dripping down them.

I step onto the shore to pull off my shorts, then head back in, forcing myself not to react to the shock of adjusting to the cold.

Beck shoots me a dangerous grin as I trudge deeper; a devilish expression that makes my skin flush despite the cool water.

I submerge up to my collarbones in an attempt to numb myself to the cold, my ponytail floating behind me. New droplets of water appear in Beck's darkened hair with each step forward, glinting in the sunshine. Just as I'm about to lose contact with the sandy bottom, I draw even with him. I reach up and tug the elastic out of my hair, letting the strands tumble free and fan around me.

We stare at each other as cold water saturates the ends of my blonde strands. I feel the hair swirl around me with each move I make.

"You're different than I expected," I blurt.

One brow rises. "What did you expect?"

"Nothing. I didn't think I'd meet you while I was here, honestly. I just…I don't know. Never mind."

I don't know how to put this fragile feeling into words. How being around him feels different than spending time with anyone else. How he's the cocky, talented superstar everyone sees but entirely different.

Beck lets his fingertips trail along the surface of the water, leaving symmetrical ripples behind. "All I know about you is that you're American, you're decent on the pitch, and you've broken a lot of hearts."

I splash him. "I'm more than decent. *Good* was the word you used, and I've never broken anyone's heart."

He raises both eyebrows now.

"Fine. Maybe I've bruised a couple of egos," I acquiesce.

Beck laughs at that, a husky sound that cuts through the cold.

"And you're hardly one to talk."

He doesn't deny it. "I was young and horny and girls were... interested."

I snort. "Was?"

"It got old."

"No strings sex? You might want to save that for a girl you didn't fuck in your club's supply closet."

"How old were you when your mom left?" He asks the question with no preamble, not even attempting to smooth the transition. Like he wants me to notice he's asking, not slowly realize we've switched topics.

"Five. And if you're going to try to turn this into some therapy session, don't."

"This isn't a therapy session. It's a date."

I blink at him. "What? No, it's not. It's...we're...this is exercising. Training."

"We're standing in water."

"This is *not* a date," I tell him firmly.

He shrugs, neither arguing nor agreeing. The ambiguity sparks some panic inside of me.

"Why didn't you let me touch you last time?" I ask, suddenly needing some answers about our...whatever this thing is.

"Why do you care that I didn't?" he replies.

I huff a sigh.

"You got off."

"Yeah, I know. *Thanks*."

Beck smirks at me, but it slowly melts into a serious expression that has my heart slamming against my ribs. "We don't have to keep score, Saylor," he tells me.

He swims away before I can respond.

I *always* keep score.

Because I hate losing.

Because I like to know where I stand with people, and especially with guys.

And because Adler Beck is the furthest thing from a sure bet.

Chapter 10

The next few weeks fly by. I guess that's what happens when you attend an elite soccer camp that believes in only one day off a week. It's exhausting in the best way, since playing is how I'd choose to spend every hour if I could.

My fellow Scholenberg attendees are tired, too. Even Olivia is too drained to make as many snarky comments. Each day, Coach Weber finds a new way to challenge us. It's a lot, and none of the other girls are sneaking around with a German soccer player on top of an already draining schedule.

Ellie is definitely suspicious about how I disappear early some mornings and in some evenings. Most Sundays.

I'm not sure why I keep lying to her. I like Ellie. She wouldn't tell anyone about Beck if I asked her not to. But if I tell her about him, I know she'll have questions. Questions I've never minded answering about a guy before. Questions I don't know how to answer in this instance.

My phone vibrates on the table that sits beside Beck's king-size bed, startling me from the relaxed haze I was enjoying. I went for a run first thing, showered, and then ended up here. We had sex—twice—and I haven't moved since. I was very close to dozing off.

Reluctantly, I drag my arm off the cloudlike mattress to grab my phone. It's a text from Ellie asking where I am.

I'm running out of excuses.

I tell Ellie I'm shopping for some gifts to bring back to the States, then toss my phone away.

"Something wrong?"

I glance over at Beck, who's lying beside me.

"No. Everything is fine," I answer, then focus on his body. We've had sex so many times, I've lost track. But Beck, naked, isn't really one of those sights you get used to.

There are other guys I've slept with more than once, but those were sporadic hook-ups spanning weeks, sometimes months, and always corresponding with some huge bash on campus. Not almost every day for weeks.

Beck mutters something in German and climbs out of bed. I sit up on my elbows. Most of the time he sticks to English around me, but there are moments when he'll revert to his native tongue. Beck pulls on a pair of athletic shorts and a Kluvberg T-shirt, and I mourn the loss of the view I was enjoying.

"What are you doing?" I ask.

Beck glances at me, and I don't miss the heat that flares in his gaze. Is it good for my ego that he still seems just as fascinated by my body as I am by his? Try fantastic.

"I forgot it's Sunday," is his explanation.

"Okayyy..." I reply, letting a question linger after the word, because that really didn't answer mine. "Are you religious or something? Because I'm not sure God would approve of how we spent the past hour."

Beck chuckles, shaking his head. "No, I'm not religious. My family does brunch once a month."

I would have been less surprised if he said he was going to church. "Oh."

"Do you want to come?"

"What?" I blurt. "To your family brunch?"

Beck nods.

"Will—uh—will your parents be there?"

Normally, meeting two professional soccer players is an opportunity I would jump at, but they're not just retired footballers. They're Beck's parents. I've *never* met a guy's parents before. And it's the fact that I *want* to, that I'm curious about meeting the people who raised him, that has warning signals singing out in my head.

"At their house? Yes, I think so."

I choose to ignore his sarcasm. "Won't that be weird?"

He shrugs. "Doubt it. I've brought girls over before."

Other women would probably wilt in response to that comment, but it prompts a rush of relief for me. I don't want this—us—to be remarkable to him.

"Okay, sure. Attire is casual?" I ask, nodding to his own outfit.

"Wear whatever you want," Beck replies in the indifferent tone most men have when it comes to fashion.

"Well, I only have one outfit, so it shouldn't be too hard of a choice," I respond, hopping off the bed to pull the dress I wore here back on.

I get dressed and follow Beck out of his apartment into the hallway. His apartment that's twice the square footage of the house I grew up in. Beck's door is the only one in the hallway. He has the top floor all to himself.

We enter the elevator, and as soon as Beck taps the down button, we drop rapidly. I expect to see the marble lobby, but the door opens to a garage instead. I follow him over to his car, which is parked in a prime spot to the left of the elevator doors.

"So, anything I should know?" I ask, as he pulls out of the garage.

"Hmm?" He keeps his eyes on the road, which I guess is a good thing.

"You said you've brought girls home before. How did they act? Am I supposed to mention soccer, not mention soccer? Is there a—"

"Just be yourself."

I eye him dubiously. That's one thing no one has ever said before. I'm used to being told to tone it down.

"And if you bring up soccer, call it *football*," he tells me.

I roll my eyes before glancing out the window.

The drive takes about an hour. I don't say anything as we roll through the open gate and along a cobblestone driveway, too busy gaping at the estate we're driving toward. I shouldn't be this shocked. Beck's apartment slash penthouse must have cost several million dollars. I know he and his family have money. Lots of it. But I'm used to modest buildings. The three-bedroom bungalow my parents bought when they got married, a dorm room, and the house I share with Cressida, Anne, and Emma that seems to need repairs constantly.

Not...this.

The Scholenberg house I'm staying in is designed in what I've come to recognize as traditional German style: brightly colored and half-timbered. But the mansion before me is much more dignified looking, both symmetrical and stately. There's a courtyard of topiaries and statues that wouldn't look out of place at a royal residence cradled between the two wings of the house that jut out to the left and right. Beck parks at the very edge of the cobblestones.

"So, is your house behind the palace?" I ask, only half kidding.

He grins. "Come on. We're late."

I follow him through the courtyard and glass-paneled doors into the marble entryway, feeling *very* out of place. One major I tried out before settling on public relations was architecture, and I feel like I've stepped inside one of the chateaus or palazzos we studied floor plans of.

There's a flurry of German, and a statuesque blonde girl who looks to be a few years younger appears, stopping at the bottom of the staircase.

"Hi, Sophia," Beck replies.

The blonde switches to flawless English. "You brought *another* girl to brunch?" She sounds thoroughly displeased about it.

At least Beck wasn't lying about his past plus ones.

"I thought you said you weren't coming," Beck replies.

"Plans change. People don't, apparently." She huffs out an annoyed sigh before holding a hand out to me. "Hi, I'm Sophia Beck."

I see the family resemblance. She has the same pronounced cheekbones and blue eyes as her older brother.

"Saylor Scott," I respond, shaking her firm grip.

"You're American," she states.

I nod. "Yep."

"Are you a model?" she asks me.

I laugh. "Ha. No. I play soccer. I mean, football."

Her eyebrows rise. "Really?"

"Really."

"Are you any good?"

"Yes," I respond immediately.

She laughs. "I like you, Saylor Scott."

I glance at Beck, then clear my throat. "Thank you?" Ten seconds ago, she was frowning at me.

"Do you not own any nice clothes?" Sophia asks Beck, wrinkling her nose as she stares at his shorts.

"Do you not own pants?" he retorts, studying Sophia's admittedly short dress.

"If I wanted your opinion, I would ask for it, Adler," she retorts.

Coming here was worth it, just to see Beck get scolded by his little sister. This is the first time I've heard anyone call him that, but I guess it makes sense. It would be strange to call someone by your own last name.

Based on the wry twist of his lips, Beck notices my amusement.

"Papa's out on the terrace," Sophia says. "Go ahead."

"Why aren't you coming?" Beck asks.

Sophia glances toward the door, shifting from foot to foot. "I might have invited Karl. He'll be here any minute."

Beck sighs. "I thought you were—"

"You do not get to have an opinion on my love life after what I've had to hear about..." A quick glance at me, and then Sophia switches to German.

Beck replies in his native language, and I'm lost, feeling like I'm stuck watching a foreign film without subtitles.

A new voice suddenly joins the conversation, and I turn to see Erika Lange—now Erika Beck—enter the imposing entryway. Beck's mother isn't in the same strata of notoriety as Christina Weber, but she's close. She still has the lean build of an athlete, and she's stunning, in an ethereal, timeless way. It's obvious where her children got their good looks.

Her tone is softer than Beck and Sophia's, but both of them fall silent as soon as she speaks. Then Erika notices me and says something else in German. Beck jumps back in, then Sophia laughs and says a few words.

I wish I could get a transcript of this conversation to plug into an online translator later, but they're speaking too fast for me to catch so much as a single word to look up.

"Hello. I'm Erika," Beck's mother says, switching to English and giving me a warm smile.

"I know," I blurt.

"You're American," she observes, echoing her daughter.

I'm guessing it means the girls Beck referenced earlier have all been German. Or at least European.

"Yes. That's why I don't know German. I mean, I didn't think I'd need to know it. I'm just here for a few more weeks." *Stop talking!* I scold myself. "I think it's a great language, though," I add.

Beck snorts, and I elbow him. Unfortunately, I think the contact hurts my arm more than his torso.

"Are you here on a university trip? Or on vacation?" Erika inquires politely.

"I'm attending Scholenberg."

Both Sophia and Erika's eyebrows rise.

"I was just planning to play socc—football. That's why I didn't learn any German. I wasn't expecting to be around so many…Germans."

There's a second snort beside me, and I jab Beck a bit harder this time.

"I'd love to hear more about Scholenberg," Erika remarks. "I haven't seen Christina in ages. She's still managing the program, yes?"

"She more runs it like a drill sergeant, but yes," I reply.

Erika laughs. "Let's head out to the terrace. It's so nice out, I thought we'd eat outside."

We walk through a tastefully decorated living room, leaving Sophia in the soaring entryway to wait for the mysterious Karl.

The terrace is covered by a wooden lattice woven with bright greenery that shades the table and chairs beneath it. It overlooks a broad stretch of grass framed by tall, trimmed hedges that block any neighbors.

Seated at the head of the table is a tall, silver-haired man who must be Hans Beck. He raises his head from the newspaper he was reading when we approach, his gaze flitting between his wife and son, then landing on me. He snaps the paper back into its original fold and tucks it under the place setting.

Beck and Sophia favor their mother in appearance. Their father cuts an intimidating figure, his domineering presence similar to Beck's, but it's a rougher one. His face is tough and weathered, and what remains of his original hair color is darker than the rest of his family's, combed back neatly to emphasize his hewn features.

"Hello," Hans greets me in a gruff tone.

"Hi, Mr. Beck." I hold out a hand to shake his. "I'm Saylor Scott."

"Hans is fine," he replies, studying me closely.

I shift nervously under his scrutiny. I don't know what is wrong with me. I'm not easily starstruck or intimidated.

"Your home is beautiful." I sweep a hand toward the yard like the Becks aren't aware their back lawn looks like it could be featured on the cover of a gardening magazine.

"Thank you," Erika says graciously. "Saylor is attending Scholenberg," she informs her husband.

Something that looks like respect glints in blue eyes the same shade as Beck's. "Congratulations. That's a competitive program."

"Thank you," I respond. "I'm a competitive person."

There's a small twitch of his mouth, and I'm fairly certain it's as close to smiling as Hans Beck gets. "The best athletes are," he replies.

I smile.

Sophia walks out onto the terrace, a guy with light brown hair right behind her. He's handsome in a sloppy way that's been carefully curated. His T-shirt has the faded logo for a band on it, and gel glints in his hair, suggesting the messy look he's sporting is purposeful.

Erika greets him first. "Hello, Karl."

There's a pause. "Karl," Hans grunts.

I watch Sophia level Beck with a sharp glance.

"Hi, Karl," he says.

I look at Karl. He's already staring at me; in a way more appropriate for a poorly lit bar than a family brunch. "Hey, Karl," I say. "I'm Saylor. Nice to meet you."

His eyes widen when he registers my American accent.

"I'm hungry," Beck says abruptly. "Is the food ready?"

"Yes, it is." Erika lurches into motion. "Take a seat, everyone."

Hans sinks back into the same chair he was seated in before. I round the edge of the table to sit on the side facing the house. There are six chairs, but only five place settings. Obviously, my attendance wasn't planned upon. I start to take the seat without a plate or silverware, but Beck grasps my elbow and pushes me down a spot to the chair that's already set.

"Take that one," he instructs.

"Wow, so you *can* be a gentleman," I whisper to him as I do as instructed.

Beck smirks as he sits in the chair next to me. "You like when I'm not a gentleman."

Yeah. I do.

"Saylor?"

I glance at Sophia, surprised she's talking to me instead of focusing on Karl. "Yeah?"

"I was wondering if you'd like a tour of the house?" she asks.

"Sure," I reply, standing and walking back around the table to the doors that lead inside. As we enter the living room, I hear Hans ask Beck something in German.

"This is the living room," Sophia announces, spinning in the center of the plush rug.

The color scheme is muted, and seems like it was crafted by a professional interior decorator. It's almost too perfect; the light grays, pale pinks, and dark blues meld together seamlessly. There's an oil painting hanging above the fireplace. Below it a series of photographs are displayed on the mantle, several staged family portraits and a few candid shots. One catches my attention. A sixteen-year-old Beck stands between his parents, beaming. I know he's sixteen because of the stadium in the background, the German flag draped across his shoulders. It's a snapshot of the moment following his breakout performance that won his home country a World Cup.

"Do your parents play football?" Sophia asks, following my gaze.

"No," I reply, laughing a little at the thought. "I don't think either of them have even seen a game."

"Not even yours?" Sophia asks, sounding surprised.

"Nope," I respond, keeping my tone light. "Did you ever play?"

Sophia scoffs. "No."

"Did you want to?"

"Not really." She glances at the photo. "They're a hard act to follow."

We head to the library next, followed by the sitting room, dining room, and an actual conservatory. Sunshine streams in through the glass, illuminating all the thriving plants.

"I feel like I'm in a game of Clue," I tell Sophia.

She laughs. "I haven't played that game in forever."

"It's my favorite board game," I admit. "I get sort of competitive. None of my housemates back home will play with me anymore."

"We're totally playing after brunch," Sophia decides, grinning.

"It's a deal," I reply, smiling back.

We walk back through the entryway, past a doorway that must lead to the kitchen, based on the flash of shiny appliances, and end up back on the terrace. Breakfast has been served. Beck's eyes dart up from his full plate to meet my gaze as soon as I step out of the house. Erika's taken the seat at the other end of the table, and I make my way around the back of her seat to sink down beside Beck.

"All good?" he asks me in a low voice.

I nod, studying the array of food spread before me. I tend to be a picky eater, and I could characterize my relationship with German cuisine as more misses than hits. There are some familiar dishes—waffles and what looks like a cheese tart with cherries—but the rest are foreign. There's some sort of smoked fish topped with a swirled cream, a green soup sprinkled with crispy brown croutons, a salad scattered with seared meat, and rolls with crispy bacon and sauerkraut peeking out.

No pancakes or eggs in sight.

I take a small helping of everything, trying to be polite.

"I ran into Headmaster Schneider yesterday," Erika states as she eats some of the green soup. "He's looking forward to the camp, Adler."

"Good. I've got four guys coming," Beck replies.

"Herrmann?" Hans asks.

"And Ludwig."

Hans nods in approval.

"What camp?" I inquire.

Everyone looks at me, but Beck is the one who answers. "It's for kids at the football academy I attended. We do a weekend clinic once a year. It's next Sunday."

"They trust you to teach children?" The words are out before I think them through.

Erika doesn't fully manage to hide her smile behind her water glass. "We're always looking for more volunteers, if you're interested, Saylor."

"Oh, um, I don't really—I've never coached anyone before," I reply.

Sophia pipes in with "If Adler can manage it, I'm sure you can."

Yup, totally set myself up for that.

I surprise myself by saying yes. Lancaster's soccer teams had to attend a youth clinic last year, but it was more a PR stunt for the university than anything. All we did was pass out water bottles and set up cones.

"Wonderful," Erika says.

"You play football?" Karl speaks for the first time since

Sophia's tour.

"Yeah, I do. You?"

"No. I'm more into music. I have a band."

"Do you play an instrument?" I ask, in an effort to be polite.

Beck sighs beside me. At first, I think it's in annoyance; but when Karl launches into a twenty-minute description of his skills on guitar, his talent for writing songs, and his lofty musical goals, I realize it was with dread. This is obviously a soliloquy the Becks have all heard before. Even Sophia looks bored.

After we finish eating, Sophia darts inside and returns with a familiar cardboard box.

"A board game?" Beck asks skeptically.

"No one invited you to play, Adler," Sophia says.

Hans and Erika rise to clear plates, and I start to as well. "We've got them," Erika says, flapping her hands toward me in a motion to stay seated. "You kids have fun."

"There's nothing fun about Clue," Beck mutters.

"It's Saylor's favorite game," Sophia states.

He looks at me. "It is?"

I nod, then shrug. "I like mysteries."

"Fine, I'll play." Beck sighs.

I don't miss the way Sophia glances between us, and I know she's misreading Beck's agreement. She sets up the board, deals the cards, and then we start to play. Despite his initial complaints, Beck is not the least enthusiastic player at the table. Karl has him beat by a mile. I guess all of his cards by my third turn, mostly because Karl keeps flashing them at me. Either he truly has no idea how the game works, or it's his attempt at flirting with me in front of his girlfriend.

Beck navigates Mrs. White, known as Frau Weiss in the German edition, out of one room, and I let out a long sigh. "You shouldn't have done that."

He glances at me. "I just did."

"But it did happen in the Conservatory."

"No, it didn't."

"How do you know?" I reply.

"Because I have the card, so I know you're just messing with me."

"Hmmmm," I say, adding a question mark next to the room listing on my sheet.

"Or am I messing with you?" Beck adds, sending me a smirk as he moves the white figurine forward.

I narrow my eyes at him.

I have to show Sophia one of my cards on her next turn, and I walk all the way around the table just to show her the illustration of a gun to ensure Beck can't peek. Out of everyone at the table, I really just care about beating him.

She shakes her head as I head back to my seat beside him. "Anyone ever tell you you're competitive?"

"Multiple times a day," I assure her.

And it's echoed again when I'm first to correctly guess the suspect, location, and weapon. Karl leaves shortly after the game ends, to get ready for a gig later.

"I think I'm done with him this time," Sophia states.

"Great," Beck says dryly. He grabs the Clue box and heads inside.

"I need to meet some new guys," Sophia tells me. "Clubbing! We should go clubbing next weekend!"

"Uh, sure," I reply, not sure what the proper response is. Meeting Beck's sister didn't occur to me when I agreed to brunch. And hanging out with her sounds...complicated. Sophia doesn't appear offended by my uncertain response, bouncing back inside while I follow.

Beck and his parents are in the marble foyer. Goodbyes get exchanged, and Erika tells me how much she's looking forward to the youth camp next Sunday. I experience another spasm of unease, remembering I committed to that. Sophia gives me a farewell hug.

I smile, and then we're back outside.

"Sophia likes you," Beck comments as we climb into his car.

"I like her," I respond glibly. "She wants to go clubbing together next weekend." I study Beck's face closely.

His expression barely flickers as he turns down the cobblestone driveway. "Not surprised," he says.

We roll through the gate and then hit cement. Beck accelerates accordingly, and soon we're speeding along back toward the city.

"Thank you for inviting me today. It was nice," I say. The words sound stiff and formal. "Your parents are really nice. It's nice you're so close with them."

Nice is the only adjective I'm capable of coming up with, apparently.

Today was a mistake. Not because it went poorly or I didn't enjoy myself, but because it complicated everything even more.

"Did you call your dad back?" The question is soft, not accusing.

"No. I didn't." I swallow. "My dad, he—he didn't deal with my mom leaving very well. None of us did, really. But Hallie and I were just kids. He was the adult. He was supposed to hold it all together, and instead he fell apart. By the time he started acting like a parent again, I didn't need one. Or want one, at least. We don't really talk and...and now he's getting remarried." I sigh. "He called the day I found out I got into Scholenberg, which kinda ruined the celebration for me. Not that he even knew what it was. I've only met Sandra—his fiancée—once, at my sister's wedding."

"How long have they been together?"

"Three years," I admit. "I don't go back home much."

"Why not?"

"It's weird. There are all these memories of the past. Before my mom left. After. My sister has forgiven him. She went through all the same shit I did, and now she's just *fine* with it all. Married with a kid, going over to his house for dinner like we were always one big happy family. I'm the resentful one stuck in the past, just getting more bitter as they move on with their lives. I don't want to deal with it, so I just avoid it. It's unhealthy, I know."

"Just because you had the same childhood doesn't mean you have to respond to things the same way. You're not the same person as your sister. I mean, look at me and Sophia. We had the same upbringing, and we're totally different people."

"I guess. I'm good at soccer. But I'm bad at feelings. And all the emotion crap."

It's an explanation. A warning too, because the lines between us are getting really blurry.

A pause, then, "You're fucking fantastic at football, Saylor."

"Thank you," I say quietly.

Unexpected warmth covers my left hand.

I focus on the German countryside flashing by, trying to shake the claustrophobia crawling over me. I just told Beck things I've never spoken aloud. Never told anyone.

This feels like more than a date. It seems like a relationship, and a boyfriend will not get me to the Olympics or on the national team roster. Signed to a professional team after graduation. Won't help me accomplish any of the lofty goals I've set for myself.

Even if I were open to having a boyfriend, Beck is the worst possible candidate for the position. Not just because he's famous. And lives in a foreign country. And goes through women at a dizzying pace. And a poster of him hangs in the bedroom across from my own.

Adler Beck is a terrible idea because I suddenly know with absolute certainty that if I let myself, I could care about him.

Like him.

Maybe even love him.

So, I slide my hand out from underneath his and pretend the pines we're passing are the most interesting ones I've ever seen, so I don't have to register his response.

Chapter 11

A door down the hallway slams. I swear, then spit out the toothpaste in my mouth. I'm texting with Emma about our lease terms. There's a week-long gap between the end of Scholenberg and the start of Lancaster's preseason. Despite the fact that we rent the house year-round, our landlord is being difficult about me moving back in a week earlier than everyone else. Supposedly because of the repairs we've been bugging him about, but I couldn't care less about the house's issues, for once. I'd rather hire a lawyer than have to go home. Emma promises to straighten it out, so I shut off my phone, then rush out of the bathroom.

I'm late for morning practice. The van must already be here, because the floor is empty.

I rush downstairs, the last one to climb into the van. Olivia rolls her eyes when I pass her.

It's sweltering today, well into the nineties. It's a relief to file into the dim room in the depths of the stadium where our film sessions take place. Coach Weber is standing at the front of the room, drawing out lines on the whiteboard next to the projector screen.

Normally, I dread film sessions. I understand the importance of them strategically, but I'd much rather be out on the field playing. Today is an exception. I sink down on the cool plastic chair with a relieved sigh. The slightly damp, musty scent permeating the lowest level of the stadium has never been my favorite, but the cooler temperature more than makes up for it. I redo my ponytail, scraping up the sweaty strands sticking to the back of my neck with the rest of my hair.

The film session lasts for two hours, then Coach Weber announces we're heading outside. Total silence follows. I wasn't kidding when I told Erika that Coach Weber is a drill sergeant. We file in line like dutiful soldiers out into the oppressive heat. The air hits in a wave of warmth like an oven door that's just been opened.

"Shit, it's hot," Ellie mutters beside me.

"You think?" I murmur back.

Our warm-up routine is a series of sit-ups, planks, burpees, and push-ups. I'm soaked with sweat by the time we finish the last set.

"Center line," Coach Weber barks. "Usual teams."

The silence holds, but Alexis huffs out a disbelieving breath to my right. Her face is the same shade as strawberry lemonade. We all follow instructions, taking our assigned positions on the field. I turn to see one of the assistant coaches wheeling out two giant trash bins. That's new.

"Are those for vomit?" Alexis asks, sounding aghast.

My stomach churns at the thought. I've thrown up during practice before. *Not* an experience I'd love to replicate. But when the bins are close enough for us to get a glimpse inside, I don't see a generic black bag. Instead, it's packed with color.

The bins are filled with a rainbow array of balloons.

"First team fully soaked loses," Coach Weber announces in the same authoritative tone that normally encourages running at an inhuman pace.

"Wh—what?" Ellie stutters beside me, and I'm equally at a loss.

Everyone else is just as taken aback, but we've all had listen to our coach drilled into us to the point that it's permanently impressed. Alexis grabs a yellow balloon; I take a blue one, and soon everyone has one in hand. I roll the sphere in the palm of my hand, feeling the liquid contents squish and contract underneath the latex skin.

My shirt is suddenly sticking to me with more than sweat, and I scowl at Olivia, my Scandinavian nemesis. Never mind the fact that the water actually feels good. I send a balloon back at her, but it hits Sydney instead, who glares at me. I shoot her a satisfied smile, and the game descends into chaos. Balloons are suddenly flying everywhere, exploding into strips of colored plastic and sprays of clear water. I don't know which side gets fully drenched first, and I don't think anyone else does earlier. We don't stop until the bins are empty.

Ellie flops down on the grass, and I lie down beside her to stare up at the perfectly clear sky.

"This is my favorite memory on this field," she says, giggling slightly.

I open my mouth to agree, then close it.

It's not mine.

Chapter 12

've just gotten out of the shower on Friday night when there's a loud knock on my door.

"What?" I call, tightening the towel around my torso. The door opens, and Alexis pokes her head in.

"Get ready, we're going to dinner and then out," she tells me.

"I was thinking of staying in tonight…" I hedge.

In truth, Sophia texted me, asking about going clubbing. Beck must have given her my number.

Alexis smirks. "Yeah, right. Cancel whatever other plans you made. Everyone's going. No excuses."

I roll my eyes. "Fine."

I text Sophia requesting a rain check and then get ready. I go for a smokey eye effect with my makeup and make the effort to curl my hair. Then slip on the strapless dress I picked out for the soccer formal last spring. It offsets my tan nicely.

An awkward silence descends when I enter the kitchen, the counter littered with alcohol. I'm honestly a little impressed by my strait-laced teammates.

Ellie breaks the quiet that follows my appearance. "Okay, that's everyone! Let's go."

We all head out of the house, where a line of several taxis is waiting. I climb into the last car with Alexis, Ellie, and a quiet girl named Alice whom I've never spoken to before but know has a mean header. Ellie spends the entire drive talking nonstop, making me think she pre-gamed hard. I might be the only sober one in the group right now.

The restaurant we stop outside is trendy and upscale. The exterior is half-timbered but painted black so that the texture differential is barely noticeable.

Based on the monochromatic exterior, I'm expecting a minimalistic interior as well. The variety of decoration inside is a bit of a shock. The floor is covered with woven rugs boasting intricate patterns. The walls are paneled with light wood. Hundreds of twinkling lights cover the ceiling, giving the space a warm, homey glow. The furniture takes the longest to absorb. It's an eclectic mix of color, weave, and, if I had to guess, century.

There's a communal feel to the large space. Long tables run the full length of the room, surrounded by chairs spanning every possible shape and color you could imagine. It's reminiscent of my high school cafeteria, but none of the food being eaten looks anything like the glop I ate for four years. I study some plates as Olivia talks to the hostess. There's some sort of fish with sectioned citrus, roasted chicken with a fancy sauce on top, and what looks like seared beef with jalapeno.

I'm distracted from my perusal when a familiar voice says, "This is a surprise."

I turn to see Coach Weber appraising our group, wearing the barest hint of a smile. It's the first time I've seen her in anything but a polo and soccer shorts. She's dressed in a pink sundress. A few middle-aged women hover behind her, looking at our large group curiously.

Since I'm the only sober one, I take the lead. "Hi, Coach."

"Scott. Ladies," Coach Weber responds, swiping her gaze across the girls behind me. "Doing some team bonding?"

"We're practicing a different kind of shots."

Ellie snorts. Alexis hisses my name.

Christina Weber has an epic poker face, but I think I catch a lip twitch. "Don't set any records. I talked to Erika Beck earlier. You're in high demand this weekend, Scott." I nod. "Have a good night, ladies. I'd recommend the chicken." Coach Weber heads for the door with her friends close behind.

"What was she talking about? Erika *Beck*?" Ellie whispers to me.

"I'll tell you later," I reply as we follow the hostess over to the large section of seats waiting for us.

Our group of thirty takes up most of the table. I opt to follow Coach Weber's suggestion and get the chicken. It's good. It comes with a cucumber salsa dressed with salt, lime, and mint, which pairs perfectly with the gin margarita I ordered.

A couple of hours later, we pile back into a series of taxis to head to our next destination.

I'm having more fun than I expected to. It might have taken six weeks, but there's finally a bit of camaraderie. Maybe it's leftover goodwill from the water balloon fight. Maybe it's because we're so close to the end. Whatever the reason, it was a relief to be plied with questions about playing in the States rather than being beamed by glares at dinner.

Taxi assignments remain the same, so Alexis, Ellie, Alice, and I are all crammed together, heading to our next destination.

"Why did Coach bring up Erika Beck?" Ellie asks.

I sigh. Was I hoping she was too drunk and distracted to remember? Abso-fucking-lutely. "I'm helping out at a youth camp on Sunday."

"A youth camp?" Alexis asks. "You?"

I should probably be offended, but I'm not. It was a surprise to me that I agreed too. "Yeah."

"Wait—but what does that have to do with Erika Beck?" Ellie questions.

The cab pulls up outside our destination before I have to answer. It's a club called Submarine that sits right along the canal. Unlike my outing with Natalie and London, the bouncer waves us right inside the packed space.

The inspiration for the name is evident as soon as we enter. The entire far wall is made from glass, and the dancing lights of the club reflect off the calm water. It's brighter inside than I expected, with Edison bulbs hanging overhead that fit with the industrial building.

Since I'm in the front of the group, I automatically turn toward the bar first.

When I push through the crowd of people to get to the long counter, I'm met by familiar blue eyes.

Beck and I stare at each other for a long moment. I recognize several of the guys behind him as other Kluvberg players and hear a few gasps from the other girls in my program as they stop behind me, recognizing the men as well. Despite practicing in their stadium six days a week, as far as I know, I'm the only one who's encountered a Kluvberg player aside from the one day their practice partially overlapped with ours a few weeks ago.

"Scott," Beck states. His tone is inscrutable, so I have no idea if calling me by my last name is an attempt to pretend he doesn't know me or to tease me.

"Adler," I reply, just as emotionlessly.

A ghost of a smile flitters across his face. "I thought you were going out with Sophia tonight."

Okay, so we're not pretending not to know each other.

"I had to cancel. We're...uh, bonding." I wave a hand toward my companions vaguely.

Beck doesn't say anything at first. He just studies me, letting his gaze drop to what I'm wearing. Azure eyes darken to near-navy.

"Have fun," is all he says before walking toward a sectioned-off area raised slightly above the rest of the club. His teammates follow.

I turn to the bartender and order a drink, suddenly in desperate need of something to do. I have no idea who chose the venues for tonight, but I'm currently two for two on people I wouldn't choose to run into on a night out. Yeah, the entire team was at that restaurant, but I've always prided myself on being the player coaches could count on. Coach Weber didn't seem overly enthused about my participation in the camp. Is it because she correctly guessed it means I'm involved with Beck?

But I'm more concerned with the most recent encounter. I had no intention of anyone knowing about my involvement with Beck. With one bar-side run-in, any hope of that is gone.

"You know *Adler Beck*?" Olivia asks incredulously. All the girls in the group are staring at me expectantly.

"We've met a couple times," I reply casually. We play in the stadium plastered with his face. Running into him there is believable, right?

"Are you interested in him?" Olivia raises one eyebrow. A challenge is dancing in her brown eyes.

"No," I lie. Or maybe it's not a lie. *Interested* seems like too small a word.

"So...you don't mind if I go talk to him?"

"No," I repeat. I don't think Beck will take her up on it, but I don't care either way. Or rather, I *shouldn't* care. Same thing.

I turn back to the bar to grab my freshly made drink. A dark-haired guy sidles up next to me and begins flirting. The first few sentences are in German, but after one clueless expression, he switches to English. I think he says he's a medical student, but I'm only able to catch every other word he says thanks to his accent and the noise in here. He's very attractive, and I'm much more focused on that than whether he's a doctor or a dropout.

He asks what I'm doing here, and when I tell him I play "football," his eyes light up.

I should see it coming, but I don't.

The next ten minutes are spent gushing over Adler Beck, and any attraction seeps away like water in a sink with an open drain.

I down my drink like a shot as he continues to praise Beck's performance last season. He's not even asking for my opinion. He's just the sort of insensitive male I usually like to shred for sport, but tonight I'm not in the mood.

Once my glass is empty, I tell him I need to use the restroom. I'm gone before he acknowledges the excuse. All my Scholenberg companions have drifted away from the bar by now. Alexis and Ellie are crowded in one of the round booths along the edge. I start toward them, only to be stopped by a sharp tug on my wrist.

Angry blue eyes meet mine.

"What the fuck are you doing?" Beck asks me.

"Walking," I answer.

He growls, an actual low vibration of anger. "You shouldn't be talking to guys like that."

"Guys like *what*?" I spit out in response. "Hot guys? German guys? Guys who learn a girl plays soccer—sorry, *football*—and start going on and on about how incredible Adler Beck is? You're going to need to be more specific."

He raises one eyebrow. "You were talking about me?"

"You done being jealous?"

"I'm not jealous."

"You're mad at me for talking to another guy. That is the textbook definition of jealousy."

"You're in a strange city and you know two German words. Leaving with some random guy is stupider than playing with a bad knee."

"I can take care of myself, Beck," I retort. "I've been doing it for a long ass time. And you didn't seem to mind when that *random guy* was you."

"That's all I am? Some random guy?"

"I..." I glance around, realizing I'm not imagining the feel of eyes on me. "People are staring."

He shakes his head, then drops his hand. "What are we doing, Saylor?"

"I don't know." I whisper the words, so low I'm not sure if he even hears them.

We've avoided—or I've avoided, and he's followed my lead—discussing it since the hiking trip he claimed was a date and I told him wasn't. We have a lot of sex and he knows me, understands me, better than most people. Better than *any* person, possibly. But he's not just an athlete, he's a celebrity. We might have both grown up in small towns, but most similarities end there. I'm just a girl trying to succeed in a sport because I can't not. Because it's everything to me, and failing would be devastating.

Hearing the question spoken out loud is a relief. It's also scary.

"Okay," Beck says, clenching his jaw as soon as the word is out, as if to restrain more from exiting.

"Okay," I repeat. But it doesn't feel like we've actually agreed about anything.

I'm prepared for this to end. I've *been* prepared for this to end. But I know it'll still hurt when it does, which has never happened before.

"I'm headed out," he tells me.

This is when I should put some more space between us. Find some guy in here who doesn't follow football, has never heard of Adler Beck, and leave with him. Show all the girls I'm here with that Beck means nothing to me. Prove it to myself.

Instead, I ask, "Do you want company?"

He studies me for a few seconds, and I'm momentarily terrified he's going to tell me no. To decide this thing between us is messy and unnecessary.

Finally, he nods.

I glance around, making eye contact with Ellie first. She's out on the dance floor with a few of the other girls, including Alexis. I tilt my head toward Beck and she nods, receiving my silent message. I mouth *Sorry* too, hoping it's a blanket apology for leaving early and for not telling her about Beck. Who I'm having sex with is none of her business, but she's my closest friend here. I'm sure she's hurt I didn't share.

We draw even more attention as we leave, plenty of drunk people recognizing Beck and calling out to him. He keeps a protective palm on my lower back, guiding me through the commotion surrounding us.

The valet pulls up his car immediately, and we climb inside. Charged silence fills the vehicle as we drive along, the tension suffocating in the small sports car. It feels like the first time we're doing this, but my body is also desperate, craving the release it's come to expect from him.

"Is it always like that?" I ask Beck as we reach his street.

"Always like what?"

"You can't go to a club without people freaking out about it?"

I was too shocked about seeing him again to really register the reactions to him the night I lied my way into his nightclub. I was mostly amused by the barista's response in the coffee shop. Most of the time we've spent together has been alone in his apartment. Or in the park. At his parents' house. I know he's famous. But I've been sheltered, I guess, from the reality of what that means in his daily life.

"I usually stay in the private section," Beck replies, not really answering my question.

"Does it bother you?"

"It's part of playing."

It's worth it, he means. The attention he receives from playing soccer—from being really good at playing soccer—is worth it. He prioritizes it, the same way that I do.

I don't ask any more questions as we wait for the door leading to the garage to open. A few minutes later, we're parked, climbing out of the car.

Beck follows me to the elevator and then down the hallway to his front door. He unlocks it, gesturing for me to head inside first. I find the light switch by feel, illuminating the entryway to his apartment. Kick off my heels and smooth the creases that collected on my dress from riding in the car.

"Nice place."

He raises an eyebrow, and I mentally shake myself for the asinine comment. I'm trying to act like this is natural and normal, and for me, that's unfamiliarity. This isn't supposed to be a place I've visited before—so many times I can find the light switch in the dark because I know exactly where it's located.

"Want a tour?"

I smirk, relieved he's playing along. "Only of the bedroom."

He erases the distance between us in one stride. As soon as he kisses me, I know we won't be making it to the bedroom.

The heat that hasn't faded flares between us again as he hauls me tightly against his body. It's a relief to shut my brain off and fall into sensation instead. To stop worrying about what I should say to him and what I should keep to myself. To stop resenting myself for being so cold while also lecturing myself for losing focus.

I pull away first, sinking down to my knees and attacking the zipper of his pants until his cock juts free. I swirl the flared tip with my tongue before sucking him deep into my mouth. Beck groans my name, his hand slipping into my hair as he fucks my mouth with rough, greedy strokes. I dig my nails into his thighs, leaving crescent-shaped marks behind before moving my hands down to cup the heavy weight of his balls.

He spits out a long stream of German as I pull away and then run my tongue along the underside of his erection. I don't understand a word of it, but the tone is impossible to miss. Dark and decadent, like rich chocolate and smoky liquor.

I've done this before—to him—enough times I've lost count. I know what will make him pull my hair harder. What will make him thrust deeper. What will make his abs clench. I do everything I can to make sure he loses his mind, relishing the power that comes along with it. Imagining the way this looks, the two of us fully dressed in his entryway like two horny teenagers racing an imaginary clock. Like we couldn't wait another second to do this even though we have all night.

The clock isn't completely imaginary, though. We have an expiration date, and I never thought that would terrify me the way it does.

Tears burn my eyes as he hits the back of my throat, my thoughts distracting me enough that I lose the pace. I take a deep breath through my nose and swallow, satisfied when I taste saltiness. His hips jerk, a few final, fast pumps, and then he's filling my mouth with hot liquid. I continue swallowing, another first of mine he's claimed.

My thong is soaked, my pussy wet and throbbing. Seeing Beck come is the most powerful aphrodisiac I've ever experienced. He hauls me upward, lifting me effortlessly as he walks us over to the sectional couch. Cool leather brushes my skin as he lies me down gently, the considerate motion a stark contrast to the roughness when I was blowing him.

I sit up before he can crawl over me, straddling his lap instead.

He lets me take control, sliding his hands up my thighs until he's bunched my dress. I reach over, grabbing a condom out of the drawer in the table where I know he keeps them. We've used one every time, because not using them would prompt a conversation I don't want to have. Letting him come in my mouth was intimate enough.

Beck removes my dress and strapless bra while I rip the condom open and roll it on him. He's still fully dressed, and there's something surprisingly erotic about sitting on his lap in just my thong. I tug the lace to the side to line his tip up with my entrance, then sink down. I'm *so* wet, but it's still a tight fit thanks to his size.

Beck grunts as I work him deeper into my swollen pussy, his hands roaming my body like he's memorizing every inch.

I moan as he spreads and fills me, a pleasure that's not just biological sparking through me. There's a satisfaction that it's *him* under me. Inside of me. He's everywhere. All that I can see and hear and feel, consuming every single sense.

"*Fuck*. You feel so good."

I lift my hips and then drop them again, swiveling my pelvis so he hits a different spot. Beck curses again, his expression pained and the tendons in his neck defined. Every time I move, my breasts brush against his cotton shirt, the soft material a tantalizing rasp against my bare skin. I can smell my arousal, mixing with the scent of his cologne and the leather couch.

His mouth lands on my shoulder, trailing hot kisses up my neck and along my jaw. He tells me how sexy I look like this. How tight and wet I am. How well I'm taking him. And God, it's too much. All of it. Everything becomes a blur. What I'm saying. What he's saying. Where I am. Who I am.

It spins into a sphere of pleasure that shatters, rendering me senseless and weightless and thoughtless as wave after wave of pleasure washes over me. It goes on and on, the contractions more powerful than anything I've ever experienced. It takes a good minute for me to regain enough control of my limbs to roll off of him and splay out on the cushions. A light sheen of sweat is covering my entire body, the inside of my thighs damp. I feel like a sponge that was just thoroughly wrung out.

Beck smirks down at me, his own expression relaxed and a little dazed.

We're athletes. Sex is a physical act. But I've slept with other guys who played sports, and it never felt like *this*.

Once my breathing has returned to normal, I ask, "Do you have any food?"

The chicken was good, but it was a small portion.

"Not any you'll like," he replies. One warm palm lands on my thigh, his thumb rubbing small circles. "But I'll see what I have." He stands up, taking care of the condom and then pulling his pants back up.

I stand too, cleaning up in the bathroom and then stealing one of his shirts rather than putting my dress back on.

Beck's peering inside the fridge when I enter the kitchen. I perch on one of the four stools that line the marble countertop. My stomach grumbles.

"So? What have you got?"

He grabs a few plastic containers and slides them down the counter to me. "Here you go. They're all labeled."

I grab one and tilt it upward. Salmon and rice—pass. "Do you have ice cream?"

He studies me.

I grin. "You do."

Beck reaches out and snags the prepared meals, sticking them back in the fridge and replacing them with a cardboard carton from the freezer.

"Yesss." I grab the spoon he offers and open the lid. "Vanilla?"

Beck shrugs as he takes the stool beside me. "It goes with anything."

"So it's not your favorite flavor?"

"Probably not. What's yours?"

"It used to be mint chocolate chip."

"What changed?"

"My mom took me and my sister out for ice cream the day before she left."

"You got mint chocolate chip."

I nod. "I got mint chocolate chip. Now I only eat it once a

year. As some fucked-up tribute or reminder, I guess." I push the tub away, no longer as hungry. "Do you have alcohol?"

Beck raises an eyebrow, but all he says is "There's vodka in the freezer."

Before I can stand, my phone rings. I slide off the stool to grab it out of the clutch that ended up on the floor.

It's Hallie. I silence it and return to my seat next to Beck. He doesn't ask, but I feel obligated to say, "My sister. I'm avoiding her calls."

"Why?"

"I'm supposed to pick out the bridesmaid dress for my dad's wedding."

"Why haven't you?"

"I don't know." It's bullshit, and Beck knows it.

"Do it now," he suggests.

"Right now?"

He nods.

"I would need another drink for that to happen."

Beck stands and grabs a clear glass bottle from the freezer. He sets it in front of me, then grabs two glasses out of a cabinet and splashes a generous amount of vodka in each.

"You don't measure? What kind of club owner are you?" I question.

"One who invested for a friend and is now focusing on practicing penalty kicks."

I laugh. "Touché."

"Prost." Beck raises the glass.

I grab the other one and repeat the toast. He laughs.

"*Prost*," Beck corrects.

"That's what I said!" I insist.

He rolls his eyes and downs the shot. I follow suit, sticking my tongue out when the liquor burns a trail down my throat.

"*Gah.*"

"You got your drink. Shop." Beck grabs a stack of papers piled on the corner of the counter and sits back down on the stool beside me.

"What are those?" I ask.

"Work stuff. Endorsement deals for me to look over."

"Don't you have people who handle that for you?"

"Yeah, but I'm not going to agree to anything without looking it over myself."

"What are—"

"Saylor." He silences me with a single look. "Shop."

I huff, but Beck's refocused on his papers. And I need to do this. I've put it off for too long, ever since Sandra called and made the request.

I unlock my phone and start scrolling through clothing sites. The longer I sit on the stool, the more uncomfortable it is. I shift, trying to find a more comfortable position. I end up wiggling my legs across Beck's lap so I can stretch out some. He doesn't even look up from the papers he's reading.

I pull up a different site. It sounds so easy: pick out a pretty dress and send it to Hallie so my father can buy it. Not just easy, fun. I spend most of my time in athletic clothes, so I enjoy dressing up for certain occasions. But I won't enjoy this occasion. Whatever dress I pick will be what I'll be wearing when my father gets remarried. I've never harbored any fantasy that my parents might reunite one day, but I guess I assumed my dad would stay forever single. I thought he, Hallie, and I would remain in the roles that, while not healthy, have been comfortable. Expected.

A stepmom and an attempt at a whole family is uncomfortable and unexpected.

I planned to only look through a couple of options and choose the one I hated least, but it's been at least an hour before I show Beck the one I settled on.

"It's nice," he says.

I snort and toss my phone on the counter. "Do you have more work to do?"

Immediately, I have his full attention. "No."

I abandon my stool and crawl onto his. His hands slide under the shirt I'm wearing—his shirt—to play with my tits. I arch my back, my body humming with pleasure and fully on board with this turn of events. But I didn't hate sitting next to him in silence either. I don't just want sex from Beck.

And I know that's why I took so long to decide on the stupid dress.

Chapter 13

Every single girl attending Scholenberg is standing in the kitchen when I walk in, still rubbing sleep from my eyes.

I halt abruptly, taken aback. "Uh, good morning?" It's not even eight; way earlier than I want to be up on a Sunday. What are they all...*oh*.

After practice yesterday, I filled Ellie in on some of what's happened with Beck, skimming over most of the details. Just telling her that I ran into him at a club and we've hooked up a few times, basically. I did tell her that he's the one running the kids' camp I'm headed to today, and that news has apparently spread around the entire house.

I sigh as I open the fridge door to grab some orange juice. If they all want to watch me make breakfast half-asleep, they can feel free.

But I'm only one sip into my juice when I hear Alexis exclaim, "He's here!"

Shit. I was banking on Beck running late. I glance at the clock on the stove. I'm not even late; he's early.

"Oh my God, it's really him!" Alexis exclaims.

I grab a breakfast bar and then call out a general goodbye before heading outside. Everyone's attention is on the front-facing windows.

It's the perfect temperature this morning. There's a whisper of warmth in the air, but none of the heat and humidity I'm ordinarily greeted by.

"Hey," I call out as I approach.

He's got the trunk of his car open, rearranging stuff.

I'm not sure how else to greet him. We don't normally kiss unless we're having sex. Not to mention I feel very on display. He offered to drive me to the camp before I left his place early yesterday morning, and I was only thinking that it would be nice not to have to walk to the stadium. Not that this would be fodder for everyone to watch through the windows.

"Hey." He holds out a hand for my soccer bag and I pass it to him.

"You should have someone give you a car with more cargo space," I say as I watch him struggle to fit it in.

"I thought my dick wasn't impressive enough for that."

"I thought Germans didn't have a sense of humor," I say.

He snorts, then slams the trunk shut. "How would you know? You can't understand a word of what we're saying."

I roll my eyes before I climb in the passenger side.

The Scholenberg van usually drops us off in front of the side entrance. Beck pulls into a private parking lot I assume is reserved for players. There's a massive coach bus taking up one side of the lot, and the other side section houses about a dozen cars.

A few men are gathered around one, another expensive sports car. Their attention turns to Beck as soon as he climbs out of the driver's seat. One of them calls out in German, then laughs. Interest shifts to me as soon as I appear, taking my bag from Beck and then following him over to the group. There are four of them: Otto, two men I've never seen before, and the one I encountered when I got lost in the stadium my first day.

My guide greets me first. "Hello. Stefan Herrmann."

"Saylor. Nice to meet you," I respond.

"We met before, no?" he asks.

I feel Beck's eyes on me. "We did," I reply. "Briefly. Nice to see you again."

He smiles, crinkling the corners of his gray eyes.

One of the men I've never met spits something out in German. It prompts immediate dislike, since I'm certain he knows I don't speak the language. Beck barks something back that causes the man to shift his gaze to the ground sullenly.

I learn his last name is Ludwig, and the final guy is Fischer. He appears to be the oldest, probably in his early thirties. We start toward the entrance that leads directly onto the field.

"What did he say?" I ask Beck in a low voice.

"Something rude he won't be repeating," he replies in a clipped tone, striding ahead through the open gate.

Well, all right then. I let him pull ahead and try again.

"Remember me?" I smile at Otto.

He smirks back. "Do you have permission to be here today?"

"Seems that way. Boring, huh?"

"I don't think anyone would call you boring."

I smile. "What did Ludwig say?" I ask Otto.

He looks uncomfortable, which confirms it was about me. "Don't worry about it," he mumbles.

"I'm not worried. Just curious." I flash him my most dazzling smile.

Otto sighs. "He said there's only a female player here because *Kaiser* can't resist pretty women."

I bristle. The only reason I'm here *is* because I'm sleeping with Beck, but that doesn't mean I'm not a damn good soccer player, one who's most definitely capable of teaching some kids to dribble. But I've still been diminished to a fangirl.

Kluvberg's field is the busiest I've ever seen it. Energy radiates and resonates across the broad expanse of grass. I can only imagine what the stadium is like during home matches. There are children everywhere, way more than I was expecting, and about a dozen adults. I spot Beck's parents talking to an older man with a bushy shock of graying hair. There's also a line of photographers holding cameras along the side of the field.

I should have been expecting press, but I wasn't. Adler Beck coaching children will probably be front-page news.

I keep forgetting he's famous.

Beck is clearly the authority figure here, and everyone pays close attention when he starts speaking a rapid stream of German. Since I can't understand anything he's saying, I study the crowd of kids that are gathered around him. I'd guess their ages range from ten to thirteen, but they've all got one characteristic in common: the awed expression aimed at Beck.

He stops speaking, and there's a flurry of movement as the kids split off into smaller sections. Otto, Hermann, Ludwig, and Fischer all walk away, and I'm left trying to figure out what the hell is going on. Beck comes over to me.

"Take that group." He points to the kids on the farthest edge of the field. "Just run them through a few ball-handling drills." He leaves without saying anything else, presumably to coach his own group. I'm torn between appreciating his faith in me and wanting to call after him to ask more questions. It's been nearly a decade since I was a middle schooler myself. I barely recall what my practices at that age were like.

But I've never been one to back down from a challenge, so I grab a stack of cones and a bag of soccer balls, pasting on my most excited smile to approach the group Beck gestured to. They study me apprehensively as I approach. Out of the coaching options, I'm most definitely the outlier for several reasons.

"Hey, everyone!" I tell my little huddle, injecting my voice with as much positivity as I can muster. "I'm Saylor."

"Why are you speaking English?" one kid asks suspiciously.

Before I can answer, another boy says, "Your voice sounds weird."

"I'm American," I reply, choosing not to mention that I don't know German. That seems like the sort of weakness I *shouldn't* share. "Okay, so we're going to start by dribbling through these cones and—"

"Boring!" a little girl, one of just two in my group, calls out. "That's so easy!"

These kids are brutal. But at least they're sticking to English.

"It's important to know the fundamentals," I reply evenly. "I'll demonstrate first. Line up behind this." I set one cone down like I'm Neil Armstrong planting an American flag on the moon.

There are some groans—and muttered German—but they all listen, lining up behind the orange marker. I set up three more cones in a straight line and then return to the first one.

"All right. I want you to dribble through on the first pass. Get as close as you can without knocking the cone over." I dribble through, brushing the ball against each cone. "Then a roll and reverse." I demonstrate, so I'm facing back in the other direction. "Alternate between step-over and scissors on the way back." I step in front, over, and behind the ball. Then, step over it, plant my foot, and pivot between the next set of cones. I execute another step-over, a second scissors, and then I'm back at the start.

The little girl who told me dribbling was "boring" is first in line. I'm used to people looking at me with envy—of my soccer skills, of the hot guy talking to me—but I've never experienced pure admiration from a child before. The awestruck look on her face makes me feel about ten feet tall.

"What's your name?" I ask her.

"Mila," she replies.

"All right, Mila, you're up first." I pass the ball to her, and she traps it neatly, then executes the drill perfectly.

"Nice work," I congratulate her, impressed. She's better than I was at that age. "Next."

All twenty of my charges run through the drill twice. I correct a few of them on the first pass, but they all have it down by the second run-through.

"Okay. Next drill." I switch up the cone formation so it's in a large circle. "Dribble through at full speed. Knock over a cone or miss one and start over."

"We did stuff like this ages ago," one boy complains.

"What's your name?" I inquire.

"Walter," he replies sullenly.

"You can go first, Walter." I smile sweetly.

He heaves out a sigh but does as I instruct. He runs through the drill without making a single mistake. I keep my expression neutral but internally start sorting through drills I did in high school. Evidently, they've surpassed the middle school level.

I have them all run through the circle twice and then announce we'll be doing one-on-one. That perks the group up.

Three duos run through the exercise, and then it's Walter and Mila's turn. I have a bad feeling about the pairing as soon as

Mila dribbles toward the two cones I set up as the goal.

Walter jostles her and kicks the ball away. I retrieve it and return it to Mila. "Start again. No contact, Walter."

He mutters something in German but doesn't touch her as he kicks the ball away for a second time, taking advantage of their size differential.

"Try again," I encourage.

"He's not giving me enough room," Mila says.

"You have to make the room." Walter replies before I can.

"You're too tall."

"You're too small," he tells her.

I ignore Walter. "Come on, Mila. Try it one more time."

She does, but the ball slips from her foot at the last minute with no interference from Walter.

"Everyone knows girls can't play football as well," Walter mocks.

This little—

I take a deep breath. "That's not true."

"Yes, it is," the insolent kid insists.

Mila's lower lip wobbles, her gaze stuck on the grass, and that's what breaks me.

I've been that little girl. I've had more guys than I can count assume they could beat me. Guys who never played soccer a day before in their life.

"Come on." I spin on my heel and start striding toward the other end of the field where Beck is gathered with his group. Either they see me as some sort of authority figure, despite being *a girl*, or they're just curious, because my players all trail after me.

Beck sees me coming. But he keeps talking, describing a drill that has all of his charges transfixed. I'm positive none of them have suggested he doesn't know what he's doing.

I let my group meld with his and stride to his side.

"Who knows who this is?" I point to Beck.

They all just stare at me.

I turn my gaze to Walter. "Who is this?" I ask him. "This football player who's a *guy*?"

"Adler Beck," Walter replies peevishly.

"And is Adler Beck good at football?"

"Yes." Walter has lost a little bit of his bravado suddenly. Either it's because we're in front of more of his peers, or because Beck is present. Since he's had no trouble tossing sass at me in front of the other kids until now, I'm pretty sure it's the latter. Which only annoys me more.

"And who am I?"

Walter looks at me with confusion. "Saylor," he mutters.

"Am I a girl?"

"I guess. A grown-up one." I almost smile at that but force my face to remain serious.

"And girls can't play football as well as boys, right?"

Walter crosses his arms. "Right."

I grin, grabbing a ball from the mesh bag set on the sidelines. "Fine."

I drop the ball and start dribbling. Belatedly, I realize I maybe should have clued Beck into my plan a little bit more, but all of a sudden, he's there, right beside me. A spin, and he's blocking my path to the goal. He's not guarding me as aggressively as I know he's capable of, but I'm having to work for every inch of ground I gain.

"Don't you dare let me win."

He doesn't reply. Maybe he's annoyed with me for turning this into a spectacle.

Out of the corner of my eye, I can see that everyone on the field is watching us. Thankfully, the photographers departed after getting a few shots. I can only imagine the headline that might accompany a picture of this.

Beck steals the ball from me but dribbles rather than steps over, and that's when I know he's playing along. He's not going to hand this to me, but he's going to let me prove my point. Help me, even.

I spin, and he jostles his forearm against my lower back. A textbook stop and go, and he's behind me. I don't hesitate, sending the ball flying. It wallops the white netting with a satisfying smack I imagine being the equivalent of a mic drop. I turn to see every single kid has their gaze laser-focused on me.

Walter looks appropriately abashed, but more importantly, Mila is beaming.

But Beck's expression is what affects me the most. He's looking at me with the same awe that's been aimed at him all morning. With some pride too. With too much I'm scared to name. My emotions are raw and all over the place. I'm so tired of having to prove myself and I'm so grateful he knew what I needed from him. We're so similar, in the most important ways.

"Thank you," I tell him quietly, then head back toward my group.

• • •

My phone won't stop vibrating on Beck's bedside table. After the soccer camp ended, we came back to his place. Ended up in his bed.

I finally grab it and answer. "Hello?" I mumble. If this is Hallie calling me to talk to Matthew Jr. again, I'm going to kill her.

"SAYLOR! OH! MY! GOD!" Emma shouts.

"Emma?" I drape an elbow across my eyes. "What is it?"

"You met Adler fucking Beck and didn't tell me?"

"What?"

"Cress just showed me an article with photos of you at some soccer field with kids. With *Adler Beck*."

Damnit. "Yeah," I admit. "He was at a soccer camp thing I went to." And is currently lying three feet away. Naked.

"And?! Did you talk to him?" Emma screeches.

"Barely," I lie.

"He didn't fall for the infamous Saylor Scott charm? The one that makes men profess their love outside in the middle of the night?"

"That happened once," I reply.

"Once more than it's happened to the rest of us," Emma shoots back.

I roll my eyes, then remember she can't see me. "I'm in the middle of something. I'll talk to you later, okay?" I hang up before she can answer and start scrolling through some of my other notifications. Most of them are from friends back home. "I've got to go," I inform Beck.

He's got one elbow tucked back behind his head, lounging in the streaks of sunset that sneak between the half-drawn shades.

Ellie's latest text asking where I am contained five question marks.

Beck sits up when I climb out of bed. "Who was on the phone?"

"A friend from back home." I clear my throat before pulling my clothes back on. "She, uh, saw some photos from earlier. The camp."

I've stared at the poster of Beck on her wall countless times.

I spend more time in Emma's bedroom than my own. I've totally lost the perspective of reality, thinking I could just casually mention who I spent the summer fucking to my best friend when I return to Lancaster's campus. She's freaking out because I was *standing on the same field* as him.

He pulls on a pair of shorts and follows me into his living room. "Is that a problem?"

"Nope. I'll just have a lot of questions to answer when I get home next week."

"Next week?"

"That's when Scholenberg ends. When I'm heading home."

An approaching date I've avoided thinking about. That I haven't mentioned. I wasn't sure if Beck knew when the program ended, but his startled expression now is telling me the answer.

There's a knock on his door.

I scrape my hair up into a ponytail as I watch him walk over to answer it. He's never had a visitor when I've been over here before.

There's a woman with black wavy hair and perfectly proportioned features standing on the opposite side of the doorway. I'm pretty sure I recognize her. She's a Russian tennis star who's dabbled in modeling. I think she won Wimbledon last year.

"Alesandra."

"Beck." She practically purrs his name.

This is good. Great. Beck obviously wasn't expecting her, based on the surprise on his face. But it's a necessary reminder. This is a glimpse of what his life will look like after I leave. Maybe this is what it's looked like this whole time.

"You've got a great backhand," I tell Alesandra as I pass her and head into the hallway. Her pretty face creases with confusion, glancing between me and Beck.

"Saylor," he calls out.

"Bye, Beck." I wave a hand, but don't look back as I walk down the carpeted hallway. My eyes remain fixed on the gleaming floor of the elevator as soon as the doors ding open.

Anything to avoid facing the fact that Beck being with someone else bothers me.

That's a problem only denial can fix.

Chapter 14

*T**his**.* This is perfection. The smell of freshly cut grass. The feel of warm sun saturating my skin. The sound of labored breaths as other players struggle to keep up with me.

I spin, elbowing Olivia as I fight to continue my progress up the field. She grunts as my arm makes contact with her stomach, but keeps pressing.

Finally, I break free—only to be stopped by the sound of Coach Weber's whistle. Followed by a second long pull.

"That's it," she announces.

I pause with my foot on the ball, pulling in deep breaths of oxygen to replenish my bloodstream.

That's it, and not just the end of the game or the end of practice for the day. That whistle signaled the end of Scholenberg. Today is our last day. The final of fifty-six days—eight weeks—just drew to a close.

The women surrounding me look just as taken aback. We've reached the end of the marathon. A finish line we all knew was coming.

Crossing it feels different. Instead of relief, I feel a sense of loss as I join in on the clapping someone started. This is likely the last time any of us will cheer each other on, at least out loud like this.

"Go get showered and cleaned up. I'll see you all tonight," Coach Weber announces.

Scholenberg is hosting a farewell dinner before we all go our separate ways across the globe tomorrow.

I head toward the tunnel, falling in line behind Ellie, but pause when Coach Weber calls out to me. It's a mirror of the first day here.

I spin and jog over, stopping a few feet away from her. "What's up, Coach?"

"I had my doubts about you, Scott," she states.

"Oh-kay," I say, taken aback.

"I knew you were talented. I expected you to skate on that, especially after an injury. But…I was wrong." She gives me a rare smile. "You're the most dedicated—not just talented—player I've ever coached. That will take you far, you understand me? You've got confidence on the field, but I also get the feeling not many people have told you this. Some players are talented. Others work hard. But it's rare—extremely rare—to have both, to never lose the drive to be better. Keep at it, and there won't be anyone left to surpass, Scott. I'm expecting to one day be known by nothing aside from the fact that I coached you for a summer."

I'm frozen. Stunned. No one has ever heaped anywhere close to the mountain of compliments she just dropped on me.

I just completed the most competitive soccer program in the world, and *Christina Weber* is telling me she expects her legacy to encompass nothing but coaching *me*. And she's completely serious.

"Uh—I—wow," I stammer. "Thank you."

"See you tonight." She pats my shoulder and then heads toward the tunnel.

I remain standing on the pitch, still shocked. Savoring my final moments on this field. I walk toward the middle, dropping down on the center line and staring up at the cloudless sky. I could be anywhere, lying on any stretch of grass. But there's a tug of attachment to this spot. Sentimentality that I've never felt on Lancaster's field after playing three seasons there.

I'm not sure how long I've been lying here when a shadow falls across my face. Somehow, I know who it is even before I shade my eyes to squint upward.

"What are you doing?" Beck asks.

"Stargazing," I say, shifting my eyes away from his imposing figure and back to the sky.

There's a whoosh of air to my left as he drops down beside me in the center circle.

"It's the middle of the day," he observes.

"So? They're still up there."

"You're done?"

"Yeah. Dinner tonight, and then…home."

A beat of silence. "Nothing happened with her."

We haven't spoken since I left him and Alesandra in his apartment.

"It doesn't matter."

"It doesn't?"

"I'm leaving tomorrow, Beck."

"What if you weren't?" he asks.

"It doesn't matter. I *am*." Hypothetical happy endings never helped anyone.

"You ever going to let anyone in, Saylor?" he questions softly.

I let him in. Way more than I meant to. It's hitting me now

how far, as I try to keep breathing through the pain of realizing this will be our last conversation. That he's never going to touch me or tease me or smile at me again.

"You're six years into your career. Mine hasn't even started." I want Coach Weber to be right about me. I want all the years of hard work to pay off, to be worth the effort. If they're not, if I waver, I'd lose my entire identity.

"You don't want distractions."

"I don't want distractions."

There's nothing else to say after that. I remain in place for a few more minutes, soaking in his presence the same way I'm absorbing the sun's rays. This is a moment I want to memorize, even if it hurts.

He sits up when I do.

"I've got to go. I'll hold the van up." I shove away from the turf so I'm standing.

Beck stays sitting. I study him, a perfect portrait framed by the famous arches of his home stadium.

I swallow. "Bye, Beck."

I've said those two words before, but they sound different this time. Finality has a bitter aftertaste that lingers in the warm air around us.

"Bye, Saylor."

There's more I could say. I've always admired Adler Beck as a soccer player. This is my last chance to tell him that, but the past couple of months have forever altered me viewing him as a once-in-a-generation athlete. We're more than two people who both love soccer. Making this moment about sport seems wrong.

So I turn and head for the tunnel without saying another word.

This is where we started.

This is where we'll end.

• • •

The farewell dinner isn't held at a fancy restaurant. It's at a tiny beer garden tucked in the midst of the city.

The relaxed atmosphere fits the shift that's taken place over the past two months. Cheerful music and reminiscing fill the air as we eat bratwurst encased in pretzel buns and gulp beer. There's a communal, celebratory mood.

Tonight, it doesn't feel like we're a hodgepodge of backgrounds and nationalities.

Tonight, we're teammates.

For the first and final time. If I'm on a field with any of these women again, it'll most likely be as adversaries.

Halfway through her first beer—which is relevant because I'm pretty sure it means she isn't drunk—Olivia gives me a hug and tells me she hopes the rest of the American team isn't as good as me at the next Olympics. Coming from her, that's the equivalent of becoming best friends.

I get drawn into a dance-off to Shakira's "Hips Don't Lie" with Ellie; a song that owns a permanent spot on my pre-game playlist, meaning I've got a full arsenal of moves to bust out as I toss my hair and lip-sync the lyrics. There's no official winner crowned by the laughing onlookers, but I'm pretty certain it's me.

Breathless and thirsty, I return to the picnic tables. I gulp some water before switching to my glass of beer.

Alexis is still in her same seat from dinner. "Did I see Olivia hug you?" she asks.

I laugh and take another sip. "Yeah. See any pigs flying?"

"What?" Alexis looks thoroughly confused, and I can't say I blame her. It's an expression I've never fully understood. If you were going to highlight the impractical nature of a farm animal leaving the ground, wouldn't it make more sense to choose the heaviest one? Like a cow? Or a horse?

"Never mind. How come you're not dancing?"

"I prefer to watch the rest of you act like idiots."

I grin. "Harsh. Come on, it's our last night. You've got something better to do?"

"Nope." Alexis takes a sip of her own beer. "Kind of surprised you're here, though."

She's studying me closely.

"I came here *for* Scholenberg. Where else would I be?"

"With Adler Beck?"

I scoff, mostly to cover the fact that the sound of his name stings like salt getting sprinkled on a raw wound. I figured me not overhearing the conversations didn't mean they weren't taking place. Between the scene at the club and him picking me up for the camp, I knew the other girls were discussing me and Beck behind my back.

"Things aren't like that between us," I reply.

"They aren't?"

"No." I drink more beer, hoping she'll drop it.

She doesn't. "You're done?"

I nod.

"Do you want to be?"

I stopped dancing for a cold drink and somehow stumbled into a therapy session. "Yes. No. I don't know." I pause. "It doesn't matter."

"Of course it matters."

"I don't—it was just supposed to be sex. I've never...cared. I shouldn't have let it happen."

"I don't think we get to choose who we fall in love with," Alexis says softly.

I flinch like she slapped me. "I didn't say anything about love."

She raises one eyebrow. "So...your plan is to never see him again?"

"I mean, I assume he'll be at the next summer Olympics."

Alexis snorts. "Right."

"Scott! Get your ass out here!" Ellie shouts.

"Be right there," I call back. "It's best this way," I tell Alexis, draining the rest of my beer.

I stand and return to the makeshift dance floor, losing myself in the music's beat.

A few hours later, the night ends with a speech from Coach Weber. I miss most of it, only registering the finality of her tone.

I was eager to come here. I thought I'd be as eager to leave. Senior year, my final soccer season, seeing my friends. Returning *home*. All things I should be looking forward to. It shouldn't feel like I'm leaving some piece of myself behind.

The beer garden's staff is happy to see us go. Not only are we a boisterous group, but Scholenberg rented out the whole place. Our exit means they can shut down for the night.

Ellie's concocting a plan to head to Submarine for some more dancing when we emerge out onto the street.

"I'm going to head back to the house," I tell her. "I'm exhausted and I've got an early flight."

"Fine," Ellie agrees with a disappointed sigh. "We can drop you off on the way."

"It's fine. I want to walk," I reply. "One last look at the city, you know?"

Ellie studies me for a minute, but all she says is, "Text me when you're back."

"I will. Have fun."

After a few more hugs, I start down the street—in the opposite direction from the building I've lived in for the past two months. It's only a few blocks to Beck's apartment.

I stop on the sidewalk outside the park across the street, staring up at the highest floor. There are a couple of lights on, not enough for me to tell if he's home or just left them lit earlier.

My time in Germany has always been finite. I knew before getting my first glimpse of Beck on Kluvberg's field that I'd leave as soon as Scholenberg ended. That departure date never changed as my feelings grew and developed.

I knew saying goodbye would hurt. But I wasn't expecting this ache in my chest. Or the echo of *"You ever going to let anyone in, Saylor?"* in my head.

I turn and continue walking toward the Scholenberg house, pushing through the pain the same way I always have. Not caring that it's begun to drizzle. Appreciating it, actually.

It hides the fact that there was already salty water dripping down my cheeks.

Chapter 15

Returning to Lancaster University for the start of senior year is anticlimactic.

The fourth time doing something is never the time remembered. At least, not the time *I* remember. This is also the final time, though, and it's not a reminder I appreciate. There have been too many *lasts* lately.

Emma harassed our landlord into letting me move in early, so I head straight to our shared house from the airport when I land.

The drive feels strange. The scenery isn't what I've grown accustomed to seeing. Connecticut looks drab and uninspired after the majestic color of Kluvberg.

The National croons "Vanderlyle Crybaby Geeks" in my ears, the melancholy melody matching my mood. I haven't taken my headphones out since I climbed into the waiting car outside the Scholenberg house fourteen hours ago. I needed to drown out the dark thoughts swirling in my brain.

The taxi I flagged down at the airport stops outside the

Colonial I've lived in since sophomore year fifteen minutes later. I hand the driver some of the dollars that have sat in my wallet for the past eight weeks. I didn't bother exchanging my unused euros for American dollars in Berlin, and the sight of the foreign currency mixed in with the green bills causes a pang in my stomach I fight to ignore.

I climb out of the back seat. The driver is already hoisting my bags out of the trunk of the sedan, and I thank him before heading up the brick walkway. I yank the heavy bags up the stairs. They thump against every step, and I curse myself for packing so much. Half of it I never even wore.

The house is empty and silent when I walk inside. Preseason doesn't start for another week, and my housemates are scattered across the country in their respective hometowns enjoying the end of summer.

I feel like collapsing in a heap on the floor, so I force myself to do the opposite. I drop my bags in the small entryway that runs between the kitchen and living room and head right back outside without venturing farther into the house.

My sneaker-clad feet pound the pavement, expelling some of the emotion simmering with each slap against cement.

I veer left, turning onto Lancaster's ivy-covered campus. My pace is fast, the burn of my calves and blur of brick buildings indications of my speed.

Campus is deserted too. There aren't any tours or summer classes being held this late in the day, and those are the only events happening around here this time of year.

It's just me and the scampering squirrels.

I run all the way past the pond to the athletic complex and sports fields, only stopping when I reach the edge of the soccer field I've spent my college career playing on. I vault over the hip-high chain-link fence onto the turf. It's a short walk out to the center of the field. As soon as I reach the heart of the pitch, I flop down.

Two days ago, I was doing this halfway around the world.

I ran for longer than I realized, because dusk has begun to fall, streaking the blue sky in shades of tangerine, fuchsia, and lilac. I stare upward for so long my eyes lose focus and the sunset twirls together like a swirl of sherbet.

He's not here. Logically, I know that. But I keep waiting, pretending he'll be standing over me any minute.

Finally, my grumbling stomach forces me vertical. I barely ate on the plane. I've barely eaten all day. Rather than hop over the fence again, I opt for the gate, walking along the path and around the bleachers to head back through campus.

"Saylor!"

I turn to see Kyle Andrews walking toward me from the sports complex. There's one SUV in the parking lot, which must belong to him.

"Hey, Kyle." I pause in place.

He flashes me a goofball grin. Kyle's known for taking nothing seriously, but he's got enough raw athletic talent to be considered my male equivalent on the men's team. Minus the national championship. "How was Scholenberg?"

"It was amazing," I reply honestly.

"Yeah, I bet. When did you get back?"

"About an hour ago," I reply. "How about you? Thought you guys start preseason next week, like us?"

"Yeah, a few of us came back early to chill before the torture starts." He gives me a sly smile. "Including Tim. Who hasn't shut up about you, by the way."

It takes me a few seconds to even remember who Tim is.

"Why don't you come over later?" Kyle suggests.

Nothing sounds worse right now. I'm totally drained, mentally and physically. Emotionally.

"Rain check?" I request. "I'm battling a serious case of jet lag."

"Yet you're out running?"

"I run every day. It's how you become a national champ, Andrews. Take notes."

He laughs.

"What are you even doing here?" I inquire, glancing around the parking lot. "I know it can't be to work out."

"I forgot my favorite shorts before leaving for break." He holds up some gray mesh material in one hand.

"Of course." I roll my eyes. "See you around. Tell Tim I'm flattered he has a crush on me."

"Tell him yourself." Kyle winks. "See ya, Saylor."

He heads for the parking lot, and I start running again.

My pace isn't quite as frantic as it was before, but I'm still pushing myself. I'm in the best shape of my life right now thanks to Christina Weber and her militaristic training methods.

My knee hasn't so much as twinged in weeks. When I departed Lancaster two months ago, that was all I hoped for. I've made soccer my top priority ever since I started playing, and anything that doesn't advance those goals doesn't matter. Can't matter.

I almost trip over my bags when I open the front door. I didn't turn on any lights earlier, and the house is dark now. I feel along the wall for the light switch and then head upstairs, leaving the heavier bag by the door. The slanting stairs creak as I drag my smaller luggage to the second floor.

Cressida and Anne's rooms are to the right, and mine is

the first one on the left, with Emma's located across the hall. I push open the wooden door, half-covered with peeling paint, surveying my room. The air has the stagnant, stale quality of that which has been sitting for a while, so I drop my suitcase and head to the solitary window, throwing the sash up to aerate.

Fresh air circulates, picking up a cross-breeze from the hallway. I'd normally describe my room as "organized chaos," but that's a stretch right now. I packed for Scholenberg in a hurry, and there's evidence of that scattered everywhere, like a tornado passed through recently.

Rather than deal with any of it, I grab a clean towel from my closet and head down the hall to take a shower. I stand under the pulsing spray for longer than usual, letting the hot water massage my sore muscles. Long showers weren't common while sharing a bathroom with six other girls.

I get dressed in a pair of sweats and a tank top, not bothering to do more than yank a brush through my blonde hair. Stray droplets follow me as I pad downstairs to forage through the kitchen.

Food options are limited. Very limited. No one has lived here since I left for Scholenberg. I finally scrounge up a packet of ramen and a bag of chips.

I make my meager meal and then raid the liquor cabinet. I drench a few ice cubes with a generous splash of gin and settle on the couch. The alcohol burns a harsh trail down my esophagus and sears my stomach as I stare at the television.

The buzzing of my phone distracts me from the fascinating task of studying a black screen.

"Hey," I answer, balancing the bowl of ramen on my knee as I tuck the phone between my ear and shoulder.

"You answered! It's a miracle!" Hallie exclaims.

"Do you know what a miracle is? I answer all the time."

"I've talked to you once in the past week."

"Fine. Half the time," I reply.

"You're back at Lancaster?" Hallie asks.

"Mm-hmm," I respond, taking a sip of soup.

"Did you unpack?" She sounds exactly like a mom, and for once, it doesn't bother me. She cares, and maybe that's something I should learn to cherish, not make fun of.

But I keep that thought to myself as I snort and answer, "Of course not."

"Headed out to party instead?" she teases.

I glance down at my sad meal and damp tank top. "Hardly anyone is back yet, Hallie." I don't mention the fact that I was, in fact, invited to one. And turned the invitation down.

"You could always come back home for a few days," she suggests. "I haven't seen you in months!"

"I'll be back for the wedding," I answer. "I've got an intense training schedule right now. It's best I stay here and use Lancaster's facility."

Hallie sighs, and I know exactly what she's thinking. "All right. Well, I'll let you go. I'm sure you must be tired. It's the middle of the night in Germany, right?"

"Right," I confirm.

"Are you all right?" Hallie asks. "You sound weird."

"I'm fine. Just…tired."

"Okay. Bye, sis," Hallie says, and the phone clicks.

"Bye," I whisper.

She's first to hang up, for once.

As soon as she does, I finish my simple dinner. Then sink deeper into the cushions and resume staring at the living room wall until I feel myself start to drift off toward unconsciousness.

• • •

Cressida, Anne, and Emma all return to Lancaster on Saturday. Cressida arrives first, and I haul my butt off the couch to greet her, abandoning the mystery book I was reading. That's all I've done for the past six days: work out and lie on the couch.

Well, that and get wasted with the boys' soccer team last night.

"Saylor!" she squeals, wrapping me up in a hug.

"Cress!" I squeeze her back.

She pulls back to study my face. "I swear, you get prettier every year. It's so unfair."

"Says the pageant queen," I reply, rolling my eyes.

Cressida is from the South, like me. Unlike, she participated in some of its more archaic traditions. She claims it was at her mother and grandmother's insistence, but Cressida is both strong-willed and loves the spotlight, so I suspect it wasn't completely involuntary.

She gives me a regal wave that ends with only her middle finger still raised. I laugh and then flop back down on the cushions that have started to mold to the shape of my body.

"I like what you've done with the place," Cressida comments, glancing around the messy living room.

"Yeah, I'll clean it up," I assure her.

"Sad I missed the party," she says, kicking a stray beer can the boys left behind. "Looked like a rager."

"Looked like?"

"I enjoyed 'Wannabe' the most," she replies, smirking.

"Fuck. I'm going to kill Kyle."

"Was he the lucky guy last night?" She winks.

I make an unintelligible sound, and Emma's arrival saves me

from actually having to answer. I didn't hook up with any of the more-than-willing soccer guys last night. I drank myself into a haze that apparently resulted in a Spice Girls concert.

Emma arrives next, bouncing into the room and leaping atop the back of the couch. Except she misjudges the distance and ends up half-smothering me.

"Emma!" I protest as her elbow digs into my left thigh.

"Miss me?" She grins, rolling back onto the cushions she was actually aiming for. "I thought you were some badass soccer player who couldn't feel pain. The way you talked about Scholenberg, I thought you'd come back wrapped in a wall of muscle or something."

"I've always been a badass soccer player," I respond.

Emma's attention shifts to the living room. "Damn, I knew I should have come back last night. You had a party without me?"

I shrug. "Just a few of the soccer guys."

Emma perks back up. "Speaking of which, I told them we'd meet them at Peak's Point in twenty minutes. Put on something other than...that." She wrinkles her nose at the sweatpants I've barely taken off this past week. "Anne's meeting us there."

I groan. "Now?"

"*Now*. It's senior year, Saylor. I don't care how hungover you are."

"I'm not hungover," I protest, even though I absolutely am.

"Uh-huh," Emma replies, giving Cressida a hug and then bouncing upstairs.

I trail after her and into my bedroom, yanking off the baggy T-shirt I paired with sweatpants this morning.

I put on a bikini and then pull the same T-shirt back on, too lazy to find something else. I twist my hair up in a messy bun, grab my sunglasses, and meet Emma in the hallway. She's wearing an emerald sarong and eyes my outfit critically.

"Don't start," I warn.

"What about that cute cotton dres—"

"It's dirty," I reply, which is true. I still haven't unpacked any of my suitcases from Germany. I'm wearing my second favorite bikini because I don't want to look at the one I wore with Beck.

Emma sighs.

I follow her downstairs, where Cressida is already waiting, always the first one ready. She's changed into a tank top that sapphire bikini straps peek out from and a pair of athletic shorts. Emma sighs again when she sees Cressida's choice of attire, and Cress and I share a grin.

It's a short trip to Peak's Point, which is a small enclave filled with brackish water. Its sandy beach is littered with enough stone to keep snobbish tourists away, which makes it a prime party location for Lancaster students. The road is lined with cars since there's no actual parking lot.

I climb out of the back seat of Emma's SUV and squint at the water before slipping on my sunglasses. We traipse along the thin trail that cuts through the greenery lining the road and then hit the rocky shore that slowly turns into more sand than pebbles. It's not just the soccer teams here. I plop down next to Sarah Hawley, who is on the field hockey team.

"Hey, Sarah." I lean back on my hands.

"Hey, Saylor," she replies. "Good summer?"

Emma snorts as she settles on my other side. "Great summer. This lucky bitch was at Scholenberg."

"Should I know what that is?" Sarah replies, looking confused.

"It's a soccer camp in Germany. They play at the Kluvberg field," Emma explains.

"Wait, isn't FC Kluvberg the team Adler Beck plays for?" Sarah asks.

I tense as soon as she says his name. It's an involuntary reaction, one I don't think anyone catches.

"Yup," Emma replies. "Saylor met him."

"What?" Sarah gasps.

"We were both at a kids' soccer camp. Not nearly as exciting as Emma is making it sound," I respond quickly.

"Wow. I'm still jealous. He's gorgeous."

"Right?" Emma replies, warming to the topic. "I have that photo of him on the—"

"I'm going in," I interrupt, standing and pulling my T-shirt over my head. I had no intention of swimming until right now, but suddenly it seems like a fantastic idea.

"Okay," Emma responds, giving me a weird look.

I stroll toward the water until it laps against my toes, ignoring the looks my body is getting from the guys. My toenails are still painted the same shade of obnoxious pink I was studying in the coffee shop when Beck appeared behind me. Barely painted, now. The nail polish has chipped, with only a few remnants of color remaining.

I wade out farther. The cool water hits my knees. Then my waist. Just below my breasts. I stare straight ahead. The curves of the cove are invisible from this angle, and all I can see is the ocean stretching ahead until it melds into the distant horizon.

Sarah's innocent question reverberates around my skull. *Isn't*

FC Kluvberg the team Adler Beck plays for?

I'm going to have to get used to it. He's not suddenly going to fade into obscurity. I'll hear his name. Watch him play. If he starts dating someone, I'll see coverage of it everywhere. If he gets engaged. Married. Has kids one day. His entire life will play out in the media, and I'll have to witness it.

I just hope I won't care by then.

"Saylor! Saylor!"

I turn in the water.

Kyle is standing at the edge, waving his arms. I splash back closer to shore.

"What?" I call.

"I need you on my team for beach volleyball," he yells back.

"Fine." I trudge the rest of the way through the water, fighting the current the whole way.

Some of the other soccer players have already set up a line of rocks I surmise are supposed to be the "net."

"Tempting some sharks?" Kyle asks me when I reach the shore.

"Statistically, it's more likely I'd get struck by lightning," I utter dryly.

"Saylor Scott: not just beauty, but brains too," Kyle announces, like he's a television commentator.

I scoff as I step into the setter's position. "Ball," I bark at the redhead holding the white sphere. I've never seen him before and there are only sports teams here, so he must be a freshman. He startles, then tosses it to me.

I spike the ball across the rocks. Since there's no visible net, I have to guesstimate on the height, but the ball arcs a good six feet before landing in the sand between two football players, who immediately start arguing about who should have been responsible for returning it to this side of the rocks. I whistle to get their attention, and one returns the ball to me. I send it sailing to the other side again, except this time one of them is quick enough to return it. I lunge forward to spike it back but am distracted when a hand brushes against my left butt cheek.

I whirl around, forgetting about the ball. "Did you just touch my ass?" I snap at the same redhead who passed me the ball a few minutes ago.

He pales. "It was an accident."

"An accident? What the fuck kind of—"

"Saylor, come on." Kyle suddenly appears at my side. "Let's grab a drink."

He basically hauls me over to the assortment of coolers spread out by boulders and hands me a can of beer.

"You probably don't need this, but it's all we brought. You good, Scott?" he asks, studying me curiously. And a little warily. No sign of his usual goofiness.

I crack the can open, making a face at the taste as I gulp down a sip. "I'm great."

"You sure?"

"Why wouldn't I be?" I challenge.

"You've just been…different, since you've been back. First you don't want to hang out, then you're downing shots like water last night. You grinded all over Tim when he first got there, then ignored him the rest of the night. He actually likes you, you know? He's not just after sex."

"Well, sex is all I do."

Kyle sighs. "Your knee is fine, right? You'll kick ass this season."

He, like everyone else, assumes nothing could bother me unless it's related to soccer.

I sip more beer. "I know I will."

There's no mistaking the assuredness in my voice, and Kyle looks even more confused. "Then what's wrong?"

"Nothing. I'm fine," I repeat, heavily emphasizing the last word.

Maybe if I say it enough, I'll start to believe it.

Chapter 16

The start of preseason is a relief, providing the exact distraction I've been craving since returning to Lancaster. I've occupied myself the past week by continuing the insanity of my Scholenberg schedule.

The rest of my teammates spend the first week of preseason complaining. Coach Taylor is intense—you don't win a championship otherwise—but she's not on par with Coach Weber. She eases us into the level of fitness we'll need once the season officially starts.

So, I spend the first week of preseason adding extra workouts to stay busy.

"You're joking," Anne comments when I come down the stairs on Friday, our fifth day of preseason training, in a fresh workout outfit. She's icing her shin on the couch, and Emma is sprawled out on the rug doing an accurate impression of a dead body.

Emma raises her head when Anne speaks, her eyebrows flying up when she registers what I'm wearing. "Are you fucking kidding me, Saylor?"

I shrug. "Not my fault you slacked all summer."

"That's what summer is for," Emma retorts before lying back down.

Cressida walks out of the kitchen holding some sort of green concoction in a glass. She studies me as she sips through a straw. "You know we have the scrimmage against Lincoln tomorrow, right?"

"That's tomorrow? I thought it was next year."

She rolls her eyes at my sarcasm. "You're not a machine. You can't keep this up, Saylor."

I don't answer, just head out the door.

· · ·

I feel nauseous.

"Saylor? Are you okay?" Emma's voice sounds to my right.

I don't bother looking up from my knees, just press my palms a little more firmly against my eye sockets in an attempt to block the world out temporarily.

"I'm fine. I just need a minute."

More whispers to the right. I hear Cressida.

"Can we get you anything? Call anyone?" Anne must be close by as well, because her voice, although low, sounds clear. Her second question is more tentative than the first. I'm guessing it's because, aside from the three of them, they would have no idea who to call.

"No, I'm good. Thanks."

There is someone I'd like to talk to right now, someone who understands what it's like to carry a thousand pounds of expectations. But I can't call *him*. I haven't contacted Beck since I left Germany, and he hasn't reached out to me.

We're done, just like I wanted. A clean break.

I peel my hands away from my face and slide off the wooden bench, ignoring the concerned stares of my three best friends. I'm sure they're all thinking *I told her so* right now, believing I've exhausted myself this past week with extra runs and workouts. If only. Physical fatigue is something I figured out how to fight through a long time ago. Mental angst is my current issue, and it's never affected me before the way it is right now.

Coach Taylor gathers us around for a pep talk I barely listen to a word of. My body knows exactly what's expected, but my head needs to get in the game. Thankfully, I feel my focus start to sharpen as I step out on the field, focusing on the green jerseys of our opponents. Everyone is going to be looking at me this game.

I went to Scholenberg.

I'm a senior.

The team captain.

This is my year to shine. And considering how successful my past three seasons at Lancaster were, that's saying something.

We lose the coin flip, but it doesn't matter. As soon as the kickoff happens, I steal the ball and bolt up the field. Lincoln is taken totally off guard. Green jerseys that were preparing to attack sprint back up the pitch, but they're too late. Defenders aren't ready. Even if they were, spinning around them would be just as effortless.

I flex the muscles of my thigh and propel my foot forward like the strike of a snake. The ball spins into a blur of black and white, landing in the back of the net a few seconds later. I lost track of how many goals I've scored in my life a long time ago, but that doesn't make it any less satisfying to add another to the tally.

The loudspeaker crackles to life, announcing my unassisted goal forty-seven seconds into play.

I smile and nod as my teammates swarm me, but I don't really register anything they're saying to me. My attention is where it should be now. I'm concentrated on nothing except winning. I'm in the sort of shape where I could run for a lot longer than I'll need to, and the mental block from earlier has disappeared, broken down by the rush of being the best on the field.

The rest of the scrimmage passes in a blur. I score once more. Emma also sneaks a shot past Lincoln's goalie. And one of our sophomores manages a half-field kick that drops right behind the goal line.

It's a dominant performance, and Lincoln trudges off the field with shoulders slumped after we shake hands, probably glad this was an away game for them.

A local reporter I recognize from last season calls my name as we file off the field. I pause reluctantly. The high of winning hasn't fully erased my weird mood, but I should be grateful the guy is here at all. Women's sports need all the coverage they can get, and this was only a scrimmage.

"Saylor, that was a very impressive performance you had out on the field today," he says.

"Thank you," I reply.

"I spoke to your coach before the start of the game, and she credited your dominance on the field to your aggressive playing style. Despite the knee injury you suffered earlier this year, you still seem to manage to find a second gear when everyone else on the field is exhausted. Where does that drive come from?"

"I've never seen the point of leaving anything on the field. If my opponent is tired, that's their problem. It just makes me run faster."

The guy interviewing me chuckles. "Well, that's certainly a mindset most athletes strive for, but few can actually achieve. I'm sure you're a role model for lots of future soccer stars out there."

Mila's face flashes in my mind.

"Are there any athletes who have inspired you?"

"Adler Beck." I don't have to think about my answer, but I wish I did.

"Really?" My interviewer doesn't bother to hide his surprise.

I'm not certain if it's because he thought I would name a female athlete, or if he expected a more original answer than the most famous footballer in the world.

Inferring it's the latter, I feel obligated to add to my response. "I was fifteen when he scored the game-winning goal for Germany in the final. I'd been playing soccer since I was five, and everyone kept telling me that I was too single-minded, that I should try other sports, other hobbies. Chill out. Be a kid. People said I was too young to be fully dedicated to something. I stayed after practice one day to keep working on a drill I messed up, and when my coach found me there hours later, he made me skip practice for a week to force me to take a break. But then there was this German guy, being idolized by millions for doing the very same thing. He inspired me."

It's the lengthiest answer I've given during an interview, and I hope that's the reason for the long pause that follows my response.

"Well, a pleasure speaking to you, Saylor, as always," the reporter finally says. "Congratulations on the win."

"Thanks," I respond, then head into the locker room.

Despite our superior performance, Coach Taylor still comes up with half an hour's worth of critiques. Ellie calls me on the drive home from the field to catch up, and by the time I hang up with her and shower, it's dinnertime.

I enter the kitchen to find Emma sitting on one stool with her feet resting on another, scrolling through her phone.

"Are you making any dinner?" I ask, opening the fridge door and surveying the variety of raw ingredients.

"I don't know. I'm not really feeling *inspired* to make anything right now," Emma replies. Even without the way she emphasizes the word, the shit-eating grin she's sporting when I spin around is proof enough she knows about the interview earlier.

I sigh. "You were eavesdropping?"

"I was across the field, Scott. It's all over social media."

Shit. "What? Why?"

"Uh, because you're hot and semi-famous and Adler Beck is hot and super famous?"

I snort. "Semi-famous? Among the hundred people who follow women's college soccer?"

Emma shrugs. "You've been in plenty of articles and magazines."

I pull a carton of eggs out of the fridge, chewing the inside of my cheek. "When you say *all over...*"

"A few million views."

"What?" I almost drop the eggs.

"And that's just this video." I didn't even know there *was* a video. The reporter was just recording my voice.

"Do you think he's seen it?" I don't have to elaborate on who I mean.

"Do I think Adler Beck has seen the video of you saying he's the reason you've become the badass soccer player you are today that has gone viral on every single social media platform and that he's been tagged in thousands of times? Hmmm... I guess

I'd go with yes. A confident yes. Like I'd-bet-my-trust-fund-and-future-endorsement-deals-on-it confident."

"I get it, Emma," I say as I set a skillet down on the metal stovetop a bit louder than necessary. "And I did not say he's the reason I'm anything."

"It was strongly implied."

Fuck. Beck hearing about my interview did not even occur to me when I answered that question. We're separated by an ocean that nothing was supposed to span.

"What's with the racket in here?" Cressida asks as she enters the kitchen. "Oh good, someone's cooking—I'm starving."

"I'm not sure if it will be edible. Saylor just learned she's gone viral," Emma explains.

"Ah," Cressida replies. "Don't look at me. I'm not responsible for the eight million views."

It's eight *million views now?*

"Was it the same video or different versions?" Emma asks.

"I watched the same one five times and then a second one once to make sure it was the same."

"That only counted as two views, then," Emma tells her.

"Even better, then. Did you hear that, Saylor?"

I don't respond as I crack a couple of eggs.

"She doesn't care about you watching it. She's worried Adler Beck saw it," Emma supplies.

I grit my teeth as they continue talking about me as though I'm not standing here.

"Why? I'm sure he's flattered," Cressida says in a reassuring tone. "I mean, no offense, but he might not even remember you. He probably does tons of those camps."

I pour the eggs into the hot skillet and start chopping fresh veggies, not trusting myself to say anything.

Eventually, the euphoria of our win earlier trumps gossip about me, and the dinner conversation is mostly centered around the scrimmage today. After we eat and clean up, Cressida announces she's invited the rest of the team over to celebrate, along with "a few other friends." From experience, I know that likely means our tiny house will soon be packed with people.

I've just finished changing into a cute dress when I hear a fresh chatter of voices echo downstairs. I swipe on a second layer of mascara and head out into the hallway, making certain to close my door behind me.

When I arrive downstairs a bunch of the juniors are hovering in the entryway. Natalie leaps on me when I hit the final step, giving me a big hug. "All hail the captain!"

We head into the kitchen, where the rest of my housemates are.

"I come bearing gifts!" Natalie announces, waving a shiny magazine cover around. "Guess who the 'Sexiest Man in Sports' is for the third year straight?"

I have a bad feeling even before I catch a glimpse of the cover.

It's a glossy photo of Beck, standing in the center of Kluvberg's field. Almost the exact spot where we laid together, and the memory is a painful twinge that feels strange to experience here.

"Shut the fuck up," Emma commands, grabbing the shiny pages and flipping through them.

I walk over to where Cressida is whipping up her customary baked goods.

"What are you making?" I ask, trying to ignore the shrieks coming from the opposite side of the kitchen. There must be more photos inside the magazine. Maybe even some shirtless ones.

"Cupcakes," Cressida replies. "And I'll be hiding them."

I roll my eyes. "Can I help?"

Both her eyebrows rise in surprise. "Sure." She hands me a bowl. "Stir this."

My hands whip frosting without any input from my brain, my thoughts spinning as quickly as the sugar and butter.

Cressida brings a tray of cooled cupcakes over to me, and we ice them with the freshly whipped frosting. We're halfway through when a phone rings. Emma leans over to one I realize is mine.

"Hallie is calling you," she tells me.

I sigh, then answer. "Hey."

"Hey! How was your scrimmage?"

"It was good." I walk over to the cabinet where we keep the liquor, tucking the phone between my ear and my shoulder. "I scored two goals."

"Congrats, sis."

"Thanks." I inhale as I measure out some gin. "How are you?"

"We're good. Matt just got a promotion, and Matthew has finally decided to start sleeping through the night."

"That's great." I take a sip of straight alcohol, wincing at the burn. "How's Dad?"

A pause, during which I roll my eyes. She could at least attempt to act like that's a normal question for me to ask.

"He's doing well."

"Great."

"Your bridesmaid dress arrived. It's beautiful."

I take another sip, wishing I could rewind and not pick it out in Beck's kitchen. It's bad enough he infected my favorite bikini and all the other clothes I wore in Kluvberg.

"You're at a party?" Hallie asks.

Natalie and some of the other girls are still squealing in the background.

"We're having some people over."

Hallie laughs. "All right, I'll let you celebrate. Talk soon, okay?"

"Okay," I reply, then hang up.

Emma calls me over with a request to autograph the magazine as an honorary German. She's drunk, and I drain my glass to make sure I'm close to getting there myself.

I take a perverse sort of pleasure in scribbling my name in black Sharpie over Beck's gorgeous face, then head into the living room.

Two shots and a game of beer pong later, I'm dragging Drew upstairs. We stumble into my bedroom, and I slip on a stray sock. I laugh like I'm watching a sitcom as I pretend to ice skate the rest of the way to my bed, flopping atop it as though I've just successfully landed a triple axel. Drew watches me with a bemused expression and then walks over to my mattress, draping his muscular frame over mine. He kisses me, and it's pleasant. Familiar. So is the way his hand wanders under my shirt to unfasten my lacy bra.

"Fuck, Saylor. I missed you." His erection presses against my thigh.

He's into this. And I'm...not. My brain won't shut up. My mind keeps spinning like the inside of a washing machine, the thoughts an endless tangle.

There's no desperation. No urgency. No eagerness.

It's not like it was with Beck.

The thought of his name is a bucket of ice-cold water, and any pleasure dissipates.

I turn my head right as his fingers reach the edge of my thong. "I'm going to throw up."

Yeah, subtlety? Still not my strong suit.

I push Drew aside and run down the hall to the bathroom, banging the door shut behind me. I hover over the toilet, waiting for my churning stomach to expel something, but nothing comes up. So, I lie down on the cool tile floor, grateful Anne cleaned it yesterday.

"Saylor? You okay?" Drew's voice comes from the hallway.

"Yeah," I reply. "I'm going to call it an early night."

Silence. "Um, okay then. Feel better."

Steps clomp back down the hallway. I sit up to lock the bathroom door and then lie down on the floor again, staring up at the ceiling. The bass beat of whatever pop ballad is blasting vibrates against my spine as I study the cracks in the plaster that crisscross in ribbons. I trace the patterns they make until I start to feel dizzy. Then I pull out my phone. The screen is covered with notifications I ignore. Instead, I pull up the web browser and type *Adler Beck* into the search bar. I disregard the first few articles that pop up, probably about the cover Natalie brought over.

I tap on *Images* and watch as photo after photo loads. Pictures of him on the field, at press conferences, ad campaigns. I keep scrolling and scrolling...until my eyes start to prickle.

I set my phone down on the tile and close my eyes, feeling alcohol and confusion course through me.

We won today.

I played the best game of my college career.

Everything I've worked so hard for is falling into place. I'm on track to accomplishing the lofty goals I set for myself a long time ago.

I should be downstairs celebrating with my teammates or in my bedroom celebrating with Drew.

But all I can think about is *him*.

Chapter 17

"**N**ice face art" is how Emma greets me when I stumble into the kitchen the following morning. "That pattern looks a lot like our bathroom floor. Oh, wait..." She taps her chin with her index finger, making an exaggerated expression of confusion.

I pass her to fill a mug with steaming coffee. "Yes, I spent the night sleeping on the bathroom floor, and it was just as uncomfortable as it sounds. Can we please move on?" I hold my face over the mug so I can inhale the scent.

"Sure—as soon as you share why you spent the night locked in the bathroom."

"Well, I don't know if you know this, but sometimes when you drink a lot of alcohol, it makes you feel like you might throw up. And I thought the best place to do that would be in the bathroom. So that's what I did. Then it seemed like too much work to get back to my bedroom."

Emma rolls her eyes at my sass, but then turns serious. "Are you okay, S? You've been acting weird."

"I'm fine," I say emphatically, taking a large sip of coffee. The bitter, hot liquid trickles down my esophagus in a rapid stream.

"Oh-kay, then."

Cressida and Anne come downstairs a couple minutes later. We all eat breakfast and then pile into Anne's car to head to practice. Since we had a scrimmage yesterday, all we have is circuit training in the gym. Which is good, because I'm not the only one who is hungover. Most of the team greets me with bleary eyes and tired smiles.

Emma's doing leg presses beside me when I finally voice the question that's been percolating in my brain all morning. "When did you hook up again after Rowan?" I ask her, referencing the frat boy she dated on and off most of junior year.

"Hello, left field," she replies, glancing over at me.

"Forget it." I shift my gaze back to the muscles of my thighs as they bunch and stretch.

"Wait. Did he ask you to find out?" she questions.

"Of course not," I scoff. "Like I would tell him, even if he did. I was just wondering."

"It was a month, I think. Grant Smith. Oh wait, no, Colby Summers. I remember because he did this thing with his tongue where…"

"I don't need details, Emma."

"You asked."

I don't reply. I sort of did.

"*Why* did you ask?"

"Just wondering." I feel Emma's eyes on me, but she doesn't say anything else.

We move on to the pull-down bar, then the Ergometer, and then we're done.

The whole team gathers around Coach Taylor. She talks through tomorrow's itinerary and reminds us about the Canadian

Football Organization Camp this weekend. Better known as CFOC, it's become an annual tradition during the past three years at Lancaster to separate the end of our preseason and start of the regular season. Each team invited only has eleven slots—the starting squad. I know Cressida, Anne, and Emma will all be on the list alongside me before Coach Taylor finishes rattling off the names.

The prospect of leaving Lancaster for a few days is a welcome one. Maybe it will help me recalibrate.

Then again, leaving the country was how I ended up in this constant state of uncertainty and annoyance in the first place.

• • •

"I wonder if we'll see a bear this year," Emma speculates from her seat beside me on the bus as we chug toward CFOC.

"I hope not," I reply, keeping my gaze trained on the Canadian wilderness. Leafy trees flash by, shadowed by craggy peaks.

"Come on, that moose was so cool!"

"The moose was cool," I admit. "It was also an herbivore."

"I could save you from a bear. We'd play it totally cool."

"I wouldn't trust you to save me from a squirrel," I retort.

"Well, this is a low point in our friendship," Emma replies, letting out an exaggerated sigh.

I smile as we pull up outside the wood lodge that houses the participants in CFOC. Lancaster sponsors many clinics throughout the year, but this one has always been my favorite. Tucked away amidst freshwater lakes and soaring pines, it's definitely the most scenic. It draws players from the best programs in North America, meaning it's a chance to settle old scores and start new rivalries each year before the season officially starts.

"First clinic starts in an hour," Coach Taylor announces from the front of the coach bus we made the trek from the airport in. "Get changed, get settled, and don't be late."

Emma files out into the aisle and I follow, trailed by the rest of our teammates. Cressida yawns widely as we pass through the automatic doors that lead into the lodge. It's welcoming and homey, with a fire crackling behind the reception desk that makes me feel like it's winter rather than barely September. There's a massive chandelier hanging in the center of the lobby, constructed from antlers. I notice Emma eyeing it and grin.

We get checked in and head upstairs. Emma and I are sharing a room, while Cressida and Anne are across the hall. Emma swipes the plastic card against the keypad, and we walk inside. It's an average hotel room, except with woolen blankets covering the bedspread and prints of snowy mountains on the walls.

"Bye-bye, summer," Emma mumbles, flopping down on the buffalo print covering her bed.

I set my duffle bag on the dresser and unzip it to grab my cleats and shin guards. "All good things must come to an end."

"Did you change your major again? Philosophy this time?"

I stick my tongue out at her and flop down on my bed. "Is it just me, or are these blankets actually really comfortable?"

"It's just you," Emma replies. "Mine's scratchy."

"I'm taking this back to school." I pat the tartan pattern I'm lying on.

"Brilliant plan. They'll never notice," Emma mutters.

I choose to ignore her sarcasm, closing my eyes and snuggling against the soft wool. What feels like mere minutes later, there's a knock at our door.

Emma murmurs something unintelligible. I drag myself vertical and stagger over to the door. I blink through sleepy eyes to see Anne and Cressida standing in the hallway.

"Told you they'd be asleep," Anne informs Cressida.

"Last time I don't bet against you, Scott," Cressida tells me.

"Let's go. Clinic time."

I grab my gear from the heap on the floor, and Emma hobbles out of bed. We all trudge down the hallway, bumping into teammates and competitors alike. CFOC's headquarters are a mere hundred meters from the entrance to the lodge. It's essentially a rectangular building constructed of galvanized metal siding meant to withstand the harsh winter. From past trips, I know the layout already. The first floor contains equipment rooms, a small kitchen, and lots of locker rooms, while the second floor is all offices. The paper posted on the front door states that Lancaster was assigned Locker Room Five and Field Three. I lead my teammates into the square room. It's minimalistic, with locker-lined walls and a couple of scarred wooden benches.

Emma, Anne, and I are the last ones to leave the locker room. Cressida went ahead with an impatient sigh. Punctual as always. We're about to exit the back doors that lead out onto the fields when I realize what I'm missing.

"Crap, I forgot my pinny. I'll catch up to you guys." I hurry back down the hallway, grabbing the white mesh jersey and pulling it on over the skin-tight polyester sports shirt I'm already wearing. I jog back to the exit leading to the fields, bursting through the doors.

Field Three is the second one on the right. Everyone has already gathered in the center, so I quicken my pace to a slow run as I near the group. Teammates part as I near, flanked by players from other programs assigned to the same first clinic. Some I recognize, some I don't.

"Sorry, Coach, I—" I freeze like I was just confronted with

the bear Emma was talking about earlier. "What the hell are you doing here?"

The words are out before I've filtered them.

Before I remember my familiarity with Adler Beck was supposed to extend no further than one brief meeting at a children's camp.

No one says anything as we stare at each other, exacerbating the awkwardness. Somehow, in the last month, I forgot how just how heartbreakingly handsome he is. How one stubborn lock of blond hair flops forward. How his presence makes my blood fizz and my heart pound.

Beck's the one who breaks the deafening silence. "Nice to see you, Saylor," he replies.

I'm pretty certain I'm the only one who catches the sarcastic undertone. I'm definitely not the only one who catches that we're more familiar than two people who met briefly once.

"Thanks for joining us, Scott. I was just introducing one of the guest coaches for the next couple days," Coach Taylor explains. "We're lucky to have his input."

I nod dumbly, still in shock.

He's here. Not in Kluvberg. *Here*, right in front of me. Close enough to touch. To talk to.

"All right." Coach claps. "Get warmed up, ladies. Ten laps."

Water bottles get tossed. Sweatshirts flung. Laces tightened. Coach heads to the edge of the field to set up a line of cones for what I'm guessing will be sprints.

Everyone moves except Beck and me. I adjust the mesh material I hurriedly yanked over my head, so it hangs correctly. "What are you doing here?"

People are staring, angling looks this way. I'm too distracted to care.

"Guest coaching."

"Because you didn't have anything better to do than attend a *women's* soccer camp in Canada?"

He's *Adler Beck*. His being here makes absolutely no sense. The guest coaches are normally former Olympians in their forties.

"Scott! Get moving!" Coach calls out.

I curse under my breath. I could count on a couple of fingers how many times I've been chastised during practice. I stay focused on the field. Always. The fact that this lapse is due to Beck makes it worse. I'm weak when it comes to him.

I shake my head and take a step back. "You could have told me you were coming."

"Would it have mattered?" He holds my gaze.

I look away first, then walk away. My steps speed to a jog, then a sprint. What the hell was I supposed to say to that?

Everywhere I look, curious glances are aimed my way. They're all starstruck over Beck, and me talking to him drew more attention I don't want.

Worse, it accomplished nothing. He's here, and I have to deal with it. Ignore it. Avoid it, the same way I've tried to stop thinking about him incessantly. But I'm cycling through reasons why he could have possibly come here, and keep coming up with only one.

Me.

Lancaster University's team attends this camp every year. He knew I would be here and chose to come.

I have no idea what the hell to make of that.

"Did your volunteer coaching gig with Adler Beck involve an international incident?" Emma questions, falling into step beside me. "Is that why you were weird about it?"

The two girls running in front of us both slow their pace as soon as she says his name. *Real* subtle, guys. A sharp glare from me has them scurrying forward again.

"What are you talking about?" I reply, my gaze dropping to the grass being rapidly swallowed by my long strides.

"He looks pissed," she tells me.

"He's German—they always look that way."

"*Saylor.*" Emma breaks out her rarely used, no-nonsense tone.

I sigh. "Fine. I fucked him a few times when I was at Scholenberg. So him being here is…a little weird for me."

Emma has some trouble staying upright. She stumbles a couple steps over nothing but flat ground before catching herself and managing to keep pace with me. I've told her some crazy things. We've shared plenty of wild nights. But based on her sudden balance issues, I'm guessing if I glanced up, she'd look pretty stunned.

She finally recovers. "I can't *believe* you fucked Adler Beck and didn't tell me until just now."

"It wasn't a big deal."

Emma snorts. "Not a big deal. Are you—"

"Ladies! If you have spare air to chat, you're not running fast enough!" Coach calls out.

Groans sound around me, but I welcome the challenge, flexing my calves with every stride to give my movements an extra boost. Ten laps fly by at the accelerated pace. Next are push-ups. Then sit-ups. Followed by burpees.

One girl throws up before we even hit sprints. Clearly her usual coach doesn't believe in conditioning the way Coach Taylor does.

Every muscle in my body is hurting by the time we get a

water break.

"I should have pretended to be sick this morning," Emma grouses.

I roll my eyes as I stretch my calf and watch Coach Taylor talk to Beck.

"Wonder what Coach is talking about with your lov-ah?" She croons the last word like she's Taylor Swift.

I shoot her a sharp look for that comment.

"Back on the center line," Coach barks. "One line of defenders. One line of strikers."

We all take our time walking back to the center of the field in a blatant attempt to prolong the short break. I end up at the front of the strikers' line, because my slow is other people's fast.

"Scott, Morgan, you're up."

I dribble over to the cone that marks the start of the drill. Coach Taylor blows her whistle, and I easily spin and sprint around my assigned defender before sending the ball into the back of the net.

"Morgan! What the hell was that? Make Scott work for it! Scott, again! This time with Adams."

I line back up at the cone, and once again, I easily skirt around my teammate and score.

Coach Taylor sighs. "Henderson! You're up with Scott. Stick to her like glue."

I line up for a third time. Janie Henderson stays with me for about twenty feet, but then I feint right, dart left, and easily outrun her. I score for a third time and expect that to be the end of it.

Instead I hear, "Adler, can you please demonstrate how to properly mark a striker, since my defenders seem to have forgotten?"

Fuckkk. I keep my gaze on the grass as I jog back to the starting cone.

I can physically feel the excitement thrumming through the assembled players as I hear footfalls approach me that must belong to Beck. Like me, they thought he was only here in an observational role. Had I known that wasn't the case, I would have let Janie keep me from scoring just now.

I can't avoid looking at him any longer without it becoming conspicuous. His blue eyes are already fixed on me as he stops about five feet away. He's shed the light jacket he was wearing earlier, the cotton jersey underneath it the same shade of dark gray as the track pants he's wearing.

We stare at each other. He's looking at me like an opponent, and I'm finally able to do the same.

Long after I should have started the drill on my own, Coach blows her whistle. I move, darting through the complicated pattern of footwork that shook off my past three defenders. Beck stays with me, just like I knew he would. He's faster and stronger than I am. But this drill isn't about speed or fitness; it's about strategy. If this were any other top-tier male footballer, I probably still wouldn't stand a chance.

But it's not. It's Beck.

Not only have I spent years watching him play and studying his technique, this is not the first time I've played with him. Against him.

I know how he thinks, how he moves. Because I've done a lot more than just play soccer with Adler Beck. My body is naturally attuned to his every shift. I can anticipate his movements before he makes them based on subtle tells most would miss. He has the same advantage when it comes to me. We practically mirror the other's movements. I spin; he turns to block me. I feint left; he goes right. I gain ground; he forces me back.

I'm so caught up in the complicated dance I startle when Coach Taylor blows her whistle. I drop Beck's gaze as soon as she does.

"Well, that was—that was something. Good work, you two. Hart, Thompson, you're up next."

I jog back to the end of the line, avoiding every gaze aimed at me.

Especially his.

Chapter 18

General exhaustion and my bad mood keep questions at bay for the remainder of the day. Just because no one says anything to my face doesn't mean I can't hear the whispers, though. They grow exponentially more annoying when we head to dinner, mostly because it's the first time all the CFOC attendees are in one place. Gossip contained to individual fields during the day's drills has its first chance to flow freely.

The lodge's dining hall is set up buffet style, with massive trays of food being warmed by kerosene candles. Tables aren't assigned, so I head for one toward the back right. The rest of Lancaster's team follows me. I set my water bottle down on the varnished wood and head for the rapidly forming line. I end up behind Samantha Cole, the captain of one of Lancaster's biggest rivals. Despite that, we've always been friendly off the field, as evidenced by the warm grin she gives me.

"Hey, Scott."

"Cole," I reply, grabbing a plate and a roll of utensils.

"I don't suppose you've suddenly started missing the net?"

"You'll find out when we scrimmage," I respond, helping myself to some salad.

Samantha sighs. "I'll take that as a no."

"Smart choice."

"Hey, some of us are hitting the pool tonight, if you want to hang out later," Samantha says as we shuffle along in line to the poutine.

"Sure, sounds fun," I reply, studying the gray sludge covering the potatoes apprehensively.

"Scott!"

I groan when I recognize Coach Taylor's voice calling my name, abandoning my spot in line to walk over to where she's standing a couple dozen feet away, next to the drink dispenser.

"Yes, Coach?"

"Do I need to be worried about you this season?" Coach Taylor fills a plastic cup with ice and then water, all while staring at me expectantly.

What?

"Worried?" I ask, startled.

"You were distracted all day."

I don't deny it. "Everyone has off days."

"They do," Coach acknowledges. "But I didn't think the player who showed up to my practice with the flu last winter lost focus when she was feeling a hundred percent." I exhale, and Coach's voice softens a bit. "I've never had to place pressure on you, Scott. Because you put it on yourself, and you excel. You're heads and shoulders above any other player I've ever coached. I don't want—"

"Hi, Elaine!" I look to the left and have to swallow a groan when I see Mackenzie Howard approaching.

"Mackenzie." Coach acknowledges her with a slight dip of

her head. She doesn't look thrilled to be addressed by her first name.

Mackenzie Howard is the current star of the US Women's Soccer League. She's two years older than me, on a professional team, and takes great pains to remind me of both every time we interact. I typically find some way to mention the national championship Lancaster won my sophomore year. Against her alma mater her senior year.

"Saylor, how nice to see you," Mackenzie says. "Can't believe you're a senior now! Two years on the Wolves have just flown by."

Yup, right on cue.

"I know!" I reply in the same upbeat tone. "Seems like just yesterday we were beating you in the national championship."

Coach Taylor's lips twitch.

"Everyone is so excited to see where you end up next year," Mackenzie states. "You know—" She stops speaking abruptly, then waves her left hand. "Beck!"

My eyes drop to my plate as I hear his steps approach. They must know each other from the last Olympics. Of course, that sends me spiraling into speculation about just *how* well they know each other. I banish the thought from my brain as quickly as it appeared. I already know I'm part of a pool—a very large pool—of women who have slept with Adler Beck. Who cares who I'm treading water next to? And...clearly I'm *far* too fixated on Samantha's swimming invite.

Don't look. Don't look. Don't look, I chant to myself.

So of course, I look. His eyes are fixed on me already, and I lift my chin as I meet his gaze head-on. Trying and failing to convince myself I'm suddenly feeling flushed because of the heat the side of the ice dispenser is radiating, not any other reason.

"Saylor." He acknowledges me and ignores Mackenzie, and I

hate how much that matters to me.

My grip on the ceramic plate tightens. "Beck."

"Oh, you two know each other?" Mackenzie looks back and forth between us. Calling Beck over was meant to be a power play on her part.

"Yes," Beck replies simply.

That's all he says. He doesn't mention I attended Scholenberg. Or the kids' camp we coached together. He gives no explanation for our acquaintance at all, leaving it open-ended in a way that doesn't sound like the clean break I thought we parted on.

"That's nice," Mackenzie says, making *nice* sound like a synonym for *boring*. "Makes way more sense why Saylor called you her idol."

My fingers clench on the plate so tightly there's a chance I might break it. But what I really want to do is fling it at Mackenzie's smug expression. She's trying to embarrass me, and it's working.

I break eye contact with Beck for the first time since he walked over, glancing at Coach Taylor instead. "Are we good, Coach?" I ask, eager to flee.

"We're good, Scott," Coach confirms. "Curfew is at ten, got it?"

"Got it," I reply hastily. "It's been a long day anyway."

"That's what you said last year," Coach replies, but her smile is amused, not annoyed. Yeah, we snuck out last year, but Lancaster still kicked ass at the camp and she only found out because one girl posted a photo the following week. "Enjoy your dinner."

I grasp the opportunity to leave. "You, too."

The line is gone, with only a few stragglers still getting food. I rejoin where I stopped, serving myself some chicken and rice, then grabbing a fork.

I stride past where Beck is still standing, talking to Mackenzie, heading toward the rows of tables and dropping my plate down next to my water bottle. I slide into my seat across from Emma. She raises both eyebrows in a silent question, meaning she saw the interaction with Beck and Mackenzie, but doesn't ask in front of everyone. The rest of the girls are talking about our scrimmage tomorrow. We're scheduled to play Montclave College, which is one of the better teams here. But assuming I can stay focused, beating them shouldn't be much of a problem.

After dinner, a few of the guest coaches make speeches. Beck isn't one of them, so I don't pay close attention. I do notice he—and Mackenzie—aren't outliers in the group the way they normally would be.

Cressida notices the same thing. "They finally recruited some guest coaches who were born in the past few decades, huh?" she whispers to me.

"Looks that way," I reply.

But I doubt recruiting them was the issue. Young, successful players do not normally jump at the chance to come to the middle of nowhere, Canada to provide pointers to a bunch of college athletes. That's why we normally get the has-beens who are wanting to relive their glory days. The fact that Mackenzie is here, plus several other pro players only a few years out of university themselves, makes me think word about Beck's presence leaked ahead of time.

Some are international players, even. William York— Britain's best hope of a world championship—is seated next to Beck.

Dinner ends with a reminder from one of the camp organizers to behave appropriately and abide by curfew.

"On that note, Samantha Cole invited us to the pool later," I announce to my teammates.

"Better plan than the campfire last year," Cressida scoffs as we enter the elevator. There might have been a minor incident with some smuggled liquor. "I'm in."

"Meet back here in a few?" Emma suggests as we reach the floor we're staying on.

Everyone agrees, and I follow her into our room, exhaling as the door swings shut and latches.

I know what's coming.

Emma takes a seat on her bed and stares at me. "Okay, spill."

"Spill?" I play dumb. Not my finest moment.

"My best friend had sex with Adler freaking Beck, and she just told me. You thought I wouldn't have questions?" There's some hurt mixing with incredulity. Out of all my friends, Emma's the one I've always shared the most about guys with. She's basically a no judgment zone.

I knew she would have questions, which is why I never told her. Not only have I not wanted to discuss Beck, it's felt like I physically couldn't. I've gotten better about burying the ache, but it hasn't faded the way I hoped. Every time I'm reminded of him, there's a twinge, just like when my knee was injured. And it hasn't healed the way that sprain did.

"It was a fling. Just some sex, then it ended."

"Two sentences? You hook up with a rich, famous, gorgeous soccer god, and all I get are *two sentences*? I have a fucking poster of him on my wall, Saylor!"

"I know. If you could take that down, that'd be great."

I've been avoiding her room for the past month for exactly that reason.

Emma's forehead wrinkles as she stares at me. "I'm confused. You bagged—no, scored, get it?"

I roll my eyes.

"With Adler Beck, and you don't want to talk about it? And you want me to take my poster down? If I had sex with him, it would be the first item on my resume!"

I snort, then head over to my duffle bag and start changing into my bikini.

"Was it bad?" she asks quietly. "Does he have a tiny dick or make weird noises or expect you to do all the work or—"

"It wasn't bad."

"Better than with—"

"Yes."

"You didn't even let me finish! What about—"

"Same answer, no matter who you say."

"Oh. *Oh*," she realizes. "Wow. So how many times did you two…"

I glance over my shoulder. "Can I ask you a favor?"

She looks confused, but answers instantly. "Of course."

"Can we talk about this in six months? Maybe a year? I'll tell you everything, I promise, I just…I need some time to pass first."

Emma studies me for a few seconds. Then half-smiles. "Yeah, of course."

I nod, then turn back around to continue changing. Emma's silent, which rarely happens. I pull a sweatshirt and sweatpants on over my swimsuit, then zip up my bag.

She still hasn't moved or said a single word.

I sigh. "Sorry. I didn't mean—"

"It's fine, S."

"It's not that I don't trust you, it's just—"

"It's hard to talk about, right?" Emma glances down, picking a stray thread on her quilt. "There was a guy I didn't want to talk about for a few months. A few years."

My mouth opens, but nothing comes out.

"You asked me about Rowan the other day? Getting over him wasn't that hard. Getting over..." She shakes her head. "I don't think I have. That I will. So, I get it. When you want to talk about—if you want to talk about it, I'll be here."

"Do you want to talk about...anything?"

"There's nothing to say. I fucked up. He hates me. The end."

A loud knock sounds on the door. Probably Cressida and Anne, impatient about waiting for us. It's been longer than a few minutes.

"Go ahead," Emma says. "I still need to get changed."

"We can wait."

"No, it's fine. I'll meet you down there."

"Okay." I nod. "As long as you're sure."

"I'm sure."

Sure enough, Anne and Cressida are waiting in the hallway, along with a bunch of other girls. I tell them Emma's coming a little later, then we enter the elevator and then make our way through the maze of beige carpeting to the section of the hotel that houses the pool.

The air is swirling with steam, excited shouts echoing off the walls. There are a couple hundred attendees at CFOC this year, and I'd estimate at least a quarter of them are in this space relaxing on loungers, sitting in the hot tub, or standing in the pool that maxes out at five feet.

A game of water basketball is already underway. I quickly shed my clothes to jump in and play. I'm using exercise as an escape right now, because the alternatives are getting drunk or sitting alone and thinking about what Emma said.

Months sounded daunting enough. Memories of Beck might haunt me for *years*?

Three games later, girls start to climb out of the pool. I'd rather continue playing, but I've also swallowed a significant amount of chlorinated water.

"Room five seventeen ladies! We've got booze!" someone calls out, prompting some scattered cheers. I pull myself up on the edge of the concrete but leave my legs dangling in the water.

"We're headed up." Cressida appears beside me, already dressed. "Do you want us to wait for you?"

"No, I'm good. Go ahead," I tell her.

She nods.

"Did Emma show up?"

Cressida frowns. "I don't know. I haven't seen her. We'll swing by your room and check on our way."

"Okay."

A few minutes later, I'm the only one left at the pool. For the first time since finding out Beck is here, I'm all alone. The steady drip of water running off my skin and back into the pool is the only soundtrack.

I knew I would probably see him again. Eventually. There are a lot of soccer players in the world. Few at his level; the level I hope to reach.

That was meant to be some distant encounter, at a huge tournament years into the future.

Not here.

Not now.

By the time I stand, my feet are pruned and the rest of my skin is dry. I towel off and then step back into my sweatshirt and sweatpants. Sink down onto one of the lounge chairs and pull my phone out of my pocket, biting on my bottom lip as I deliberate what to say. If I should send anything. The last text I sent him was one asking what time I should come over. So, so different from the place we're in now after a month of silence.

SAYLOR: Field twelve.

Ball is in his court. Or at his end, rather.

I smile grimly at my lame sports joke as I stand, leaving the humid air behind and weaving my way back down the hotel halls and through the lobby. No one stops me. Technically, all attendees have a curfew that went into effect an hour ago, but any authority figures will hopefully be distracted by the party happening upstairs and not me taking a walk.

The automatic doors glide open, providing me with a soundless exit—into a deluge of water. It's not raining out—it's *pouring*. I'm soaked after a few steps and debate turning back, but I press on. At least it'll wash the chlorine out of my hair.

Everything glints under the natural light of the moon and the artificial ones lining the path that leads from the lodge to the fields, coated with a sheen of water.

I don't stop walking until I reach the center line of field twelve. A stray soccer ball got left behind from the drills earlier. I step on it with my sneaker, a high-pitched squeak sounding as my sneaker struggles to get purchase on the slick surface.

This was dumb. I could get hypothermia or something, standing out here in the rain. It's not that cold, but still.

My soccer career is my most prized possession. I guard it against anything. Except the first time I met Adler Beck, I put my eligibility in jeopardy so I could beat him. That should have been my first clue to stay far away. Warnings only matter if you heed them.

"No stargazing tonight?"

I spin to face him. Beck's wearing all black, his blond hair and tan skin the only parts of him not blending in with the night.

"The grass is a little wet for it."

"I noticed." His clothes are soaked, just like mine, rivulets of water rolling down the chiseled planes of his face.

I stare at him and he stares back at me and it feels like eons have passed since we laid together on Kluvberg's field and stared up at the sky. Somehow, it also feels like that was yesterday.

"You still want that rematch?" I ask.

I planned to ask him why he was here, again. But now that he's standing in front of me, that seems less important. He's here. The *why* doesn't matter as much.

Beck arches an eyebrow. "It's raining."

I smirk. "I noticed. Only the best conditions for the *Kaiser*, is that it?"

He swipes the soccer ball out from under my foot, forcing me to stumble. Then he's off, racing across the soggy ground toward the nearest goal.

I sprint after him, and we start to play.

I'm sure we must look ridiculous. Playing soccer in the pouring rain, wearing wet clothes with our hair plastered to our heads. Both of us were already soaked, and pretty soon we're both splattered with mud as well.

We're making a mess of the field too. I leave a foot-long gouge in the ground after slipping, my sneakers ripping up the grass and my sweatpants finishing the job.

Beck doesn't ask if I'm okay or offer me a hand to stand up. He keeps running toward the goal, not waiting for me to catch up.

And I love every disordered second of it.

I don't think about technique or angles or strategy. My only purpose is keeping the ball moving through and around the puddles dotting the ground. I watch ribbons of rain run out of Beck's hair, absorb the intensity in his blue eyes, and I don't move away when his warm body jostles mine; the contact somehow searing through the waterlogged layers we're both wearing.

He plays with me like we're equals, and that's all I've ever wanted to be. I'm not keeping track of the score, which has never happened before. Even during scrimmages or practice, there's a constant clicker in the back of my head.

I love soccer, and it's amplified around Beck. By Beck.

Because we're the same when it comes to this sport, in comparison to all the ways we're different outside of it.

Because he makes me better without saying a single word.

Because I love *him* too, I think, not just the game we're playing together.

The rain gradually slows to a trickle.

"What time is it?" Beck asks.

I pull my phone out of my pocket to check. "After midnight."

We've been out here for more than an hour.

He nods, rolling the ball under his foot. "I've got a call at one."

It takes me a couple of seconds to realize what he means. Our middle of the night is Germany's morning. "Oh. Right."

God, I don't know what to say. Or do. He came here. I texted him. I'll be back at Lancaster in two days. He'll be back in Kluvberg.

"I'll see you tomorrow."

"Beck."

He stills immediately. Then turns back around. Like he was expecting—hoping—I might stop him.

I swallow. "We had our first preseason match a few weeks ago."

"I know."

There's a sinking sensation in my stomach. "You, uh, saw the interview I did, then?"

"After. They didn't include it in the game coverage."

Game coverage? "Wait, you watched the game? *My* game?"

"Yes." He says it simply, like it should be no surprise.

"Why?"

"I wanted to see you play."

"You've seen me play."

"Not at home, with your team. I was curious."

He didn't forget about me the second I left, at least. "That interview...it was stupid. I didn't think you'd see it. That anyone would see it. It was a surprise any press even showed up for our scrimmage—it used to be a struggle to get them to come to our playoffs game—and I was distracted and just said the first thing that popped into my head and I didn't know it would become a thing that—"

"Did you mean it?"

I swallow. "Yes."

He clicks his tongue like he's disappointed by that answer.

"It wasn't supposed to be about anything related to what happened between us," I continue. "Just, you know, you as an athlete. It was a *compliment.* I'm sorry if you're mad that I—"

Once again, he interrupts. "I'm not mad."

"You seem mad," I state.

"It would have been nice if you'd told me that yourself, is all."

"Told you *what?* It's news to you that other soccer players have followed your career? Surprise, you're famous."

He scoffs. "It's news to me that *you* followed my career, Saylor."

"So have millions of other people!" I don't get why he's fixated on this. Because I never acted like a fangirl, he assumed I had no idea how successful he's been?

"You're not millions of other people to me."

That pulls me up short.

"*You* watching me play, *you* following my career, *you* saying I inspired you—that's different from *millions of other people* doing those things."

Fuck. Fuck. *Fuck.* I know exactly what he means. It's the same feeling I just experienced when he told me that he watched my game. I knew he had that power over me. I had no clue I had that power over him.

The silence between us stretches longer and longer, me scrambling to figure out what to say.

Beck speaks first. "Otto hung a sign that says, 'Saylor Scott's Inspiration' above my locker."

I appreciate his attempt to lighten the mood. "That's kind of funny."

It's also bittersweet, learning more of the ways my presence in Germany lingered even after I left.

"He's still sore he never got a shot with you," Beck tells me.

"Goalies aren't my type," I manage to say. Truthfully, Beck was the only guy I looked twice at, the whole time I was in Germany. In the month since I've been back.

His phone rings, breaking the resulting silence. He pulls it out. Glances at the screen. "I have to take this."

Beck starts toward the lodge, speaking rapid German.

And all I can wonder, watching him walk away, is if he ever felt this awful any of the times that I did.

Chapter 19

'm exhausted the following morning, snippets of my conversation with Beck playing in my head all night and making it hard to sleep. I down two cups of coffee between bites of cereal at breakfast, determined to fight through the exhaustion like I always do.

We head toward the fields, sorted back into our teams, any alliances formed during last night's fun falling apart. First up on the schedule is an hour-long scrimmage, followed by rotating between clinics. This game won't count for anything, but pride is on the line. We'll play most of these teams, including our opponent today, Montclave College, during the regular season. This is our opportunity to warn other schools they shouldn't be clearing any space for a national trophy.

Samantha holds out a hand as we meet with the ref, which I shake.

"Looking forward to kicking your ass, Scott," she tells me, grinning.

I smirk back. "It'll be fun to watch you try, Cole," I reply before calling tails.

I choose correctly, and it sets off a domino effect of luck. Emma slides a kick behind their goalie when she thinks Emma is going to pass to me instead, and then Natalie manages a wicked header. I make a half-field shot that results in a lot of wide eyes on the field. Cressida lets one goal in, but we still emerge victorious.

Then, it's onto the rotation of drills. My eyes seek out Beck as soon as the final whistle blows. He's talking to William York again.

The station Mackenzie is in charge of is the first one we rotate to after a water break. She gives me a condescending smile as we gather around. I smirk back at her. If she wants to challenge me, soccer is *not* the way to do it. She hasn't seen me play in two years, and I was the victor of our last match-up then. Confidence counts a lot more if you can back it up.

The drill Mackenzie describes is similar to the one Coach Taylor had us running through yesterday. Except instead of starting from side-by-side cones, we're facing a defender already in the penalty box and a goalie in position.

"I'll demonstrate one round," Mackenzie announces. Her gaze roams across the group. I know she's going to pick me long before she says my name. "Saylor. You're a striker, right?"

"Right." I keep my response short, and I hear Emma muffle a snort beside me.

Mackenzie knows exactly what my position is, and feigning forgetfulness isn't the upper hand she thinks it is.

"Are you willing to help me demonstrate?" Mackenzie asks sweetly.

I tighten my ponytail. "Sure."

She passes me a ball, and I trap it neatly, waiting for her to get into position. As soon as she's in place, I strike, racing forward. I don't head straight toward her, jutting out to the edge of the box so she has to come to me. As soon as she leaves her position, I employ some of the footwork I can thank Christina Weber for. Mackenzie tries to copy me, but she slips.

As soon as she does, I send the ball into the netting, easily outsmarting the goalie. It's not the most satisfying goal I've ever scored—not by a long shot—but I still enjoy watching her squirm when I turn around. "Was that what you had in mind?"

"Good work, Scott," Mackenzie mutters through gritted teeth. "Two lines, everyone."

After Mackenzie's, we cycle through three more drill clinics. We're only one away from Beck's.

William York is in charge of this one, and there's a fair amount of whispering going on between the girls surrounding me. He's the most popular—and good-looking—guest coach so far. He has a charming British accent and the implied importance of a member of the royal family. William seems oblivious to the attention as he talks us through a combination passing drill.

A few players struggle with the fast-paced weaving once we start.

I'm not one of them, and William comes over right after I finish.

"Excellent work out there," he tells me, flashing a cheeky grin.

"Thanks." My tone is polite, but don't smile back.

"You're the girl who went to Scholenberg, right?"

I don't love knowing I've been gossiped about among the staff. "One of them, yeah."

"The only one here," he replies, still grinning.

I nod.

"Beck said you were amazing."

I falter at that for a split-second. I've seen him and Beck talking twice now. They're friends...maybe? Colleagues? Did Beck actually say that, or is William just joking around?

"That was nice of him."

"Maybe even inspiring." He winks, then moves on.

Seems like I might be the only person on the planet who hasn't watched the clip of me praising Beck.

A few minutes later, we're switching again.

Beck's wearing all black today, just like he was last night. The dark color emphasizes his golden looks.

Those whispers about William York? Absent. You don't gossip about Adler Beck when he's standing in front of you—you stare at him.

Nothing but wide eyes and awed silence surround me. Plus a few glances between me and Beck, confirming there's still speculation about our private conversation on the field yesterday.

Wonderful.

Beck's body language is as intimidating as his looks. He's planted in place, arms crossed. His presence isn't charismatic; it's commanding. He barks out rapid instructions for the drill, and I'm not surprised to hear they're twice as complex as every other clinic we've completed so far. After our scrimmage earlier, most of the guest coaches have been taking it easy on us. At least for now, this afternoon will probably be a different story.

The exercise requires receiving a flighted ball, dribbling on the attack through a series of grids, and then taking a shot on goal.

Based on the uncertain expressions around me, most are unsure about how to execute it.

Beck catches the confusion. "Would a demonstration help?"

Heads bob around me, but mine doesn't move.

"Saylor?" He addresses me directly, and it catches me off guard. I wasn't expecting him to single me out today.

"Yeah, Coach?" I don't miss the way a muscle in Beck's straight jaw jumps, but I hope everyone else does.

"Do you know what you're doing?" he asks.

"I always know what I'm doing," I reply, projecting my usual confidence.

How ironic that I'm saying that to the one exception.

"Show me," he says.

Not them. *Me.* I have no idea if that means something or if I'm so tired, I'm reading into nothing.

I nod, walking forward and then speeding up to a sprint when I reach the first grid. Beck sends me a flighted ball, and I send it straight into the goal.

He doesn't congratulate me, just nods.

Like a perfect play is exactly what he expected.

Somehow, that's better than any praise.

I move to the back of the line, letting the other girls in the group go ahead with the drill, with varying levels of success. Beck corrects every error. He's a good coach, stern but fair.

Before I have the chance to go again, a loud horn sounds across the field, signaling the end of the clinics and the break for lunch.

"Thank God," Cressida announces beside me. "I'm starving. Who thought those little boxes of cereal were breakfast? Give me some waffles and bacon."

"It's a soccer camp, not a vacation," I reply, laughing, although I'm just as hungry.

"Why can't it be both?" Cressida challenges.

I'm following Anne off the field when Beck speaks. "Saylor?"

I pause as everyone looks at me. "Yeah?"

"Can I talk to you for a minute?"

I bite my bottom lip before turning and walking back toward him. "Fun drill," I say, once I reach him.

Beck shakes his head a little, the corners of his lips barely lifting as he rakes a hand through his hair. "I'm leaving," he tells me.

"What about lunch?" I ask stupidly.

Another head shake. "I already stayed later than I should've. I have to be back tomorrow."

"Oh." Part of me was already making plans for what I'd text him tonight. I thought we'd *have* tonight. "Is that what the phone call was about?"

He nods once.

His season has started. It's shocking he was able to come at all, not that he's having to depart early. But I'm still…I thought we'd have a tiny bit more time.

Beck's staring at me, waiting for me to say something.

"I'm leaving tomorrow. Heading back to Lancaster. You're going back to Kluvberg. So…nothing's changed?"

He's still staring. "You tell me."

I clear my throat. "Nothing's changed."

"You asked me why I came—you didn't need to. You know the answer. I came to see *you*, Saylor."

I close my eyes. "Beck…don't. This is hard enough, okay?"

"Is it hard for you? Because I can't figure out what I am to you. *If* I'm anything to you. You left after Scholenberg like it was nothing. Like it was easy for you."

"I left like it was the only option. My entire life is in the US. My school, my friends, my family…"

That last excuse is flimsy, considering everything he knows about me. But the rest is valid. What did he expect? For me to move to Germany?

"You could have called, or texted, *once* before last night. I came all this way and..."

"And *what*?" I ask. "Are you mad you didn't get laid on this trip, or something?"

Beck just shakes his head again, looking disappointed. That's worse than him appearing angry or annoyed. He knows me well enough to tell I'm deflecting. To get that I'm avoiding admitting the truth to him.

My voice lowers. "I thought–I thought we were just having fun..."

"I'm glad you enjoyed yourself." The words are inscrutable.

I huff. "Like you didn't."

He steps closer, and I pull in a quick breath. "Of course I did. Of course I want to fuck you again. But it was more than sex for me. I let you walk away because I thought it was a lost cause. But then you did that damn interview and I thought..." He runs a hand through his hair. "I thought that maybe it was more for you too. I guess I was wrong."

"You weren't wrong. But I..." I chew on the inside of my cheek. "I don't know how to do this, okay? Not at all, and definitely not with you."

Twin lines of confusion appear between his eyebrows. "What are you talking about?"

I roll my eyes. "You're *Adler Beck*."

He looks even more confused. "I know."

"You don't just live in Germany. People there call you *Kaiser*. You're not just relevant when there's a World Cup. You're super famous all the time."

His brows rise. "The attention bothers you?"

"It's just more complicated."

Most of me loves that Beck is such a major part of the soccer world. That he shares the same competitive fire. That he gets what being an athlete is like entirely, without me having to explain anything. That he easily accepts what others have called me crazy for.

But it comes with one major downside. The attention one interview I mentioned his name during was overwhelming. I can't imagine what it would be like on a larger scale. It's what I'll be known for. Any article about my career will include some reference to him. Dating Adler Beck would become my biggest accomplishment.

That's a sacrifice for me, one I'm not sure I'm willing to make.

Instead of telling him any of that, I say, "A lot of women want you."

"*I* want *you.*" Three short, simple words that say so much. That he flew over a thousand miles to tell me.

"Beck!"

I swear under my breath as Mackenzie jogs over to us. She has the worst timing.

"Your car is here," she informs him.

Shocking, that she decided she needed to be the one to come tell Beck while we're having a private conversation.

Beck nods, and I know that's it. He has to go. He's leaving, when I've barely registered he's here in the first place, and I'm less certain of where we stand than before he arrived.

"I'll let the driver know you're coming," Mackenzie says. "He's worried about traffic."

I snort as soon as I'm reasonably certain she's out of earshot. "Unless there's a moose crossing, you should be fine."

When I glance at Beck, he's smirking.

"What?"

"Nothing."

"Sorry if you're, you know, friends."

His smile only grows. "She's not my type. I prefer strikers."

"She *is* a striker, Beck."

He shrugs. "I didn't know that. Should tell you everything you need to know."

"Uh, fly safe."

Beck reaches out and tugs the end of my ponytail. It's an affectionate gesture, a little teasing. But the last time he pulled my hair, his dick was in my mouth.

Heat flares in his gaze as we stare at each other, and I'm pretty sure he's thinking the same thing.

"Bye, Saylor."

"Bye, Beck."

He turns and strides away, leaving me standing alone. I watch him walk away, left with the paralyzing sensation of uncertainty. Wishing I said more. Wishing I cared less.

I like things to be black and white. Adler Beck is a whole lot of gray. Overwhelming, confusing gray.

And I don't know what to do about it.

If I should do anything about it.

Chapter 20

The plane aisle finally clears. I hop up, eager to stretch my legs and breathe something other than recycled air for the first time in two hours.

I've been dreading this trip, but there's a rush of nostalgia when I walk out of the automatic airport doors into the Georgia sunshine. Hallie snagged a prime spot at the front of the line. I stick my suitcase into the trunk of her white SUV and climb in the passenger seat to give my sister a hug. She squeezes me tightly, smelling like sunshine and applesauce.

My chest clenches like it's being squeezed by a rubber band. I might complain about Hallie's constant check-ins, but she's the one person who's always been there for me. The one family member who's never abandoned me, either physically or emotionally.

I missed her. I love her, even though I'm shitty about showing it.

"Happy wedding weekend!" she cheers when we pull apart.

"Please don't try to make that a thing," I reply, rolling my eyes at the cheerful expression emphasized by the colorful silk scarf Hallie tied around her ponytail. It practically smacks me in the face as she spins to refasten her seatbelt.

"Well, *someone* has to counteract all the negative energy you're exuding," she replies, as I click my seatbelt into place.

"I had to get up at five to go for a run before leaving for the airport. They messed up my coffee order, and the row behind me contained not one, but two screaming children. Please excuse me if I'm not the picture of joy and excitement."

"Right, because otherwise you would be," Hallie remarks dryly as she pulls away from the curb. I don't deny it. She knows exactly how I feel about this weekend.

"Speaking of screaming children, where's yours?" I ask.

Hallie manages to give me side-eye while navigating a roundabout. "With Matt and his family. They're staying with us."

"What? Why?"

"Because they're *Matt's family*. You can always stay at Dad's."

I huff out an annoyed breath. "So Jackson is also staying at the house?"

"He's my brother-in-law, Saylor."

"Which makes the fact that he does nothing but hit on me all the weirder."

"Well, *you're* not related to him," Hallie points out.

"Legally, I am."

"He's just trying to be friendly."

I laugh. "Thank God you found Matt in pre-algebra. Jackson asked me out to dinner at your wedding, Hallie. That's not just being *friendly* to your sister-in-law's sister."

She doesn't argue with me. "He's harmless."

"I know. Doesn't mean I want to spend the next couple days

fending off his advances."

"Would it be that terrible to be in a relationship?" Hallie asks. "Not with Jackson, but someone else," she adds hastily, completely misreading my silence.

"I don't have time for it."

"You make time for it, Saylor. There's never been a guy who made you consider it?"

I'm focused on the line of palm trees we're passing by. "Maybe. I don't know."

"Don't know what?"

I sigh. "It's complicated."

I haven't seen or spoken to Beck since he left CFOC. I can't reach out to say *nothing*, and that's currently all I have to share. Talking to him is a leap I'm scared to make for many reasons, chief among them that I'm scared to fall. So I've focused on soccer and dreading this trip ever since returning to Lancaster, rather than dealing with any of it.

"Relationships are complicated. Doesn't mean they're not worthwhile."

"We weren't in a relationship," I tell the trees.

"Oh. Okay."

"I think I'm in love with him, though." Shocked silence follows. "So that's...inconvenient."

"Does he go to Lancaster?" Hallie asks tentatively.

I didn't plan to discuss Beck with her. But talking about it is easier than I would have expected. "No. He plays professionally." I pause, then add, "In Germany. I met him over the summer, when I was at Scholenberg."

"Ah. So it's a distance thing?"

"Partially. He's also kind of...famous."

"*Famous?*" Hallie sounds amused. "For *playing soccer?*"

I scoff, unsurprised by her reaction. "Yes."

"What's his name?"

"Why?" I ask suspiciously.

"Why do you think, Saylor? I want to look him up."

"That's totally unnecessary."

"*Saylor.*"

I sigh. "Fine. His name is Adler Beck."

Hallie slams on the brakes. *Slams.* We're approaching a red light, but still. Way more force than was necessary. "*Adler Beck?*"

"You know who he is?" I'm shocked. Hallie has never expressed any interest in soccer. She once asked me how many touchdowns I scored in a season.

"Of course I do," she says, sounding less like my serious older sister and a lot more like a preteen at a boy band concert. "He's famous!"

"I know that he's famous. I just told you he's famous, and you laughed."

"I just didn't, I—wow. Okay. That's...wow. You should have invited him to the wedding."

I snort. "Yeah, right. We're not...I'm not cut out for a relationship."

"Of course you are," Hallie responds. "Do you think I planned to end up married with a kid at twenty-seven?"

"Um, honestly? Yes," I reply.

Hallie and her husband Matt had one of those insta-love connections that were all the rage in middle school but rarely lasted past puberty. They spent the entirety of their high school and college years attached at the hip. I would have been more surprised if she'd told me they *weren't* getting married when she made the announcement three years ago.

Hallie's eyes are on the road, but I have a feeling she's rolling them. "Well, I didn't. I mean, maybe I liked the idea of having the stable family we didn't, but that was also why I was terrified. Worried Matt and I might end up like Mom and Dad."

"You were?" I ask, surprised.

"Yeah, I was," Hallie confirms. "And the point is, I realized it. I moved past it. I'm not sure if you have."

"I don't need a psychology degree to know I've got trust issues because Mom left, Hallie. That's my shit to figure out... sometime."

She's quiet for a minute. "Don't let her take anything else, Saylor."

We're both silent after that. Any mention of our mom tends to have that sobering effect. Losing a parent is traumatic under any circumstances. Having them purposefully abandon you? I'm not over it. I'm not sure I ever will be.

. . .

I'm expecting Hallie to pull up in front of the bungalow she and Matt bought when they got married. Instead, she stops and parks in front of a long, industrial-looking building on the fringes of town.

"Where are we?" I ask.

"They moved the farmer's market here last year," Hallie tells me as she shuts off the car and opens the driver's side door. "If you came home more frequently, you'd know that."

I ignore the dig as I climb out of the vehicle. "What are we doing here?"

"I need a few things for dinner. You can browse the booths. They have crafty stuff for sale too."

"Crafty stuff?"

"Yeah, knitwear, embroidery, artwork. Stuff like that."

"How exciting," I deadpan as we walk inside.

I trail after Hallie, glancing around the booths as we pass them. There's fresh bread, slippers, cheese, wooden bowls, and even a table selling homemade dog treats.

I stop at one displaying framed paintings on a wire wall. They're mostly watercolors. My gaze lands on one of a soccer field. The watercolor effect makes it look like it's raining.

An elderly woman appears at my side. "Can I help you find anything, dear?"

"I—no." I look at the painting again. It reminds me of my favorite painting in the art museum in Kluvberg. Also of a rain-soaked field in Canada. "Are you the artist?"

"I sure am," she says proudly. "Painted this one while I was watching my grandson's soccer game."

"It's beautiful."

"Thank you."

"I'll take it," I say impulsively.

"Wonderful! Let me wrap it up for you."

I watch as she carefully folds a few sheets of tissue paper around the painting and then sets it in a box. I pay and thank the woman, then continue walking. Hallie is browsing through bouquets of flowers several booths down.

"You bought something?" she asks, spotting the box I'm carrying.

"Yeah. Found a painting I liked."

She raises an eyebrow but doesn't comment. "Can you hold these?"

"Sure," I say, tucking the box under my arm and taking the flowers from her.

Hallie finishes her shopping and then we head back out into the parking lot. It takes several minutes to load all the groceries she purchased into the back of the car.

"Hi, Hallie!" A blonde woman stops by the trunk.

"Hi, Stephanie. How have you been?"

"Busy," the woman replies with a smile. "Simon is teething."

"Oh, no," Hallie responds.

I feel like saying the same thing, except in relation to this topic of conversation.

"Yup, it's been an experience. Hoping I'll have some wisdom to pass along by the time Matthew hits that stage."

Hallie laughs. "That would be wonderful."

"Who's this?" The woman turns her attention to me.

"Oh, sorry. Stephanie, this is my sister, Saylor. Saylor, this is my friend Stephanie," Hallie says.

I transfer the last bag into the trunk and turn around. "Nice to meet you."

"Oh my goodness, I can't believe I'm meeting the famous Saylor!"

"Famous?" I look at Hallie.

"Your sister talks about you all the time at our meetings," Stephanie informs me.

"Meetings?" I echo.

"Yes, we're in the same book club."

I bite my bottom lip to keep from laughing. "Really?"

"Hallie's our newest member, but she contributes a lot."

"She usually does," I reply.

"Well, I've got to get going, but great to see you, Hallie. Nice to meet you, Saylor," Stephanie says before she keeps walking down the line of cars.

I head to the passenger side, and Hallie climbs in the driver's seat.

"You're in a book club?" I laugh.

Hallie glares at me. "It's my one night out of the house, okay?"

"I wasn't judging." I totally was. "I just find the thought of you in a book club amusing."

"It's fun, okay? We have interesting discussions."

"Oh yeah? What was the last book you read?"

Based on Hallie's expression, that is the last question she wanted me to ask. "*The Duke Who Defiled Me*," she mutters.

"I'm sorry, what?" I giggle. "Are you serious?"

"I didn't choose it."

I'm laughing too hard to reply.

"We can't all have thrilling lives in reality, Saylor."

The serious note in my sister's voice is the only reason I'm able to regain my composure. "My life isn't thrilling, Hallie."

She snorts, dubious. "If you say so. Just don't judge my life."

"I wasn't, Hallie."

But I have. I've always viewed quiet and settled as the antithesis of everything I ever wanted mine to be.

She's still doubtful. "Sure."

"Just because I don't see myself with a husband and kids doesn't mean I judge you for choosing those things. You're my sister. I'm happy for you."

"I know you don't. I—I shouldn't have said anything. I've just been stressed making sure everything is all set for the wedding."

I grasp the peace offering. "Well, I'm here now. I want to help."

Hallie smiles. "You're going to regret saying that."

She pulls into a driveway behind two other cars ten minutes later.

I grab my luggage, the painting, plus a paper bag from the farmer's market and head inside.

The bungalow is homey. I've only seen photos, and Hallie's redecorated since the last ones I saw. The living room is scattered with baby toys, and beneath them, a brightly patterned rug. The walls are decorated with vibrant prints. The framed pieces are interspersed with family photos, and I'm surprised to see how many I'm featured in.

"Hallie?" a male voice calls as we head toward the back of the house.

"Yeah. We're back," she announces as we walk into the kitchen.

Matt is sitting at the round kitchen table, bouncing my nephew on his lap. An older couple I recognize from Hallie's wedding as Matt's parents are seated across from him...along with his brother Jackson.

"Saylor!" Matt greets me enthusiastically as he rises to give me a hug. "So good to see you."

"You too, Matt," I reply. "The house looks great."

"Thanks." He gives me a boyish grin, then holds up my nephew. "Want to hold Matthew?"

"I—well—it's—"

Matt doesn't really wait for a response. He passes me the baby, and it's either grab him or let him drop.

I clutch Matthew tightly to my chest, terrified I'm going to mess up holding him. He appears unconcerned about that possibility, blinking up at me innocently as he waves his little hands about. I stare down at him. He's so...tiny.

My nephew yawns, then his brown eyes shutter shut. "Um, he seems tired?" I say.

"Wow, he hardly ever falls asleep while he's being held," Hallie comments, coming up beside me. "Impressive. We'll have to fly you down to babysit on a regular basis."

"Hilarious," I respond.

Hallie takes Matthew from me and transfers him to a small cradle tucked in a corner of the room. Matt's parents and brother stand from the table to greet me. I force myself not to yank my hand away when Jackson's handshake lasts twice as long as necessary.

"I'll get the couch made up for you as soon as I get these groceries put away," Hallie tells me, unloading the paper bags from the farmer's market.

"Oh, Saylor should take the guest bedroom," Matt's mother says.

"No, it's fine," I tell her, because what else can I say? *Actually yes, I'd love to have four walls enclosing my sleeping space that aren't part of a communal area.* Hallie would kill me. "I'm going to go for a run."

Hallie eyes me, frowning. "I thought you went for one this morning."

"I did, but I'm missing practice today," I reply. "So I should go for a second one."

"Mind if I join you?" Jackson asks, rising from the table and shooting me a grin. "I need to get in shape for lacrosse."

"Saylor runs fast," Hallie says. "Just a warning."

Jackson's smile only grows. "I'm sure I can keep up."

I doubt it.

Jackson is tall, but his lanky frame lacks muscle. I'd be shocked if he's in shape enough to jog more than a couple miles. I can't recall the last time I ran less than five, but I've been inside this house for about ten minutes, and he's spent eight of them looking at my long legs. Decimating oversized male egos is my favorite hobby. If it keeps him from bothering me the rest of the weekend, that's just a cherry on top.

Hallie sighs. "Have fun."

I'm already wearing my standard athletic apparel and sneakers. "Ready?" I ask Jackson, pulling my hair up in a bun.

"Yeah, sure," he replies with overdone casualness.

We head outside. I suck in deep breaths of humid air as I stretch my calves on Hallie's front lawn.

Then I start running.

Jackson attempts to make small talk with me for the first block but runs out of breath a couple later. We've barely made it to the park—less than a mile from Hallie and Matt's house— when he collapses on the side of the sidewalk. "Holy shit. How far was that?"

"Not far," I respond, standing over him. "Want me to come back for you?"

"Yeah, yeah, go ahead." He waves an arm and then lets it drop, breathing heavily. "I'll catch up."

I cover my snort with a cough, then continue running through my hometown, staying away from the downtown section and instead weaving through the residential neighborhoods. About a half hour later, I circle back to the park. Jackson is still there. Standing now, at least.

"Wasn't sure if you were coming back." He chuckles.

"Just had to get in five," I reply.

"Five? You just ran five miles?" He gapes at me.

"Uh-huh." I turn back toward Hallie's. Jackson trails after me. Calling his pace a jog would be a compliment, but he makes it.

We return to the kitchen to find the scene virtually unchanged from when we left. Matt's seated at the kitchen table with his parents, Matthew is asleep in his crib, and Hallie's making sandwiches for lunch. With the exception of the baby, they all look at us as we enter.

"You good, little bro?" Matt asks Jackson. He appears amused, which makes me like him a little more.

"Great," he wheezes, dropping down in the open chair. Hallie gives me a *look*.

I head to the fridge, grabbing a couple bottles of water. I hand one to Jackson and then drain most of the other one. I'm soaked with sweat, but I feel better.

"How far did you guys go?" Matt questions.

I wait for Jackson to answer. "I only made it to the park. Saylor ran five miles after."

Everyone gapes at me.

"It's less than I would have run at practice," I say with a shrug.

"My goodness." Matt's father chuckles. "Guess you won't be able to complain about lacrosse any longer, Jackson."

It's impossible to tell because his face is already so red, but I'm pretty sure Jackson is blushing.

"I'm going to shower," I announce.

"Towels are in the closet," Hallie informs me as she spreads mayonnaise on bread.

"Great." I grab my duffle bag and head upstairs, already deciding to make my shower last as long as possible.

This is going to be a long weekend.

• • •

"It's *so* nice to see you, Saylor," Sandra tells me. For the fourth time.

She showed up an hour ago to pick up her wedding dress from the closet where Hallie has apparently been storing it for her, took Hallie up on her offer of a glass of wine, and has stayed for three. Glasses, not hours. Although it does feel like it's been three hours.

I paste a smile on my face. "Nice to see you too."

Hallie jumps in. "These cookies are fantastic, Sandra."

I look at the clock: ten-thirty p.m. A reasonable time to announce I'm headed to bed, right? Matt's mom went to sleep a little while ago.

Too bad we're hanging out in my bedroom.

"Thank you, Hallie," Sandra replies, beaming.

"They are good," I admit, taking another bite.

They're fudgy and peanut butter-y. Cressida would probably love the recipe.

"How are your classes going, Saylor?" Sandra asks, chugging right along on the try-to-get-to-know-you train.

"Fine, I think," I reply. "I've only been to one in the last couple weeks."

"One?" Sandra replies, looking startled. "Were you sick? Marcus didn't mention..." Her voice trails, ending in the awkwardness of us all knowing my dad is not exactly well-informed about my life.

"No, I just had soccer," I respond matter-of-factly.

Sandra looks to Hallie for backup, but Hallie just sighs and shrugs.

We've had this argument many times before.

"I'm sure your professors—your advisors—they must know how important your classes are," Sandra says. "You're at school to receive a degree."

My shoulders tense. "My professors and my advisors would rather I win another national championship than attend class. I'm at Lancaster on a full athletic scholarship. I'm there to *play soccer*."

Sandra frowns. "Surely they don't expect every student who's on an athletic team to give up every other aspect of their college experience."

"Saylor takes soccer very seriously," Hallie says, shooting me a warning look when I open my mouth.

"That's...wonderful," Sandra tells me, sounding uncertain that's the right adjective. "I was never that athletic myself, so it's hard for me to imagine that dedication."

I take another bite of cookie.

"Well...I should get to bed," Hallie says. "Matthew will most likely wake me up in a few hours."

"Oh, of course." Sandra stands. "I'm sorry to have imposed for so long."

"Not an imposition at all." Hallie rises also. "The dress is in Matt's office. Here, I'll show you."

"Good night, Saylor," Sandra tells me.

"Night," I reply, before they head upstairs.

I'm already wearing my pajamas, so I just have to duck into the half bath to brush my teeth before climbing under the covers on the couch. I close my eyes and inhale the unfamiliar scent of whatever laundry detergent Hallie uses.

Low voices converse a few minutes later, then I hear steps head down the hallway. The front door opens and closes.

More footsteps. Closer. "Saylor?" Hallie whispers.

I don't answer.

There's a sigh. "Goodnight."

I lie there for a while before I finally fall asleep.

Chapter 21

This is only the second wedding I've ever attended. The few friends I have who are in relationships are still a long way away from what's meant to be a lifetime commitment.

My mother is an only child, and the few hazy memories I have of her side of the family turned to wisps of smoke around the same time she disappeared. They didn't keep in touch, much less invite us to any celebratory events.

And rather than relying on his family after becoming a single father, my dad retreated from his. Maybe we do share some DNA after all.

I'm surprised to realize that rift seems to have been restored when I enter the old white church where my father is getting married today.

There are still a couple of hours left before the start of the ceremony. Hallie refused to agree to show up a half hour ahead of time like normal wedding guests. Since she's my mode of transportation, I didn't really have a choice except to show up this early too.

Now that we're inside the church's lobby, which is bustling with extended family I haven't seen in years, I get that it might have been a bit awkward for us to show up an hour and a half from now. But not as uncomfortable as having to interact with virtual strangers who share my last name.

"Hallie!" A stout, white-haired woman sweeps my sister up in a hug, crushing the bag containing Hallie's bridesmaid dress between them.

I watch Hallie surreptitiously shake it as soon as she's released.

"Where's Matthew? Both of them!"

"They're at the park with Matt's family. They'll all be here soon. Saylor and I wanted to arrive early so we could help out."

Big of her to include me in that offer. And Hallie's also drawn our grandmother's attention to me.

"Saylor!" She moves forward slightly, then shifts back, and the uncertain motion is worse than a bone-jarring hug. My own grandmother is apprehensive about showing me affection. Maybe I really am the cold-hearted bitch I've been called.

"Hi, Grandma. I like your dress," I lie.

It's an aggressive shade of periwinkle, accented with what I think is meant to be a fascinator but looks more like a bird nested in her hair that left a few feathers behind. I doubt critiquing her outfit is going to dissipate any of the tension hanging in the air.

"Why, thank you, dear. I got it on sale!" Her thick southern accent emphasizes each syllable.

"Really?" There's a hint of sarcasm in the word that my grandmother doesn't catch.

Hallie does, mouthing *Stop it* at me.

"I hear you're quite the soccer star, Saylor," my grandmother says. "If I had your looks, I would just sit around and wait for some handsome fella to sweep me off my feet."

"How progressive of you," I reply sweetly.

"We should really go check on some...things." Hallie smiles. "We'll see you later, Grandma." She grips my bicep—she's stronger than I would have guessed—and pulls me away. "Really, Saylor?"

"I'm not going to apologize for being a feminist. I should *sit around and wait for a guy*? What decade is this?"

"Grandma went to debutante balls, and our father's wedding isn't the right time to lecture on feminism—even if it's the only time you're home to talk about anything."

Great. Another guilt trip. "Am I supposed to apologize for going to college? For pursuing a professional soccer career?"

"Plenty of people go to school and have careers and *also* keep in touch with their family."

"Less than you'd think," I mutter. It's true. Giving your all—absolutely everything—requires just that: everything. Not worrying about others' feelings. Not coming home for holidays. Sequestering every ounce of energy and bit of brainpower. "And I'm not interested in being 'plenty of people.' I want to be the best."

Hallie says nothing. No matter our shared experiences— growing up motherless, our father checking out, and a small town that loves to gossip—we're very different.

Soccer is my escape.

Hallie wants to fix it all, make peace with our past. She married the perfect guy to be a father. She's the perfect mother. She showed our hometown a Scott woman can be reliable and genuine. She talks to our father and extended family.

I fled as far and fast as I could.

We enter the aisle of the church. I didn't grow up devout.

The last time I was inside a religious building was when I was here for Hallie's wedding. I glance around at the varnished wood trim, stained glass, and symmetrical pews. The scents of incense and fresh flowers mingle in the air, swirling around our strides toward the altar. Garlands of daisies, peonies, and ranunculus hang along the end of each pew we pass.

"Looks like we missed the decorating," I state. "Bummer."

"I'm sure there's still work to be done," Hallie informs me. "Let's go hang up our dresses."

I heave out a sigh but follow her out of the aisle toward the back of the church.

We run into our father on the trip down the hallway. I freeze as soon as I see him, nerves dampening my palms with sweat.

"Oh, good. I wasn't sure what time you girls were going to arrive." He gives me a nervous glance that seems to be my only greeting.

"I told you we'd be here by one, Dad," Hallie replies, giving him a hug. I stand by, feeling more awkward with each passing second.

"Well, something always seems to go wrong at weddings, and nothing has yet." My father frets, glancing upward like he's expecting the roof to cave in at any moment.

"Everything will be fine," she says soothingly.

"I guess I'm a little nervous." My dad fiddles with his cufflinks.

"That's normal. Totally normal. Everything is going to be perfect. And Sandra is wonderful."

"Plus, she seems like a low flight risk," I add.

Hallie sends me a sharp look for that comment, but my father chuckles. Makes an actual sound of amusement.

I can't recall the last time that happened. Probably because we barely speak.

"I know–I know I put you girls through hell back then. If I could go back and do things differently, I would. I hope this can be a new chapter. A fresh start for our family." He pauses, and when he speaks again, his voice is thicker. "You two mean the world to me. I hope you know that."

The words are meant more for me, but Hallie is the one who responds. "Oh, Dad." She hugs him, and I watch them share a moment I'm meant to be included in.

She forgave our father a long time ago. All three of us know that. I'm the one entrenched in the past.

Holding grudges.

Forcing friction.

Because I believe people should be held accountable for their actions. Because actions have consequences. Because I've prioritized scoring goals over being daughter or sister or granddaughter or aunt of the year, and this trip has thrown that into glaring clarity.

My father releases Hallie and then takes a hesitant step toward me. Then another. And another. He wraps his arms around me and gives me a small squeeze. I lift my own arms to touch his back, but don't tighten them.

It's barely a hug, but it's something.

"Marcus! There you are!" A harried-looking woman wearing a pantsuit appears at the end of the hallway. "We need to go over some reception logistics."

She must be the wedding planner.

"Go handle that, Dad. We've got to get ready for photos," Hallie instructs. Then she starts striding down the hallway.

"See you later, Dad," I say, and then I literally have to sprint after Hallie since I have no idea where exactly we're headed.

"Sheesh! Are you training for a speed-walking competition?"

Hallie snorts. "Says the girl who runs five miles a day."

"I thought we got here ridiculously early to *avoid* having to rush. What's with the sudden hurry?"

"Well, we have to make sure Sandra's not gassing up a getaway car."

I sigh. "Hallie, it was a *joke*! I'm not allowed to have a sense of humor?"

"We're in a church, not a comedy club."

I fake gasp. "Is that why there are crosses every two feet?"

Hallie slants me an unamused glance as she stops outside a carved wood door. "I hope you got the sarcasm out of your system. Sandra will take anything you say seriously, and I'm sure she still feels bad about last night."

"Fine," I mutter as we head inside a room that finally makes me feel like we're in the current century.

The walls are covered by the same dark wood paneling as the hallway and pews, but there's a sectional couch in the corner upholstered with blue cotton. Sunshine streams in through the windows, beaming directly onto the folding table that's been set up in the center of the space. Only small sections of the scratched plastic surface are visible. Most of it's covered with bobby pins, hair ties, tissues, water bottles, Band-Aids, and a lot of makeup. A couple room dividers are set up, screening off parts of the space from view.

"You're here!" A figure in a pink robe barrels toward us. Sandra stops just a couple of feet away. "Thank goodness."

"Didn't I say we'd be here at one?" Hallie asks.

"Yes, you did," Sandra confirms. "Everyone's been asking when Hallie and Saylor would arrive, though!" She lets out a nervous, tinny laugh. "I guess we know who the real stars of the show are!"

I'm not surprised Hallie's arrival was anticipated. I am surprised mine was, but I'm guessing there's a fair amount of intrigue about my presence. I haven't been back home since graduating high school, except for Hallie's wedding.

"This is the famous Saylor?" Another woman appears at Sandra's side, one who looks enough like her, I'm certain they are related. "My goodness, you're gorgeous, dear."

"Uh, thank you," I respond. I'm sporting oversized sweats and a bun so messy it seems an insult to the hairstyle to even call it one. I figured I'd have plenty of time to get ready.

"I'm Sandra's sister, Sally," the woman explains.

"Nice to meet you," I reply with a polite smile.

"It feels like we've already met. I've heard so much about you from Marcus."

An interruption saves me from having to respond. The door reopens, and a woman with auburn hair sticks her head in the room. "Photos in half an hour," she announces, holding up the camera strapped around her chest.

Sally leaps into action. "Take a seat, Sandra. I've got to finish your hair!"

A temporary vanity covered with beauty products has been set up in one corner. Sandra settles into a director-style folding chair, and Sally continues winding Sandra's shoulder-length brown hair around the barrel of the curling iron.

Hallie hangs her dress bag up on a curtain rod and unzips it. "You should get dressed," she tells me. "You heard the photographer."

"Wait, I'm supposed to be in the photos?" I whisper.

"Yes." She shoots me a *Duh* look.

"Why didn't you say that earlier when I was complaining

about leaving so soon?"

"I did," Hallie replies as she pulls her black bridesmaid dress out of the bag. It's a sensible A-line style that's knee-length. "Good to know you weren't listening."

I scoff as I grab my dress. Once I've changed, I head over to the full-length mirror to apply some mascara and lip gloss.

I still love the dress I chose at Beck's kitchen counter. It's a one-shoulder design with a tight bodice. It's floor-length, but the flowy chiffon is asymmetrical, showing off flashes of my legs every step I take.

"Everyone ready?" Sally calls from the vanity. She's changed as well, into a cap-sleeved dress that falls to mid-calf. Sandra is wearing her wedding dress, which is a simple white slip with a lace overlay.

"Ready!" Hallie replies.

We file out of the room and back into the hallway. There's only one door farther down the hallway on the opposite side. Sally heads through it first, revealing that it leads out into the gardens behind the church. There's a stone courtyard in the center, surrounded by an explosion of lush greenery with some scattered dots of color provided by the few remaining blooms.

My father is standing in the courtyard, along with my Uncle Jerry and two older men I vaguely recognize as his business partners.

"Isn't it bad luck for the groom to see the bride before the wedding?" I whisper to Hallie.

She gives me a dubious glance. "You're superstitious?"

"I'm an athlete." Still a blank stare. I sigh. "Never mind."

The photographer's instructions stop any further conversation. I'm handed a bouquet of roses and told to smile. We take individual photos, group photos, candid shots, posed shots. I lose track. I just keep smiling, and no one seems to notice the expected expression pasted on my face is mostly fake.

The wedding planner finally tells us to head inside and take our places for the ceremony. The building echoes with audible chatter as we walk down the hallway toward the front of the church. My father and his groomsmen split off to enter the front of the altar.

There's a man who looks close to eighty waiting in the church vestibule. The front doors to the chapel have been closed, and the oak ones leading to the aisle are shut as well.

Strains of organ music drift beneath the ancient wood, halting the chatter that was previously echoing. The older man introduces himself to me and Hallie as Sandra's father, and the two of them take their place at the back of the line. The music swells and transitions to a melody even I recognize.

The doors in front of me open, and Hallie starts walking. I count to ten and then follow her down the aisle.

A hush fell as soon as Wagner began to play, but there's a low hum of voices filled with excited energy as we walk forward. I reach the end of the aisle and take my place beside Hallie at the foot of the altar. Sally takes the next spot, and then I watch the whole congregation rise as the music reaches its crescendo, perfectly coordinated with Sandra's arrival.

She's beaming, her smile giddy as she floats down the aisle on her father's arm. She doesn't look like someone who's done this twice before.

Everyone's focused on the bride's arrival. I'm the only one who glances at my dad, taking in his expression. His smile is soft and a little stunned. A reaction I might have made fun of, once upon a time. Before I saw that same look on Beck's face, aimed at me.

My mom took a lot when she left, just like Hallie said. She stole my belief that everything would be okay. Taught me that things don't work out. Since I was five years old, I've reserved trust and faith in anyone except myself. You can't let yourself down.

And then I met Beck, and that changed. I'm *realizing* it changed, right now, as Sandra reaches my dad's side and the ceremony begins. I'm not assuming my father's second marriage will fail, that the love and happiness on his face will fade over time.

I'm cynical, but I'm not certain of collapse.

Because of Beck.

Because...he makes me believe happy endings might be real.

And I wish he was here, instead of so far away, so I could tell him that.

Chapter 22

The country club where the reception is being held is only one block away from the church, but Hallie insists on driving. I don't protest; mostly because my feet are killing me from standing in heels. I stare out the window, smushed in the back next to the car seat, as Matt and Hallie talk about how smoothly the ceremony went.

We pass the small downtown area—library, post office, general store, and high school—before arriving at the country club. It's not nearly as posh as it sounds. It's simply an oversized building set behind an ornate gate and before the golf course.

The front lobby is minimalistic, with a flawless floor and muted colors. The ballroom is located just past a double set of doors. It overlooks a stone patio surrounded by the lush grass of the golf course, and the entire room is decorated in creams and golds that make me feel like I'm stuck inside a giant wedding cake. Round tables dot the hardwood floor, decorated with dishes and floral arrangements I recognize from the ends of the pews. Guests are milling about, claiming seats with wraps and clutches. I head toward the first empty one I see.

"Where are you going?" Hallie asks, grabbing my arm.

"To get a table," I reply.

"We're sitting up there." She nods to a long rectangular table next to the dance floor, positioned as the center of attention.

I sigh but follow her over to it. My grandparents and Sandra's parents are already seated. I take the chair at the farthest end, next to the highchair that's been set up for Matthew Jr.

"When is dinner?" I ask Hallie. I'm starving.

She rolls her eyes. "It's drinks and appetizers first. Then the first dance. Then dinner. Then cake…"

"Okay, okay," I reply. "No dinner yet. Got it."

There's a round of applause, and I turn to see my dad and Sandra are entering the room. They're quickly swallowed into the crowd. On cue, servers start to spread through the room with trays. Twinkling lights turn on out on the patio as dusk begins to fall.

"I'm headed to get sustenance," I inform Hallie.

"Alcohol or food?"

"Both." I stand but only get a dozen feet before I run into my Great Aunt Eloise.

"Saylor! So wonderful to see you, darling. How is school?"

I learned my lesson on this question last night. "It's great."

"And you're still playing soccer?"

"Yes."

Despite my efforts to offer the simplest answers possible, Eloise manages to draw our conversation out for a good ten minutes. As soon as I finish talking to her, I run into another distant relative. Then another. And another. By the time I make it out onto the patio, half the hors d'oeuvres are gone.

I snag a few mini bruschetta and strike up a conversation

with Ashley Martin. Her father works with mine, and we were friendly in high school. We've barely started chatting when Hallie appears.

"Here you are! Come on, we need you at the table."

I groan. "Nice to see you, Ashley. Bridesmaid duty calls."

I follow Hallie as she weaves through the tables back to ours. My dad and Sandra are standing from their seats at the head table and making their way out onto the dance floor. I plop down on my chair to watch them waltz, realizing I never even grabbed a drink.

I remember my father having no sense of rhythm, but apparently it's something he rediscovered along with some paternal instincts. They sway in time to some song with a melody that sounds familiar but I can't name.

The music ends, and Sandra walks over to her father. He rises, takes her hand, and they head back out onto the dance floor. I expect my father to walk over to his mother's chair, but instead he strides in the opposite direction.

Toward my end of the table.

Toward *me*.

"Dance with your old man, Saylor?"

My gaze swings to Hallie, but she doesn't look the least bit surprised. She knew. She knew he was going to do this, and I feel a little betrayed by the lack of warning.

"Sure," I say, standing. What else can I say? We're in front of a couple hundred people. On his wedding day.

We head out onto the dance floor, and my father's lost his newfound rhythm. We sway awkwardly together.

"I'm happy for you, Dad," I finally say when the silence is so thick, it's choking me, and I feel like I have to say something.

"Thank you, Saylor. That means a lot," he replies, the corners of his eyes crinkling.

Silence falls between us again.

"Maybe we'll be doing this again one day. At your wedding."

I tense. "I doubt it."

"There's no...special guy?" my father asks, and if I wasn't so uncomfortable, I would laugh. My father checked out back when I thought boys had cooties. We've *never* had a conversation about a guy. I doubt his rediscovered parenting skills would be thrilled to know about the ways I took advantage of his absence during my high school years.

"Nope." I almost leave it at that, but then I add, "Not a big fan of relying on people."

"You don't have to do everything alone, Saylor."

"Well, I didn't really have a choice."

He sighs. "I know. But I hoped you'd learn from my mistakes."

"I *have*."

"Relying on people is not a mistake. Relying on someone who doesn't rely on you is. That's what happened with your mother and me. I relied on her for everything, and she didn't rely on me at all. You're strong, Saylor. So, so strong. You don't need someone to hold you up, but it's nice to have someone to lean on." He looks over at Sandra, who's laughing at something her father is saying. "It's really nice."

I say nothing.

Wisely, my father opts to change the subject. "Sandra and I were talking about taking a weekend trip to Lancaster this fall. Hopefully catch a soccer game?"

"You want to come to one of my games?" I don't bother to hide the shock in my voice.

He nods once.

"*Why?*"

"Well, I've never seen you play in college, and—"

"Exactly. You've *never* seen me play in college." *Or high school. Or middle school.* Pretty sure the last time was in elementary school. "Why now?"

My father shifts uncomfortably while dancing. "I'm trying to do better. Be better. If you don't want me—us—to come, that's... understandable. Just say so."

"No, it's fine. You can come. Just let me know which game you want the tickets for."

"We can buy our own tickets. I want to support your team."

I snort. "The entire season is sold out. You won't be able to get into the game unless I request them for you."

"*Oh.* I didn't realize..."

"That other people care about seeing me play?" I let a little bitterness seep into my voice.

"No," he insists, although I'm certain I'm right. "I just—you always said women's sports don't get enough attention."

"They don't. I'm trying to change that."

My dad looks at me, and it's not with the uncertainty or discomfort I'm used to seeing. There's pride etched in the lines of his face, and it feels good.

Despite our difficult relationship—if you could even call it one after years of animosity—it feels really good for him to look at me like that.

I resent him for a lot. But he's trying, and it's harder to ignore that up closer. Harder to avoid eye contact than to not return a phone call.

I clear my throat. "I'm sorry for not calling much. The summer was...busy. I've been busy."

"It's okay, honey."

The song ends before either of us can say anything else.

Which is not a terrible note to end on.

When I return to my seat, dinner has been served. Hallie keeps glancing over at me, and I can tell she's dying to ask what me and our dad were talking about, but she restrains herself.

After dinner, I make a beeline for the bar to finally get a drink. I've just ordered a gin and tonic when I hear a familiar voice.

"Well, well, well. If it isn't the famous Saylor Scott gracing us with her presence."

I turn to see Andy Jacobson has appeared to my left. "Have we met before?" I tease.

The lopsided grin many high schoolers fangirled over appears. "Nice to see you haven't changed. Still breaking hearts, Scott?"

"Are you volunteering yours, Jacobson?"

His dimples deepen. "Nah. I learned my lesson."

"That why you're stalking me at my dad's wedding?"

Andy clutches his chest in mock outrage. "Stalking? That's harsh. I'm here to catch up with old friends."

"Oh yeah? Who would that be?"

"Who wouldn't it be? The whole town is here."

"Yeah." I let out a long exhale as the bartender hands me my drink. "I noticed."

"Rare to have a celebrity in our midst."

I scoff.

"I'm serious," Andy insists. "You're huge. My buddy's cousin goes to Lancaster and said it's nuts there. You're ranked first in the country!"

"Yeah, I know," I say before taking a long sip of my drink.

His words aren't terrible for my ego, though. Nice to know someone here appreciates what I've accomplished since leaving.

"Hooking up with you in high school earned me some major cool points at college, by the way."

"Still a gentleman, I see."

Andy grins. "So, what's it like—"

"Saylor! We need you for the cake." Hallie appears.

I let out another long breath, trying to summon some patience. Talking to Andy was the first time I was semi-enjoying myself all night. "Why? Do I have to cut it up?"

Andy snorts. Hallie glares.

I down the rest of my cocktail like a shot. "See you, Jacobson."

"I'll save you a dance, Scott," he calls out as Hallie hauls me off.

"Maybe there could be *one* part of the wedding I don't have to be front and center for?" I suggest.

"It's not particularly fun having to track you down for every event," she retorts.

"Then don't," I reply, a bit sharper than I mean to. "And don't think I don't know you had something to do with the dance."

"If I don't, then Dad will be upset. Now Sandra too. And if I'd told you about the dance, you probably would have hidden in the bathroom or something."

"Yeah. Obviously."

"Was it really that bad?" she asks.

"It was...weird." The strangest part being that it felt like dancing with my dad. Not a stranger. Not a source of strife. The closest to a normal moment we've shared in a long time.

We reach the dance floor, which has been cleared for the cake. It's three tiers that match the room décor perfectly, all white with flowers that have been dyed gold. Or are made of gold-colored frosting. Cressida could probably tell.

Champagne is passed around, and Sandra's father makes

a toast. Rather than the customary sip, I drain the entire glass as my father and Sandra make an impractical team attempt at slicing through the dessert.

I snag another glass of champagne as everyone oohs and aahs over the slow process.

"How many of those have you had?" Hallie looks over and eyes the glass flute in my hand.

"Not enough." I take a sip of fizzy liquid.

"Don't be selfish, Saylor."

It's amazing how, after twenty-one years, Hallie still doesn't know people pushing me only makes me push back. Harder.

I grab a second glass from the display, double-fisting champagne.

"Me? Selfish? Never." I take a sip and send her a sweet smile. At least I own up to it.

Hallie backs down and looks away, just like I knew she would. I also know it's not because she doesn't care. She just avoids confrontation the same way I seek it out.

Plates of cake finally start to disseminate amongst the crowd. I grab one and, with another full glass of champagne, head outside. The patio is empty now. I'm guessing it's the lack of appetizers combined with the slight chill in the air. Coming from Connecticut, the temperature still feels tropical to me.

I settle on one of the concrete benches and stare out at the manicured golf course.

The pristine grass reminds me of a soccer field.

Reminds me of Kluvberg's field.

Reminds me of lying on it with Beck.

I gulp down the rest of the bubbly alcohol and spin so my feet rest on the opposite end of the concrete bench. My stilettos fall to the stone floor as I stretch my toes, luxuriating in the freedom the lack of a pointed prison allows for. Champagne fizzes in my stomach, making me feel restless and relaxed.

I pull my phone out, rubbing a sore spot on the arch and my foot, and it turns out there *is* something I would do drunk I wouldn't sober. Or maybe I'm just using alcohol as an excuse.

It rings once, and I take a bite of cake. A choice I regret when he picks up on the second ring.

"Saylor?" His voice is raspy and rumbly, and it takes me approximately ten seconds to realize how I fucked up. It's getting late here. It's much, much later in Germany.

I don't reply at first. I *can't*, because there's a lump of flour and sugar blocking my windpipe.

I wash the cake down with some more champagne.

"Saylor?" he says again, tone more alert and softer. "Is everything okay?"

"Yeah. Sorry. I didn't mean to wake you up." Silence, while he's likely wondering why I'm calling, and I savor the sound of his even breaths in my ear. "I'm at my dad's wedding."

"How is it?" There's a soft rustle in the background, like he's moving between sheets.

"It's...weird. A lot of people I haven't seen in a long time. And my sister basically has a second child to look after this weekend. But my dad seems happy, so that's good."

"Are you drunk?"

"No." I pause. "Maybe a little."

"Is that why you're calling?" Beck asks.

"No. You said I didn't call. So I'm...calling."

"It's been two weeks."

"I've been busy," I tell him. Same excuse I gave my dad. Truthfully, I don't know *how* to draw boundaries between soccer and the rest of my life. I've never tried to.

"I know. Nine goals. Impressive."

A warm flush spreads across my skin that has nothing to do with the drinks I've been downing. He's been checking my stats. "Does that mean you didn't change your mind?"

"Change my mind about what?"

"About me. About wanting me."

He doesn't reply right away, so I brace myself for the worst. "I'm never going to change my mind about wanting you, Saylor."

This time, the lump in my throat is all emotion. It takes a lot longer to get rid of. "I miss you," I whisper.

Hallie chooses this exact moment to burst out onto the patio. "We need you for another round of photos."

Out of all her interruptions tonight, this one is the worst. It anchors me back to reality, reminding me that I'm at my father's wedding—a dad I barely talk to. That my relationship with my sister is complicated at best. That I've been avoiding this exact situation—falling in love—for a reason. That the reason I woke Beck up is because he lives far, far away. That me admitting I miss him might have just been torture for the both of us, and I should keep that bottled up so that he *can* change his mind about me.

"I have to go. Sorry for waking you up." I tap the end button before Beck can reply, shoving my feet back into the stilettos and wincing as my feet protest.

"Who were you talking to?" Hallie asks as I approach her.

"No one."

Despite the literal impossibility of my answer, Hallie doesn't press. Instead, she apologizes. "I'm sorry about before. I know today is tough for you."

"It's fine," I mutter as we head back inside the country club. I owe her an apology too, but right now my emotions are all over the place.

It's strange, being in my hometown, surrounded by family, seconds after talking to Beck on the phone.

It's a collision of two worlds: the Saylor Scott who grew up in a tiny town with a broken family and the one who fought for relevance until she ended up training with the best.

The girl who grew up convinced love was a legend and the woman worried she might have found it.

We take more photos, there's another round of dancing, and then my dad and Sandra disappear in a shower of grains of rice and a deluge of well wishes. They're headed straight to the airport to depart on their honeymoon in Lisbon.

The drive back to Hallie's from the reception is silent. Either she's still annoyed with me or simply too tired to talk. I'd guess it's a combination of the two.

The porch light is on when we arrive back at the bungalow. Matt left the reception early to bring Matthew Jr. home and put him to bed.

"Night," Hallie tells me when we walk through the front door. She heads straight upstairs.

I was exhausted earlier, but suddenly I'm not. I head to the couch and grab sweatpants and a sweatshirt out of my suitcase. I change and then walk into the kitchen, swinging the fridge door open and hauling myself up on the edge of the countertop to survey the contents.

Wasteful? Yes.

Convenient? Also yes.

I'm not hungry. I've had enough alcohol to know more is a bad idea, but also enough where I'm not thinking logically. I compromise by grabbing a bottle of beer and a can of seltzer. Then stroll out the door off the kitchen, onto the deck, and down into the yard.

The lawn feels like home. I've spent more hours on grass than I could ever count, but mostly wearing cleats. Crushing blades of grass is much more satisfying when it's with your bare feet.

There's a hammock strung up between two broad beech trees, and I flop down atop it, beverages in hand. I can't see anything through the canopy of leaves, and I prefer it that way. Stars have a way of suggesting too much. The vastness of the universe makes me feel small, inconsequential. Like maybe the decisions I have to make aren't quite as massive as I've made them out to be.

In the context of the world, they're definitely not.

In the context of my life, they're trajectory. They'll send me down one path. There will be other choices further in the future, but no chances to return to where I am right now. That's what has me paralyzed in place, scared to take a step.

I toss the drinks on the ground, belatedly realizing that means they'll probably explode whenever they're opened. Too tired to care, I push off from the ground so the hammock I'm lying on starts rocking back and forth.

I'm asleep before it stills.

• • •

"If only I had a camera on me."

I squint upward and find Hallie's smirking face, rubbing a hand across my eyes. "Why have a hammock if you're not going to use it?"

"We use it plenty. We just don't sleep in it."

I stretch, relieved to discover a bird didn't decide to crap on me overnight. My muscles are stiff, but I've definitely woken up feeling worse. I'm not even that hungover. "You should. Switch things up a bit."

Hallie rolls her eyes, suggesting she's taken my words as a personal affront, an assertion that she plays it safe while I dance with danger.

I sigh. "Look, Hallie. About last night. I'm sor—" I don't even get the full apology out.

"It's fine, Saylor. We're good." Hallie loves to sweep anything uncomfortable under the rug. It's why she's on a joking basis with our father whereas I can barely exchange a dance's worth of words with him. Avoidance versus grudges. I'm not sure either approach is healthy, but I know Hallie's means me pressing things will only end with us on worse terms. "Do you want breakfast?"

"No, I'll get something at the airport."

"Okay. Your flight's at eleven, right?"

"Yeah."

Hallie heads back inside.

I pick up the beer and seltzer I never opened and walk up the steps after her. The kitchen is chaos. Matthew Jr. is screaming. Hallie and Matt are grabbing toys and food, trying to calm him. Matt's family is eating breakfast at the table. No one except Jackson acknowledges my entrance.

I stick the drinks back in the fridge and help myself to a banana. I contemplate changing my outfit as I peel the fruit and then decide against it.

"You ready, Saylor?" Hallie asks, handing Matt a bowl of the cereal that seems to have halted the shrieking.

"Yeah," I respond, heading into the living room to zip up my suitcase.

Once I make certain that I have everything, I return to the kitchen to say goodbye to everyone. Matt suggests slash forces I hold Matthew Jr. again. Thankfully, he starts screaming after a few seconds, so it's a short farewell to my nephew. Saying so long to everyone else doesn't take that much longer.

Hallie and I head for her car. When she brakes at the stop sign at the end of her street, I suck in a deep breath.

"Can we stop at the post office?"

"Uh, sure."

The town's tiny post office is just as quiet and empty as one would expect early morning. I don't realize until I'm outside the doors it's because it's closed.

It's Sunday.

I'm not shipping life-saving medication. There's no real urgency. But I am worried I won't send it if I don't do it now, that I'll talk myself out of it.

There's a jangling sound to my left, and I glance over to see a man unlocking the side door tucked around the corner. I'd guess he's in his late twenties, and he does a double-take when he glances over and sees me.

"Hi! Could you do me a massive favor?" I ask, walking over to him.

He doesn't answer right away, looking a bit stunned. I don't recognize him, so I don't think he recognizes me. Maybe he's just taken aback that I'm here. Most people probably remember post offices are closed on Sundays.

"Well?" I ask.

"Uh—um, I'm not supposed to—I mean—sure."

A rush of relief overtakes any annoyance with his slow reactions. I follow him inside through the door he was unlocking.

I have Beck's apartment address memorized, and I pay the exorbitant fee required to ship the box with the painting I purchased to Germany after relaying it to the postal worker.

"Thank you," I tell him, paying after he's completed the shipping slip.

My chest feels a little lighter when I leave the post office. I'm bad with words. With feelings. But I saw the painting and thought of Beck, so I'm hoping he'll look at it and think of me. Some physical acknowledgement that the time we've spent together mattered to me. That *he* means something to me.

I'm a mess who's done nothing but complicate things between us. Continue to complicate things. If my departure from Germany damaged us, we're in tatters post-Canada. But the dysfunction doesn't diminish what we shared.

Maybe that's what my mother meant about broken beauty.

Or maybe she was referring to herself.

If she hadn't left, I'd probably ask her.

Chapter 23

The next two weeks follow the same pattern every fall has for as long as I can remember. The official season starts, and everything but soccer fades. I barely attend class, I stop attending parties, and I don't answer the three phone calls I receive from a German number.

But I do answer calls from my father. Ever since the wedding, he's made a point to check in once a week like he's worried if too much time passes, we'll revert to silence. Each conversation, we muddle through a few mundane topics: the weather (different in Connecticut than Georgia), hometown news (nothing's changed), and how I am (busy). Despite the repetition, he keeps calling. And I keep answering.

And now, he's here. He followed through on his plan to come see me play, surprisingly. He ended our last phone call by telling me that he and Sandra were planning to come to our next home game. I didn't miss that meant he actually took the time to look up my soccer schedule.

They made the puzzling decision to make the fifteen-hour

drive rather than fly and were supposed to arrive an hour ago.

I sit in the locker room, listening to the chatter of my teammates around me as I tighten the laces of my cleats. Anne keeps looking at me out of the corner of her eye.

"You really need to work on your subtlety," I inform her, spinning around on the bench to face my locker.

"What?" she asks innocently.

"You've been making worried faces at me for the last five minutes. Cut it out."

"Are you okay? Normally you're more hyper before games."

She's not wrong. I usually take on DJ responsibilities and blast a pre-game playlist or something.

"I'm fine. Just...my dad is here."

Anne fumbles for words. "Your–your dad? I didn't, I mean... you've never..."

"Yeah, I know I've never mentioned him. We're...not that close."

"Oh. Wow. If you want to talk about it..."

"I'm good, thanks. Ready to play." I stand, stretch, and yank my jersey on over my sports bra.

Most of the team is already huddled around Coach Taylor. There's no pep talk. We had a three-hour strategy session yesterday afternoon, and everyone knows what is expected of them today. This is just another game. It's not a championship or even a playoff match.

No one wants to risk our perfect record so far this season, but even playing at the highest level of collegiate athletics feels mundane after a certain point. I couldn't have even told you what day we were playing Northampton back when our schedule was announced.

Coach Taylor finishes explaining our warm-up drills, and we

file out onto the field one by one.

After attending my first football game at Lancaster freshman year, I sweet-talked the guy who announces the football players as they run out of the tunnel to do the same for the women's soccer team. And not just the starters—the entire team.

It was a genius move, if I do say so myself. Not only because it pumps up the crowd, but because it's fantastic for team morale.

I mean, who *doesn't* want to run out on the field as their name is announced on a loudspeaker to a chorus of cheers?

No athlete I've met.

Coach tugs at my sleeve as I pass her. "You good, Scott? You look a bit like you're headed into a cage match."

"To win it, right?"

Coach gives me a rare smile. "Give 'em hell."

"That's the plan." I head down the tunnel after Emma.

"You're in a weirdly good mood," she says as I stop beside her.

I tighten my ponytail. "I'm always in a good mood."

Emma snorts loudly. "Uh-huh, sure."

"Number twelve, Emmmaaa Waattkkkiinnnssss!"

"That's my cue." She grins and jogs out of the tunnel.

"And last, but certainly not least, we have our captain. Lancaster's leading scorer. Number twenty-two, Saayyyllloooorr Sccccccooootttttt!"

I sprint out into a wall of noise. The stands are full, and I don't bother to scan them. It's a perfect fall day, warm with a crisp edge. The game is supposed to start at three, and the sun is bright but not blinding.

The sound of voices and the smell of concession stand snacks mingle in the autumn air, but I don't pause to take in the atmosphere. I'm laser-focused on lunges, toe touches, and scoring sprees.

Warm-ups end, and I call heads. We win the coin toss, opting to take the kickoff.

I'm addicted to this moment. Some players love the euphoria of scoring a goal or the thrill of being ahead when extra minutes end.

For me, it's the start of the game, when anticipation's built to a breaking point.

I love scoring and I love winning. But in those moments, I already know what I've accomplished.

I know the ending.

Right now, I have a chance to determine it.

I'm in motion as soon as the ball leaves Emma's foot, sprinting upward with the other forwards. I challenge the Northampton player who has possession, a sharp jab of her elbow landing on my ribs, letting me know she doesn't appreciate the crowding. Too damn bad. The hit offers me an opening. I spin, taking the ball with me, and start running in the opposite direction from where she was headed, back toward Northampton's goal.

Cassidy Jones is waiting for me. She was at CFOC; we chatted between clinics, but she's no longer a friendly face. She's nothing but a barrier now.

I kick the ball to Natalie, and she passes to Emma. After years of playing together, we're in perfect sync. Emma sends the ball back to me before I enter the penalty arc. I take advantage of the split second of confusion among Northampton's defenders as they scramble to keep up. A few seconds later, I score the first goal of the game and receive a whole lot of appreciation from the crowd.

Northampton doubles down after that, barely letting us past the center line. The only upside is they're so focused on keeping us from scoring, they're unable to press themselves.

The scoreboard is still displaying 0-1 when we leave the field for halftime. I take a seat on the bench and drink slow sips of water. Coach Taylor has her trusty whiteboard out, talking through suggestions of plays. I watch her marker slash, circle, and squiggle, the hectic motions as discombobulated as the thoughts in my head. They bounce between my dad and the game and the missed calls on my phone. I never used to consider myself a coward, but I'm now certain I am one. I'm fearless on the field. Off it, I'm scared to even answer a phone call.

I push thoughts of Beck away as I stand and return to the pitch. But they'll only go so far. He's a distraction, just like I told him I didn't want.

We weren't the only team discussing strategy. Northampton opts for a very different approach in the second half. They're more aggressive, pushing toward the end of the field they were formerly protecting.

Anne and our other three defenders have their first real tests of the game as I try to slow Northampton's offense along with the rest of the midfielders. The girl I'm marking passes to a teammate, and Emma is too far away to stop the ball. The Northampton player sends it flying toward the net, but Cressida is ready. She snags the ball midair, and I let out a long sigh of relief.

I turn to head back to the center line. It takes a while for everyone else to follow, and I frown as Emma falls into position beside me for the kickoff. We've still got a half hour of play left, but Northampton's shot on goal seems to have invigorated my teammates.

Suddenly, it feels like we *are* playing in a championship. That extra gear I always find as I near the end of a game, like a shark moving in for the kill? I'm not the only one shifting, and Northampton is totally unprepared for us to all start sprinting faster and pressing harder. It's an onslaught that earns us two more goals: a header from Natalie and an impressive scissors kick from Anne.

When the final whistle blows, I'm expecting the team to flock around Cressida, who managed a shutout, or Anne, who scored the most recent goal. But they don't. They throng around me.

Once we finally disentangle for handshakes, Natalie falls into step beside me. "Three zip against Northampton? They might as well inscribe the championship cup already."

I laugh. "If everyone keeps playing as well as they did today? Definitely."

"Not much we wouldn't do for you, Captain."

"What do you mean?"

"Anne said today was a big deal to you. That your dad is here?"

An unexpected lump appears in my throat as Natalie looks at me curiously. There's no worship in her eyes right now, just friendship.

"Yeah, he is," I finally manage as we fall into line for handshakes.

I walk back to Lancaster's bench to grab my gear and then spot Anne, who's grabbing her own stuff. She looks a little nervous as I approach, so I pair the "Thank you" I was already planning on with a hug.

"Anything for you, Scott," she replies with a smile.

I pretend to wipe tears away from my eyes, and she shoves my shoulder.

"Forget it. I take it back."

I'm grinning as I head into the tunnel. The mood in the locker room is electric. Northampton is normally one of our toughest opponents. We just destroyed them. It bodes pretty damn well for our championship chances, which already looked excellent.

I shower and change into jeans and a T-shirt. I texted my dad earlier, letting him know where to pick up the game tickets, and also told him where we could meet after the game. He's right by the oak tree I described when I leave the locker room, just to the left of the field's exit.

Cressida, Anne, and Emma all trail behind me. I definitely didn't buy Cressida retying her sneakers twice in an effort to delay leaving until I did, but I can't blame them for being curious. I've met all their families. I spent a week with Emma's two summers ago when my own family thought I was still at the U20 team training camp.

Most of the crowd has cleared by now, but there are still a few streams of students leaving the stands. We're stopped several times, which only increases my anxiety. I'd rather get this over with.

We finally reach the shade of the oak. "Hi, Dad. Hey, Sandra."

"Saylor!" Sandra speaks first. She steps forward to give me a quick hug. "What a fantastic game!"

"Thank you," I reply, my gaze bouncing back to my father.

He doesn't say anything.

"Uh, these are my teammates and housemates: Emma, Cressida, and Anne." I point to each of them as I say their names.

"It's so nice to meet you, Mr. Scott...and uh, Mrs. Scott," Emma says.

The last two words are a bit of a question, and yeah...I probably should have provided a bit of context. They know nothing about my mom leaving, about the family trip two weeks ago actually being my father's wedding.

"Nice to meet you two." Cressida jumps in, smoothing over the awkward moment, and Anne echoes the sentiment.

"Lovely to meet you all. And my goodness, you're all so gorgeous!" Sandra comments.

"So kind of you to say that," Emma replies. "It's really hard on our egos, being friends with *the* Saylor Scott."

I roll my eyes. "The trip here was okay?" I finally address my dad directly.

"Yup. Quick and easy," he replies. I don't know how you could categorize a fifteen-hour drive as *quick*, but I don't challenge him on it.

"That's good."

Silence falls over our little group.

"Are you free for dinner?" my dad finally asks. "Your friends are all welcome to come too, of course."

It's just past five, which is awfully early for dinner, but I'm starving, so I nod. "You guys want to come?" I ask them.

They all stare at me, obviously trying to suss out whether or not I mean the offer. I nod again.

"Yeah, we'd love to!" Emma answers for all three of them. "Tony's?" she suggests, referring to the local pizzeria just on the edge of campus.

"Are you good with pizza?" I ask Dad and Sandra.

"Sure," Sandra replies, looking overly thrilled about it. Since I know she's not a huge sports fan, she's probably happy that part of the visit is over. Or maybe she's trying to encourage my dad, who hasn't said much.

Sandra's enthusiasm carries us through the walk to the restaurant. It's mostly filled with her rapid questions about

Lancaster. I answer the ones posed at me directly, but let my friends pick up some of the slack in the conversation.

Tony's is packed, like usual. The commotion is welcome, washing away some of the awkwardness between me and my dad, but I didn't think through how many students would be here, fresh from the game.

Normally, I'd enjoy the attention, but in front of my dad and Sandra, the constant congratulations are kind of embarrassing.

Jason Williams leaps up from a table filled with his frat brothers to give me a bear hug. "Scott! Way to kick ass! You better come to Kappa tonight to celebrate. I even got gin and—"

"Jason, this is my dad," I interrupt, raising my eyebrows meaningfully as I nod at my father.

"Oh. Hi, Mr. Scott. Nice to meet you." Jason switches from partier to polite with a charming grin.

"And this is my stepmother, Sandra," I add. It's the first time I've called her that, and it feels weird.

"Are you two...dating?" Sandra asks, her eyes on the arm Jason has slung over my shoulder.

"Plead my case, Mrs. Scott," Jason says. "I've been trying since freshman year, along with every other guy on campus."

I twist out of his grip. Trying to get me in bed, maybe. Since my body doesn't seem to want anyone except Beck, his chances have only gotten worse. "Go eat your pizza, Williams."

Sandra continues to ask most of the questions as we find a table and order food. People stop by our table periodically, and each time someone does, I experience a flash of annoyance and pride.

Annoyance, because it's one more person who's made a mention of my performance today aside from my father, who supposedly drove over a thousand miles to see it. Pride, because the surprised, delighted expression on his face every time someone stops makes it pretty clear he's impressed.

He doesn't know how to tell me he's proud of me. I've purposefully made it hard for him, as some twisted penance for all the years he wasn't around to say anything at all. He made sure there was food in the fridge. Drove us to the mall to get new clothes. If I hadn't gotten a full ride here, he would have paid for my college the way he did for Hallie's. But he was never there. Never present. Never engaged. I don't know when that started to change, but it was long after I'd become accustomed to his absence. Years after I'd learned to live my life parent-less.

We finish our early dinner and then start walking back to the soccer field's parking lot. Right as we reach the edge of campus, my father finally addresses me directly.

"Saylor, could I talk to you for a moment?"

"Sure." I halt, noticing Sandra has slowed to read the plaque on the side of the English building.

Fluent in social cues, my friends say their goodbyes and then keep walking toward the parking lot.

"I..." My dad clears his throat.

I drag my gaze up from the leaves beginning to coat the brick pathway to his face.

"I just wanted to tell you how fantastic you were today, honey. I can't believe—I can't believe I've never seen you play before. It was—you are—extraordinary."

There was a time—a very recent time—when I would have replied with some harsh words. Maybe a pointed *What can't you believe?*

There wasn't a damn thing keeping him from attending one of the hundreds of soccer games I've played in.

He wasn't deployed overseas. He wasn't working three jobs

to support Hallie and me.

He was locked in his study, drinking scotch. Or at some fancy restaurant in Savannah with a twenty-six-year-old.

I'm bitter about that. Maybe I always will be.

But...I'm also sick of carrying the anger and bitterness around.

"Thanks, Dad." I scuff the toe of my sneaker against some dead leaves, causing them to crinkle. "And, uh, thanks for coming."

"Of course," he replies.

There's no *of course* about it, but I don't say that either.

Sandra catches up with us and smiles at me. "What a beautiful campus. You must love it here, Saylor."

"Yeah, I do," I respond. "Emma drove. So I should..." I jerk my thumb toward the parking lot, where my friends are waiting for me. "Are you guys staying for long?"

"No," Sandra answers. "I have to be back for school on Monday." She's a teacher, I recently learned. Guess that's why she was so stunned by my disinterest in academics. "We'll drive back tomorrow morning."

"Oh, okay," I respond. The round-trip drive will last longer than the time they've spent here.

"We can stop by in the morning before we leave?" my father suggests. "Hallie gave me your address."

Of course she did.

"Yeah, that's fine," I reply. "I'll be up early for practice anyway."

"Okay," my father says. "We'll see you tomorrow, then."

"Okay," I repeat. "Night."

I turn and head for the parking lot. No one says anything as I climb into the car. Emma starts driving around the sports complex, then turns onto one of the side roads that leads back to our house.

"Your dad seems nice," Anne says as we reach our street.

"Yeah," I say, staring out the window.

My feelings about my father are all over the place right now, and I let them churn inside of me until we reach our house. Knowing I should forgive him is different from actually doing so.

I head upstairs as soon as I walk through the front door, changing into my comfiest set of pajamas. I debate flopping down on my bed with the new murder mystery book I downloaded last night, but decide to head back downstairs to make some tea first.

Emma's standing at the counter, mixing one of her infamous cocktails. She studies the peach-patterned cotton I'm wearing. Hallie bought them for me as a joke, but they're so soft, I wear them more than I planned to.

"You're staying in tonight?"

"Uh-huh," I say, starting the kettle and then climbing up on the kitchen counter to lean my head back against the upper cabinet.

"Jason will be disappointed."

"He'll get over it," I tell the ceiling.

Emma hasn't pushed me on Beck since CFOC, and her poster of him magically disappeared the day we got back. I'm guessing her mention of Jason is her way of asking if I'm still needing time. The answer is yes.

Cressida enters the kitchen in sweats and a face mask.

"Wait—you're not going out either?" Emma exclaims.

I straighten my head to see Cressida shrug. "Not in the mood."

She comes over to the cabinet next to me to grab the flour.

I know what's coming next, so I slide off the counter so she can grab the sugar from behind me, relocating to one of the stools.

Emma huffs as she measures out tequila. Then squeezes two lemons. Then adds some orange juice.

I turn my attention to Cressida as Emma returns the ingredients to the fridge. "What are you making?"

She eyes me apprehensively. "Sandra's brownie recipe. She gave it to me at dinner."

"Oh."

"Did someone drink the tomato juice?" Emma inquires with her head inside the fridge.

"Please tell me you're not putting tomato juice in *that*," I reply, nodding to the cocktail shaker.

"What? It's fruit. And healthy." Emma heaves out a disappointed sigh that suggests she didn't find the tomato juice.

I'm almost certain it's on the top shelf, but I keep that to myself.

"Emma, *no*." Cressida backs me up. "That's disgusting."

"Fine." She sighs again, grabbing some ice from the freezer and shaking the mixer. She snags a glass and pours some out.

The kettle shuts off, so I grab a mug out of the cabinet.

"Here. Try some." Emma holds a glass out to me.

"What? No."

"It's good."

I doubt it, but I take the glass. It's better than I expected, probably because I know it could have been *so* much worse. "Fine. It's not awful."

Anne enters the kitchen, also in her pajamas.

"Are you kidding me?" Emma exclaims. "*No one* is going out tonight?"

"I'm tired," Anne says. "And full." She pats her stomach.

"Unbelievable." Emma huffs.

"Stay in with us," Cressida tells her. "I'm making brownies."

Emma groans, but leaves the kitchen. Probably to get changed. Sure enough, she returns in a silk sleep set, her hair up in a messy bun.

"So, are we talking about dinner or pretending it didn't happen?" Anne asks, taking a seat on the stool next to mine.

I play with the string of the teabag. "Thanks for coming, guys. I know it was awkward."

"It wasn't awkward," Cressida says.

At the same time, Emma asks, "Why was it so awkward?"

I laugh, then sober. "My mom left when I was five. My dad basically checked out after that. We've never had much of a relationship—definitely not a good one—and he's trying now, I guess. It's weird with him and it's weird with Sandra. I barely know her. They only got married a couple of weeks ago."

"That's why you went home," Emma realizes.

"Yeah," I confirm.

"I'm sorry, S."

I force a smile. "It's fine. It'll work out. Or it won't. Whatever."

There's a pause as they all decide what to say in response.

"Brownies are in the oven," Cressida announces, breaking the heavy moment and gaining my eternal devotion as a result. "I'm going to watch a rom com."

"Can we watch *Sweet Home Alabama*?" Anne asks eagerly.

Emma measures out more tequila, then divides her cocktail into four glasses. The drink is mostly alcohol at this point, which helps with the flavor.

Thirty minutes later, we're all sprawled across the living room, brownies in one hand and tequila in the other, watching *Sweet Home Alabama*.

I laugh so hard my sides hurt. Emma squeezes my hand when Melanie makes jam with her mother. Anne ruins all the best lines by saying them a few seconds too early.

And it's probably my favorite night in college.

Chapter 24

wake up on the living room floor. At least it's an upgrade from the bathroom tile.

I sit up, rubbing sleep from my eyes. Emma is sprawled out on the couch. Anne's in the recliner. And Cressida is lying on the opposite corner of the rug.

Emma snores loudly. I grin, grabbing my phone so I can record her.

"Shit!" I shout when I catch a glimpse at the screen.

"What?" Anne startles awake, glancing around the living room wildly. Her red hair is a snarled mess.

"It's almost eight," I reply.

"Oh, shit!" Anne says, standing.

"Cressida! Emma! Wake up!" I holler, running into the kitchen to start brewing coffee.

"What's going on?" Emma calls out.

"We've got practice in twenty minutes!" I call back.

I dump the grounds into the coffee maker and dart toward the stairs. I whirl around my room like a hurricane, almost toppling over as I rush to change out the pajamas I'm wearing into shorts and my practice jersey. My hair goes up in a messy ponytail, and then I sprint across the hall to brush my teeth and wash my face.

Slams and bangs around the house suggest everyone else is getting ready just as quickly. Coach Taylor does *not* love tardiness.

I sprint down the stairs, cleats in one hand and sneakers in the other. "EMMA! ANNE!" I holler. "We've got to go!"

"I'm coming!" Emma shouts back.

"Why is no one else *ever* ready?" Cressida asks from the front hall, exactly where I knew she'd be. Her usual routine is to lean against the cubbies and watch us all dart around desperately. "Practice is always at the same time. It doesn't magically move up just to catch y'all off guard."

"You could have a little more sympathy this morning," I retort, hopping on one foot as I put on my shoes.

"Even less. We all woke up at the same time. *I'm* ready to go."

"Start driving yourself, then!"

"No way. Watching y'all race around is too much fun," she replies.

The frenzied sound of running footsteps echoes upstairs as Anne and Emma hurry about.

"Especially hungover."

"Can you at least check if Jenny is here to pick us up?" I ask.

Cress rolls her eyes, but heads for the front door. "She wasn't a minute ago—*holy shit.*"

"What?" I reply, lacing up my left sneaker. "Did she leave without us? I can drive, I just need to get my keys from—" I glance up as I grab my right shoe and freeze in place. Thoughts screech to a stop in my head. I might be hallucinating.

Adler Beck is in my house, standing five feet away from me.

He's wearing a tracksuit, Kluvberg's blue with the club emblem embroidered in white. A jacket is tossed across the top of the leather duffel bag he's carrying. He must have taken a red-eye to be here this early, but his are perfectly blue, without any dark circles.

"What are you doing here?" I choke out.

"I got your gift," Beck states.

I stare at him. Thanks to the large amount of tequila I drank last night, it takes me a good minute to realize he's talking about the painting I sent. "A thank you note would have sufficed. You didn't need to fly across the Atlantic."

"If you'd answered any of my calls, I wouldn't have had to fly across the Atlantic."

Shit. I have no good excuse for not answering and no idea what him coming all this way means.

"I didn't, um, I—"

Loud steps pound behind me, followed by an even louder "Oh my God" in Emma's voice.

Some of the shock is beginning to ebb away, letting details trickle in. Cressida is standing by the front door, her mouth literally open. If I glanced behind me at the stairs, I'm sure that Anne and Emma look just as shocked. When Emma and I discussed Beck, I definitely didn't mention he might show up here sometime.

I can't believe he's here. That he came *all this way.*

Last night's drinking and lack of sleep are catching up to me. My temple starts to throb.

There's a knock on the door. I think it must be Jenny—wondering what the hell is taking us so long—when I hear my dad's voice. "Saylor?"

My headache gets worse. I totally forgot he and Sandra were

stopping by this morning.

"We'll, uh, be in the car," Emma says, basically dragging a shocked Anne out the door. After a few seconds, Cressida unfreezes and follows them outside.

"One second," I tell Beck, then pass him.

My dad and Sandra are standing just past the steps. I paste a smile on my face as I approach them.

"Good morning!" Sandra says cheerily.

"Morning," I reply.

"Looks like a busy one," my dad says.

Jenny is here, her car loitering along the curb next to my dad's. Emma, Cressida, and Anne are cramming themselves inside. We always squeeze in more than the number of seatbelts for the short trip.

"Yeah. I've got practice, so..."

"Right, of course. You mentioned it last night."

I nod.

"Well, enjoy practice and we'll talk soon, okay?"

I nod again. "Okay."

"Hopefully we'll have the chance to come up again before the end of the season."

"You don't have to do that, Dad. It's a really long trip."

"I want to," my dad tells me. He glances at Sandra, who smiles encouragingly. "We want to."

I swallow hard, then clear my throat. "Okay. Just let me know which game, and I'll get you tickets."

"Sounds good." He steps forward and gives me a hug. That, I'm expecting. The whispered "I love you, sweetheart," I'm not. If he's said that to me before, it faded with memories of my mom.

I'm not ready to say it back, but I squeeze him a little tighter. I hug Sandra too, and then they're leaving, heading for the car parked behind Jenny's.

I suck in a deep breath, then walk over to the driver's side window. "Go ahead," I tell Jenny. "I'll meet you guys there."

She looks surprised. "You sure?"

"Yeah." I avoid the stares from my housemates in the backseat, then head back toward the house.

Beck has moved into the living room. He's standing by the couch, studying the plates littered with brownie crumbs and the glasses that still smell like smoky tequila. His gaze swings to me as I enter the room, and his presence hits me all over again. It still doesn't feel real that he's here. That he dropped everything and flew to see me—again. I'm flattered. I'm also anxious, registering what that means. He takes soccer as seriously as I do. Yet he came all this way—while in season—to talk to me. I'm not the only one strongly affected by this thing between us, like I'd selfishly assumed. Him telling me I matter to him was a lot to take in. Him showing it by coming to Lancaster is even more shocking.

I'm a little better with actions than with words. So instead of saying anything, I walk right up to Beck and kiss him. I try to pour everything I'm feeling into it. Everything I haven't found the words to say to him.

It takes him a few seconds to react. Then he's kissing me back, and I rapidly lose track of…everything. I didn't forget what this heat between us was like, but my memories don't compare to the real thing. To his smell and the softness of his warm lips pressed against mine. Kissing him makes his presence feel even more real.

"Was it me you missed, or this?" he asks when we finally separate, his hands roaming my back and tangling in the end of my ponytail.

I think he's teasing, but we haven't gotten to that easy place yet, so I'm not sure. I don't miss the pointed reference to the phone call that was our last conversation.

"Can it be both?" I reply, smirking. "I haven't gotten laid in a while."

I haven't gotten laid since him.

"Been a while for me too," Beck tells me.

Hopefully as long as I've been gone, but I don't ask for those details. "I'm *really* late for practice. I'll be back in a couple of hours, and then we can talk."

"Can I come?"

I blink at him. "You want to come to my practice?"

Beck nods.

"They'll, uh, they'll recognize you."

We've had spectators at practice before: parents, friends, siblings. A few high school teams. Never any world-famous soccer phenoms.

"Are you embarrassed by me?" I think he's teasing, but again, I'm not really sure.

He's the one who's going to leave this time, because he lives on a different continent and the entire country would notice his absence. And I'll be the one stuck answering questions about him, because my teammates will all be curious about my fling with a hot celebrity and won't even consider Beck meant anything more to me.

Rather than tell him any of that I just say, "No."

"Then let's go."

I grab my keys and my gear, then lead the way outside. Beck leaves his bag in the entryway. I haven't asked any of the important questions, like how long he's staying, yet.

He climbs into the passenger seat without comment. I twist the key in the ignition, and the engine flares to life. Loud pop music blares through the speakers. Beck smiles a little as I turn the volume down and reverse out of the driveway.

"I'm sorry I didn't answer any of your calls," I say, breaking the silence between us.

It's the truth, and not only because it's landed me in the predicament of showing up at practice with Adler Beck in tow. His presence will overtake the Trey Johnson incident to claim the number one spot involving gossip about me, I'm sure.

"Don't apologize if you don't mean it."

"I *do* mean it. I just felt...silly for calling you. It was nice hearing your voice, but it also...it hurt. I wasn't thinking straight, and I was missing you, but it felt like I just made everything worse. So I've been avoiding you since, trying to take that back, and I *am* sorry about that."

A long pause follows. "I need to know if you're letting me in or shutting me out, Saylor. Because the back and forth...I can't keep doing it."

I've been waiting for him to say some version of that. For a while, I was *hoping* to hear it. If he'd ended things before we went hiking, before I met his family, before I left...that would have been a clean break. I would have healed. Would have been fine.

Instead, there's this searing agony in my chest fueled by panic. Time apart hasn't weakened my feelings toward Beck. It's strengthened them.

"Now you only want me if it's convenient?" I snap.

I'm hurt, and I hate that I'm hurt. He's given me so many chances, and I've blown every single one of them. Of course he'd reach a breaking point eventually. We all have one.

"I will *want* you, regardless. But I can't be in a relationship with someone who doesn't answer my calls for two weeks."

Him dropping the r-word startles me into silence. The way

he drops it so casually, the way he implies we're already in one. I focus on driving, turning into the soccer field's parking lot a few seconds later.

I toss Beck my car keys, then grab my bag from the back, ignoring the feel of his eyes on me the entire time. "Lock up if you go anywhere."

I climb out of my car and jog toward the field. My teammates are all clustered in by one of the benches, meaning I missed warm-ups. My pace quickens to a flat run as I head for the huddle.

Coach Taylor glances my way as I approach, everyone else following her attention. "Scott! So generous of you to grace us with your presence."

"Sorry, Coach," I clip, dropping my bag by the bench. I'm angry at myself for being tardy. And I'm more than a little distracted by the lingering emotions following the conversation I just had with Beck.

"Ten laps," she tells me.

I nod, then start running again. Warm-ups are usually only eight, but I don't have to ask why two more got added. I've never been late for practice before—not *this* late, at least.

By the time I finish my laps, the rest of the team has moved on to drills.

"Everything okay, Scott?" Coach asks, coming up beside me.

"Everything's fine," I reply. "Just overslept. It won't happen again."

She nods. "Join the purple group."

I nod back, then snag a purple pinny and jog over toward the cones that have been set up. I join the line behind Jill, one of the freshmen.

"I swear it's him," she's saying.

"Where?" the girl in front of her asks. Her back is to me, so

I can't tell who she is.

"Bottom left, beside the bleachers. Right by that tree that—"

"Oh my God. You're right. It does look like him."

"It doesn't just *look* like him. It *is* him," Jill insists.

"What would *Adler Beck* be doing here?" the other girl asks. She turns. It's one of the sophomores, Jasmine. "Does that look like Adler Beck to you, Saylor?"

I exhale, allowing my eyes to wander to the sideline for the first time since I got to the field.

He's attempting to be inconspicuous, but it's not really working. There are a handful of people in the stands, watching. A few students passing by on their way to the athletic complex. One gorgeous German, leaning against the metal side of the bleachers.

I hope he remembered to lock my car.

"It does, yeah," I say.

"Do you think he's participating in a clinic here, like he did at CFOC?" Jasmine asks excitedly.

"You met him, right?" Jill questions. "At Scholenberg this summer? Can you introduce us? I want his autograph."

"Autograph?" Jasmine grins. "I want his number."

I pray the line will move faster so I'm no longer trapped in this conversation. But everyone's moving slower than usual. Jasmine and Jill aren't the only ones whispering. I catch Emma looking over at me from her spot across the field.

Practice *finally* ends, and I take a seat on the grass to stretch my tired muscles. Between trying to ignore the gossip and the fact Coach Taylor doesn't believe in the concept of an easy practice, I'm exhausted. And I had no time to plan out what to say to Beck with everything else going on around me. I'll have to wing it, which has never gone well for me in conversations.

I hate the paralyzing feeling that accompanies uncertainty. I can feel it creeping over me right now, making my skin itch and my insides crawl. Ending things with Beck would be best. He's a distraction I don't need. But I *want* him, distraction or not, and I realized how much when he issued the ultimatum in the car. Having him in my life won't help me win games. But he'll be someone to call after each victory or loss. I've never had that support. Never realized it was something to look for until I found it.

My teammates are slow to leave the field, most of them hanging around the benches drinking water. I focus on finishing my stretches, relieved that no one has come over here.

A few minutes later, I hear some commotion. When I glance up, there's a new figure on the field, way taller than any of my teammates. Beck pauses to say something to Coach Taylor but continues toward me less than a minute later. A few of my remaining teammates exchange shocked glances. They might have been angling for an introduction, but they all assumed Beck was here in some professional capacity.

Beck drops down on the grass beside me without speaking a word. But it says a whole lot. He had to have noticed all the looks at him during our practice. Maybe he could even hear the speculation about why he's here from where he was standing. Him coming over here sends a very clear message—he's here for me.

He tilts his head back, staring up at the blue sky. "Your left touch could use a little work," he tells me without glancing over.

I scoff, straightening from the lean over my left leg. "I only take advice from soccer players who have won a gold medal."

Germany got silver two years ago.

Beck grins at me, an easy, carefree one that lightens a little of the weight on my chest.

I lean over my right leg to stretch that hamstring.

"Thank you for the painting."

"You're welcome. I just saw it and thought…"

"It looks just like the field that night."

I clear my throat. "Yeah."

"I didn't come all this way to thank you for a painting, Saylor."

"I know. You came to issue an ultimatum."

"It's not an ultimatum."

I straighten. "It sounded like an ultimatum."

"Well, it wasn't one." His hand lands on my knee, a warm weight I don't want to shake. "Me wanting you doesn't mean much if you don't want this too. Me coming here doesn't matter if you keep running away."

I glance around the field. Everyone has gone now, thankfully. I grab his wrist and lie down, pulling him with me.

"No stars again," Beck comments.

I laugh. "Shut up."

"I missed you too," he says. "You hung up before I could say it."

I gnaw on the inside of my cheek. "Hallie was calling me to take more photos. I didn't call planning to hang up on you, if it makes any difference."

"That was your dad earlier?"

"Yeah. He came up for a game, with his new wife."

"About damn time." There's bitterness in Beck's voice—bitterness on my behalf—and it hits me square in the center of my chest.

I'm used to Hallie coaxing me toward peace. My best friends spent last night making polite chitchat with my dad. No one has ever told me my resentment toward my father is valid. With three words, Beck just made it clear to me that's how he feels. I knew he understood my commitment to soccer. But it's hitting me all over again, how he really knows *me*.

I clear my throat. "How's your family?"

"Good. Sophia asks about you a lot."

"Is she still dating Karl?"

"No. That appears to have ended for good, thankfully. She's talking about taking a break from boys, but that's never lasted long in the past. Sophia is...Sophia." Affection floods Beck's tone. "She wants to text you, but I told her not to. Guess she listened, for once."

"Why not? She can text. It'd be nice to hear from her."

"Because you talking to my sister but not to me would have been terrible for my ego."

"*Please.* Your ego is just fine."

He rolls his head toward me. "Do you think I do this shit with other women, Saylor? Because I don't."

"You brought lots of other women to meet your family. You told me. So did Sophia."

"That was different. There were a few years...a few years where I needed the distraction. When it was way easier to bring a girl over to my parents than talk to them about how overwhelmed I was. I was a kid. Those girls...none of them meant anything to me. I knew you'd be different the second you commented about my shoulder."

"You were that sure I'd go for the asshole, *how dare you talk to me* act, huh?"

"I've never been sure about anything when it comes to you, Saylor, except you're the one person who can make lying in the grass feel more thrilling than skydiving."

My eyebrows rise, surprised. "You've been skydiving? Or is

that a metaphor?"

"Once," he tells me. "It was a rush."

"You weren't worried about breaking a leg?"

"No. And you wouldn't be either. You're fearless."

I shake my head. "I'm scared."

His expression softens as he realizes I'm no longer talking about jumping out of a plane. Falling for him feels far more terrifying, and I'm fighting every urge to flee from it.

"I don't want to go skydiving with you, Saylor. I want to be the person you rely on when you're acting like you can do everything on your own."

His words remind me of my dad's, and I push back the same way I did at the wedding.

"I *can* do everything on my own," I insist.

"There's a difference between wanting to and having to."

I swallow. "Relationships hardly ever last."

"Which you know from the many you've been in?"

"I didn't need to get nailed in the face with a soccer ball to know it was going to hurt," I retort.

That earns me a wry smile. "You're equating me swallowing my pride and flying almost four thousand miles to being on the receiving end of a wayward kick?"

We're talking in circles, and I like to run straight. I sit up and then stand, brushing some stray grass off my shorts.

Beck sits up too, draping his elbows over his knees and watching me cautiously.

"Do you still want that rematch?" I ask. "I'll let you pick the prize this time."

He looks at me like I'm insane. "There's no goalie."

"So?"

"So, there won't be a winner."

I grin. "That's the sweetest thing you've ever said to me."

Beck is arguably the best soccer player in the world. Yet he's never once made me feel inferior, treated me as any less because I haven't signed a pro contract or because I'm a woman. It's one of many attractive things about him.

He grumbles as he stands. "You're not tired from practice?"

I shake my head. "You know me better than that."

"I *do* know you." His blue gaze is intense, burning right into me.

"I know," I say.

"You told me you don't do rematches," he reminds me.

I swallow, holding his gaze. We've played soccer together since I said that. Had sex. Those moments have meant more with him than they ever have with anyone else. "I do a lot of things with you that I don't do with anyone else."

"Scott!" A male voice interrupts the intense moment. I smother a sigh, glancing over to see Kyle Andrews jogging this way. "Congrats on the win yesterday. Heard it was fucking epic—*holy shit*. That's Adler Beck." Kyle glances between me and Beck—twice. "This is Adler Beck."

If I were in a lighter mood, I would laugh.

"You're—I mean, man. I'm a huge fan! We always watch the Kluvberg games. I can't believe—I wish…" Kyle glances around like he's waiting for someone to appear with a camera to commemorate the moment. Hopefully he won't pull his phone out for a selfie.

I take pity on him. "Beck, this is Kyle. He's on the men's soccer team."

"I'm the captain, *actually*." Kyle gives me an affronted look.

"The *captain*, then. I wasn't sure if you wanted to take credit for going one and three," I say sweetly.

Kyle glares at me, but it morphs into an awed expression when Beck holds out a hand and says, "Nice to meet you."

Kyle looks a bit dazed as he shakes Beck's hand. He fanboys over him for a few more minutes, then finally leaves.

"He's going to tell the whole school you're here," I inform Beck, passing him the ball. "So we'd better make this quick unless you want to start signing autographs."

"What are we playing to?" Beck asks, shrugging out of his jacket.

"Five? Like before?"

He nods. "And what are we playing for?"

"Your pick, remember?"

"And what are my options?"

"Well, you already told me what you want, so you can stick with that."

His eyebrows rise. "You?"

"Are you asking me or telling me?"

"I'm trying to figure out how you plan on 'winning' yourself."

I'm not planning on winning at all, but saying so would ruin the surprise of what's probably a stupid gesture. At least I warned him I'm bad at this. I've never hidden any part of myself from Beck, never attempted to act like someone I'm not.

I pass him the ball. "Just take the first shot."

He makes it, unsurprisingly. We're standing fifteen feet away from a wide-open net and he has better shot accuracy than a sniper.

I make my shot. He makes his.

We volley back and forth like that, until it's my last one. Since he hasn't missed a shot, not like he did last time, I can't win.

If I make it, we'll tie.

If I miss it, I'll lose.

Since I'm competitive, I kick it toward the corner flag, smiling when it lands just inside the line. It couldn't be more obvious I missed on purpose, and I watch that register on Beck's face.

"I'm not running," I tell him. "Want a tour of campus?"

Chapter 25

Beck's sitting on my bed paging through a book when I walk into my room.

After we left the field, I took him on a brief tour of campus. He got a phone call right as we returned to my empty house, so I decided to take a quick shower. Between sleeping on the living room floor and practice earlier, I felt gross.

Beck isn't talking to anyone now. He's staring at me, standing in a towel with dripping wet hair.

"Everything okay?" I ask, shutting the door behind me.

"Yeah." He closes the book—one of my mysteries—and sets it on the bedside table. "Just Wagner, checking in."

"He mad you're here?"

"He's not…thrilled."

I walk closer, catching the bob of his Adam's apple as I approach. "How long can you stay?"

"My flight leaves first thing tomorrow. I'm heading straight to Berlin for a match."

I'm expecting the answer. Even before his coach called, I

knew there was no way his absence wasn't being missed. Beck's not just famous, he's important. People pay to see *him* play, not to attend a soccer game.

"First thing tomorrow is...soon."

He nods. "Best I could do."

I take another step, then abandon the idea of personal space altogether, climbing right into his lap. The thick span of his thighs spreads mine, tugging the towel so high it's barely covering any of my legs. Some beads of water fall from my hair and land on him, but Beck doesn't seem to notice. Or care. His hands land on my waist, tugging me even closer to his chest. His mouth lands on the curve of my shoulder, pressing a warm kiss to my damp skin.

It's heaven, him touching me like this. Our physical attraction has always been a noticeable presence between us. It's impossible to ignore right now. It feels like forever since we shared a moment like this. For a while, I was convinced we would never share a moment like this again. That heightens every sensation now.

"*Saylor...*"

I shiver at the way he says my name, filled with so much longing and lust. Like he's dying to touch me. Desperate to fuck me. Beck's looking at me like *I'm* the important, beloved one. Like I'm the center of *his* world.

"Have I mentioned how happy I am that you're here?" I ask, lifting the hem of his T-shirt.

Beck smirks as he helps me pull the fabric over his head. "You've yet to mention it, actually."

He's teasing, but he's also right.

"I warned you—I'm bad at this stuff," I say, running my hands down his pecs and across his abs. Enjoying the feel of hot, firm skin pressed against my palms. "I freak out. I shut down. I run. But...I'm trying. I promise I'm trying."

Beck kisses me, the towel I'm wearing falling apart following one firm tug. His hands slide up, leaving a trail of goosebumps behind, until he reaches my boobs. I moan into his mouth when he cups them, the jolt of pleasure sudden and consuming.

He flips me effortlessly, so that I end up on my back beneath him.

I push my fingers into his soft hair.

Trail my fingers down his neck.

Dig my nails into his back.

I was overwhelmed before; I'm drowning now. Sinking through ecstasy and euphoria. Beck kisses me urgently, fervently, fiercely. His tongue and lips assault my breasts, my neck, my chest. All while rubbing his massive erection against my inner thigh. Teasing me.

"Beck, please." I let him hear the desperation in my voice. It's not like he can't tell I'm a wanton, writhing mess beneath him.

"Do you want me, Scott?" He's never called me by my last name in bed, and the sound of it falling off his lips is surprisingly erotic.

His fingers trail enticingly down my ribcage, and I arch against him. "What the fuck does it seem like?"

There's a flash of humor on his face, but it's quickly overtaken by heat. One hand slides between my thighs, and my hips jerk upward from the additional stimulation. If this were anyone else, I wouldn't capitulate.

"I want you more than I've ever wanted anyone," I tell him, laying myself bare in more ways than one.

Beck unrolls a condom and then thrusts inside of me. I muffle my moans against his shoulder, having no idea when my housemates will be home.

Thoughts flee like dandelion pappuses in the wind. All that remains is sensation.

I'm aware of everything and nothing.

Thoughtless and overstimulated.

There's the heat of his skin. The ripple of his abdominal muscles pressed against my stomach. The thick hair my hands are tugging at.

I'm close, feeling trickles of ecstasy, when he slows, pumping into me at a leisurely pace. Languidly. I clench my inner muscles and feel the muscles in his back ripple as he responds.

He slides out of me, teasing me with the bulbous tip of his cock, and I let out a throaty gasp. Then he plunges back inside, and I'm over the cliff. Liquid hot pleasure courses through me as I light up like a supernova.

I watch Beck's face tighten and then relax as he finds his own release.

He drops onto the comforter beside me a few seconds later, both of us breathing heavily. Beck gets up to take care of the condom, then lies back down beside me. His fingers start sifting through my hair, the slight tug on the strands somehow reassuring.

I speak first. "I never told you that you inspire me as a soccer player because you haven't been *just* a soccer player to me since we met. I used to watch you play and admire your skill. Analyze your strategy. Those aren't the things I'd notice now. And I didn't know how to admit that you mattered, or if I even should, so I said nothing. Then that guy asked during the interview and it just...came out. People cared, so much more than I thought they would. I didn't even think, before I said it. Didn't know someone was filming me. But do you know how many *millions* of views that video got?"

I pause, but Beck's fingers keep brushing through my hair.

"Being known because of you is not the career I was after," I tell him. "Which is selfish of me, because I know it's not something you have control over. But I'm worried, if people find out about us, it's all I'll be associated with. It'll be just like at the camp you brought me to. Everyone will know I'm only there because of you. I want to earn my accomplishments, not have them handed to me because of what you worked for. Does that make any sense?"

"It makes a lot of sense," he replies. "But no one could watch you play and say that you don't deserve a spot on any football field. That's what Herrmann said, after that camp ended. What Otto told me, after he saw your penalty kicks."

"Really?"

"Really. I resent the attention sometimes, and maybe it's selfish of *me* to ask you to deal with it too. But you can use it, Saylor. If they pay attention to you because of me, use it however you want."

"True. I could get a Nike deal out of dating you. Or at least an Italian car…"

He pinches my side. I giggle, rolling onto his chest and tracing circles above his heart.

"You live in Germany," I state.

Beck doesn't just live there. He *is* German. His family lives there. His friends. His team, the only one he's ever played for. None of those are easy ties to sever. I'm not even sure they're ones he *could*. He's under contract with FC Kluvberg, and I'm positive they're not looking to offload their star player.

His fingers migrate to my arm, tracing patterns on my skin the same way I'm touching him. "I'm aware."

"That's far from here."

"The flight wasn't short."

He knows exactly what I'm alluding to, but is going to make me say it.

"I could come visit Kluvberg after my season ends...but that won't be for months." I feel shitty saying it, after he came all this way during his season. But I'm striving for total honesty. This is me letting him in. Staying in place instead of fleeing. "The team's schedule is intense. *My* schedule is crazy. It's my senior year. I want another championship. So...I just want to make sure you know what you're getting into."

He stares at me for a few seconds, then reaches toward my bedside table and grabs his phone.

"Sorry, am I boring you?"

Beck smirks, then taps the screen. My phone lights up on the charging station where I left it. "Go ahead. Answer it," he tells me.

I roll my eyes, but reach over and grab it. "Hello?"

He hangs up, then sets his phone back on the table. "That's all I need you to do, *Schatz*."

"What does *Schatz* mean?" I ask.

He just smiles. "Still not fluent?"

I toss my phone away and flop back down. "It's a difficult language," I grumble.

Beck's grin remains in place. He's in a better mood than I've ever seen him, and there's a warm glow in the center of my chest, realizing it has to do with me. "I'm not asking you to choose between me and football. I love how focused and dedicated and motivated you are. You inspire *me*. And I know exactly what I'm getting into."

"You were right," I say.

He hums. "About what?"

"It *was* stupid of me, playing in the park before I got cleared. The only reason I did was…well, I wanted to play with you. Wanted to more than being careful or playing it safe."

Beck smiles, tenderly tucking a piece of hair behind my ear. "I overreacted. I was so scared I hurt you. And that took me off guard, because I never cared about anyone else on the field like that before."

"I won't tell your teammates."

He chuckles.

"What about…what about next year?" I ask. "I planned to play…here." Beat Mackenzie Howard in another championship. I know some players opt to play overseas, but I never pictured myself being one of them.

"We'll figure it out."

"Don't make it sound easy," I say. "It'll be hard."

"I know it'll be hard. You don't walk on the field knowing you're going to win, Saylor. You earn it. Fight for it. That's all I'm asking. For you to try."

His phone rings before I can formulate a response.

Beck groans, then glances at the screen. "I have to take this," he tells me apologetically.

"It's fine," I say.

He sighs before answering, running a palm over his face as he listens to whatever's being said. Then replies in German.

I stand and pull on some clothes, then point toward the door and mouth *I'll be right back*. Beck nods before I slip out of my room and head downstairs to grab a snack. We got some lunch on campus, but I skipped breakfast and am currently starving.

I'm spreading peanut butter on slices of apple when I hear Emma's voice. "Hello! Anyone home?" She appears in the doorway to the kitchen a few seconds later, with Cressida right behind her.

They both stop and stare at me.

"Hey," I say, continuing to spread peanut butter.

"Why haven't you been answering any messages?" Cressida asks. "We were worried."

"My phone died," I respond. "I normally charge it overnight, and there wasn't exactly a cord on the living room floor."

I got thoroughly distracted after plugging it in, but I don't mention that.

Emma glances around, then stage-whispers. "Where is he?"

I smirk. "Upstairs."

"Upstairs? Is he...*staying here*?"

"Yeah. Just for tonight. He's leaving tomorrow. Where's Anne?"

"She has a study group thing," Cressida answers. "Now, can you explain what the fuck *Adler Beck* is doing in our *house*?"

I glance at Emma, since she already knows part of the story. "I had a...thing with him over the summer, while I was at Scholenberg. And now I think I might be dating him."

"*What?*" Cressida gasps.

"Saylor's in *lo-ve*," Emma sings. She beams at me. "I'm so happy for you, S."

"Thanks," I say.

"You knew about this?" Cressida asks. Looks at me. "You told Emma?"

"She barely told me anything," Emma states. "I didn't get

any dick details at all."

"How disappointing." A male voice joins our conversation.

I laugh at the expressions on Cressida and Emma's faces as Beck walks into the kitchen. They both look too stunned to introduce themselves, so I do it for them. "This is Beck. Beck, this is Cressida and Emma."

Beck smiles. "Nice to officially meet you. I've heard a lot about you both."

Neither Emma nor Cressida say anything; they just gape at him.

"Don't make it weird, guys," I say, adding more peanut butter to the knife.

"Well, I'm going to, uh, do some laundry," Cressida says.

Emma shrugs. "I should do some homework."

I smirk at Beck once they're both gone. "They're big fans of yours."

He rubs the back of his neck, shaking his head a little.

I push the plate toward him. "Want some apple?"

. . .

Anne walks into the kitchen right as I'm starting to cook dinner. She looks behind me at the stairs. "Whe—uh, where's Beck?" I can tell she's trying to sound nonchalant, but she falls spectacularly short.

"In the shower. How was your study thing?"

Anne rolls her eyes. "You're *dating Adler Beck*, and you want to know about my marketing class?"

She's obviously talked to Emma or Cressida recently.

"He's just a guy."

She scoffs. "Fine. He's just a guy. You're in a relationship? Half the campus is going to enter a state of mourning."

I shake my head. "Are you done?"

"I'm happy for you. I'm just *shocked*. Him being here is like..."

A long pause follows, during which I raise one eyebrow. "Like what?"

"I don't know. I can't think of a good celebrity equivalent."

I snort. "Where are Cressida and Emma?"

"Trying to fix the television before *Twenty-Five to One* is on."

"Of course they are."

"Don't think I didn't see you watching last week," Anne replies.

"It was impossible to ignore. I didn't think it was physically possible for someone to cry that much." I open the fridge door to survey the contents.

"Are you making dinner?"

"Yeah," I reply, pulling a package of chicken out of the fridge and turning on the oven.

"Can I help?"

"Sure, thanks. I haven't started the salad, if you want to do that."

Anne pulls greens and veggies out of the fridge. We talk about our next game on Tuesday as we prep dinner. Cressida and Emma return to the kitchen a few minutes later, still bickering about whatever is wrong with the television.

It feels like an ordinary Sunday night.

Until the sound of footfalls comes from the stairwell. I glance up, taken aback by how right Beck strolling into my kitchen wearing athletic shorts and a T-shirt with wet hair looks. I get why my housemates are freaking out about him being here. But to me, the sight looks normal. Appears perfect.

Emma and Cressida keep arguing in an overdone attempt to act casual as Beck saunters over to my side. "Smells good."

"I can cook."

"Can you?" he asks, leaning against the counter.

"Mm-hmm."

We stare at each other, and it's the first time I wish I lived alone. Emma, Cressida, and Anne are my best friends. They're a friendly spotlight, but it's still attention I wish wasn't on us. The time I have with him is so limited, more slipping away every second.

Beck has one of those faces that looks better the longer you stare at it. I get lost in familiar azure depths, so adrift I startle when Anne says my name.

"Saylor?" she repeats.

"Yeah?" I tear my gaze away from his.

"The timer just went off for the chicken."

I grab the potholders off the counter and pull the pan out of the oven. Juice bubbles and crackles in the bottom of the dish. The surface of the meat is crispy, cooked to a perfect shade of light brown. I grab the meat thermometer from the drawer to check, but I already know it's done.

Anne grabs plates, Cressida gets the silverware, and Emma makes one of her gross drinks. We all sit down at the table together.

My three housemates have either gotten over the shock of Beck's presence or are getting better about acting normal around it. None of them have any shortage of things to say during dinner. They chatter about such a range of topics I can barely keep track. Most of my focus is on Beck's hand, resting on my thigh beneath the table. He doesn't move his fingers, just leaves his palm there. Touching me like he's just as aware of the time ticking away and wants to make the most of every minute.

The food is good—if I do say so myself—but I'm barely tasting what I'm eating. We finish dinner, and Cressida offers to do the dishes.

"It's fine, Cress. I know you want to watch the show. I'll clean up."

"What show?" Beck asks, speaking for the first time since we sat down at the table.

"*Twenty-Five to One!*" Emma exclaims. "Have you seen it?"

I snort and Beck glances at me.

"What is it about?" he asks.

"It's a reality television show about finding love," Cressida replies.

"Filled with unnecessary drama and toxic personalities, and fueled by too much alcohol," I add.

"Do you watch it?" Beck questions.

"I mean, sometimes. If it's on…" I hedge.

"She watches it," Emma confirms, and I glare at her.

"Okay, let's watch it," Beck states.

I glance at him. "Seriously?"

"Why not? I'm definitely not playing Clue with you again."

I fight the smile, I really do. But I don't win. "Fine."

We all head into the living room, Cress deciding to do the dishes later, just like I knew she would. They'll probably sit in the sink until tomorrow. I end up smushed next to Beck on the couch that's not really large enough for four people, which I'm not complaining about.

The show starts with an elaborate montage replaying last week's most shocking events.

"That's the guy they're all fighting over?" Beck whispers to me as the new episode starts.

"Yup," I reply. "Not your type?"

Beck chuckles, and I lean a little closer to feel his chest vibrate. "Nope. Yours?"

"I prefer blonds."

I look away, back at the screen, which is currently depicting a hot-air balloon ride over a field of wildflowers. The hot-air balloon lands in the field, and the couple disembarks to discover a picnic that's already been prepared. "Seriously? How unrealistic," I grumble.

"Saylor! I can't hear what they're saying," Emma complains.

I sigh as I settle back into the soft cushions, watching as the lead and his current date make contrived conversation, biting back more sarcastic comments. And then Beck's left hand settles on my knee, and I lose all interest in what's happening on the television.

I glance over at him, but his attention seems to actually be on the show. His thumb traces small circles on my skin, and zings of arousal shoot up my thigh. I bite my bottom lip and shift closer to him. Beck's arm slides down my back, dipping underneath the hem of the crewneck sweatshirt I'm wearing. I have nothing on underneath, and he discovers that.

Rough callouses scrape against my lower back as his palm drags across the skin, leaving goosebumps in its wake. I lean into him even more, and Anne's pretty much got the center of the couch to herself. I'm partly on the cushion, mostly on Beck's lap. He keeps rubbing his hand against my skin but doesn't venture any farther north.

Beck's eyes don't waver from the television, which makes it even hotter. Either he's completely oblivious to the effect his touch has on me, or he's actually paying attention to the show.

I stopped paying attention to the show a long time ago.

I close my eyes, inhaling his familiar scent as I rest my head on his shoulder.

The next thing I'm aware of is whispers.

"...leave her down here?" Cressida's voice.

"She spent last night on the floor. This is an upgrade." Emma this time.

I groan, unwilling to open my eyes.

"I've got it from here." Beck.

"Great. I'm going to bed," Anne says. "Practice earlier kicked my ass."

"Imagine how terrible it would have been if we lost yesterday," Cressida comments. Her voice is fading, and I don't hear anything from Emma, so she must have already gone upstairs.

My eyelids crack. It's just me and Beck in the living room.

"Ready for bed?" I ask.

"You obviously are," he replies, smirking.

I roll my eyes before I stand and stretch, then head toward the stairs. Beck follows.

The upstairs hallway is empty, all the doors except mine shut. I enter my room, with Beck right behind me, closing the door behind us.

Not bothering with much modesty—or pajamas—I slip out of the sweatpants I put on earlier. Pull off my sweatshirt—flashing him—before climbing into bed wearing my underwear and a T-shirt I left in the sheets.

Beck strips down to his boxer briefs, then climbs into bed with me.

Before he turns the light out, I say the words I've been afraid to utter until right now. "*Ich liebe dich.*"

Beck is a stunned-looking statue beside me. "What?" His voice comes out choked.

I don't even think he's trying to draw this out or get me to say it again. I think I genuinely took him completely off guard. Or my pronunciation is so terrible he's trying to figure out what I'm saying. *"Ich liebe dich,"* I repeat, more carefully.

It comes out easier this time. I'm jumping. Falling. Flying. And it's scary. But not as terrifying as it could be, because I trust Beck to be there when I land.

"You learned German," he states.

"Three words. Not that impressive."

He sucks in a deep breath. One that sounds unsteady. I've witnessed Beck angry and confused. Teasing and turned on. Sweet and understanding. I've never seen him look like *this*. His features sharpen, emotion making them appear more severe and sculpted. "I love you, Saylor Scott."

I hoped he did. I wanted to tell him, regardless of whether or not he said it back. But I thought I was prepared, if he did decide to say it.

I'm not.

Because it's one thing to hear others exchange those words, or to say them in different combinations.

It's another matter entirely to have someone say them to you.

To hear them ring with sincerity.

"You don't have to say it just because I did," I tell him.

"I'm not. I've wanted to say it for a long time."

"Yeah?"

He leans down to kiss me. "Yeah. *Ich liebe dich auch.*"

Turns out my pronunciation *was* terrible. I'm surprised he managed not to laugh.

Beck turns out the light, then lies down beside me. I snuggle into his chest, closing my eyes. Relaxing against his body.

I don't deflect.

I don't flee.

For the first and final time, I let myself fully fall.

Epilogue

Beck

You could hear a pin drop in the silent living room of Saylor's childhood home.

I've never understood that expression. Not until right now, when it's so quiet I can hear the rasp as I rub my sweaty palms against the cotton fabric of my shorts. Catch the steady *whoosh* of my own heartbeat. Marcus Scott takes a sip of water from the glass he's holding, and I swear I can hear him swallow. His wife, Sandra, shifts beside him, looking as uncomfortable as I feel.

My usual confidence has dried up into nothing but uncertainty, trying to decide how to ask this. If I even should.

The back door opens and closes, the scuffle of shoes and babble of a toddler filling the formerly quiet house.

I'm caught somewhere between relief and dread at the sounds. Maybe it's a sign. This was my one chance to talk to her father alone.

Hallie appears in the doorway a minute later, her son propped on one hip and her husband right behind her. Her eyes bounce around our awkward trio, Marcus and Sandra on the couch, me sitting on the armchair next to the fireplace that looks like it's never been used.

"They took the tent," she announces.

Marcus glances at his older daughter, and I take the opportunity to pull in a quick breath. My lungs feel tight and constricted, like an invisible fist is squeezing them.

"Great. Thanks, honey."

Hallie's attention is back on me before her father has even finished speaking. "Everything okay in here?"

"Adler wanted to have a quick word." Marcus refocuses on me as he speaks, his expectant expression a reminder I said that and then haven't managed to verbalize much else.

"Oh?" Hallie's eyebrows rise as she studies me, not even flinching as Matthew Jr. grabs at her hair with his small hand.

"We should get going," Matt says, bailing me out. "Little guy missed his nap, so there's a high chance of a tantrum any minute."

The understanding look he aims my way doesn't appear to have anything to do with his kid's sleep schedule, though.

Maybe I should have asked Matt for advice on how to do this. Presumably, he had a similar conversation with Mr. Scott before proposing to Hallie.

But Hallie has a very different relationship with their father than Saylor does. And Matt and Hallie have a very different relationship than Saylor and I do. Plus, Matt didn't live in another country.

So I'm not sure his advice would actually be all that helpful.

Hallie nods, but it's reluctant and her expression remains wildly curious. "Party went great, Dad. I think Saylor really enjoyed it and it was awesome that—"

"I'm going to ask her to marry me."

Finally, the words that have been circling my mind for the past ten minutes—the past few months—come out.

And as soon as they're out there, lingering in the air, we're back to pin-drop silence.

I clear my throat, the next words flowing a little easier now that the first sentence is out. "I want her to know I'm *in this*, certain about us, before she has to make decisions about her future. Now that she's graduated, Saylor can sign a professional contract. I'm hoping she'll consider a German team. It's not that difficult to get a work permit, but it would be even easier if we're..."

I let my voice trail and exhale.

"The logistics don't really matter. The point is, I love Saylor. I want her to achieve everything she's ever dreamed of. And I want to be next to her when she does. I want her to *know* I'll be there, no matter what happens."

I aim a meaningful glance Marcus's way, hoping he'll understand what I mean without me having to spell it out more than that.

I want Saylor to know I'm not going to abandon her the way her mother did physically and her father did emotionally. And while a marriage license is no guarantee, it's the best I have to offer her aside from the time and promises I've already made.

Marcus's expression is neutral, carefully so. I've never had the easiest time reading him. If he's shocked, he's hiding it well. He's not looking like he's inclined to throw another party, either.

And I realize I never asked a question.

"So, what I'm saying is—"

"They're resurfacing Sumter Street." The door bangs open,

a gust of warm wind finding its way into the living room before it slams shut again. "Construction vehicles everywhere and cops blocking it off."

Saylor appears a second later, kicking off her sneakers and pulling out the elastic holding her blonde ponytail in place simultaneously. Always in motion, always looking for the next challenge to tackle.

I swallow the unease that realization comes with.

Saylor Scott is *it* for me. No other woman will ever compare. She's been in my life for almost exactly a year, and I can barely remember what it looked like before we met. Before she beat me in a shoot-out, women were just...there. The attention and the games were fun. Flattering. Mutually enjoyable.

But it lost any appeal when Saylor appeared in front of me with all the subtlety of a supernova. Our long-distance relationship has never felt like a sacrifice, because I don't want anyone else. I could name a thousand reasons why I'm certain she's the one, but none of them—or all of them—would articulate the way I feel about her quite right.

"Whoa." Saylor's glancing around the living room with a furrowed brow, her expression puzzled. "Weird vibe in here." She pulls her jacket off and tosses it on the arm of the couch, her gaze settling on me. "Everything okay?"

"We were just talking about what a success the party was," Hallie says. "The whole town showed up for its sweetheart."

Saylor's nose wrinkles as her blonde hair falls around her face. "Is that seriously what anyone calls me? The *town sweetheart*?"

Hallie grins. "Well, no one who knows you."

Saylor scoffs as she plops down on the couch. "Most of them came to see Beck." She turns her head to smirk at me, and I manage to smile back.

She's teasing.

But I know she gets frustrated by the level of interest and attention I draw. Saylor wants to be well-known—on her own terms. For her own skill. She wants women's football to receive more attention because of her talent, not because she's associated with me.

"Only the women," Hallie says.

Saylor rolls her eyes.

I know she cares about me. She's told me she loves me, and she's shown it.

But I'm not certain where I fall on her priority list when football is involved. We're at two very different places in our careers. Hers hasn't reached its peak. And as much as I like to pretend otherwise, mine possibly has.

I have no doubt Saylor will accomplish everything she's hoping to.

Me? I've hit the milestones. I've proven myself. And while I have no intention of retiring anytime soon, that means some of the pressure is off. Saylor doesn't share the same mindset.

We haven't discussed many details regarding her next move, only spoken in abstract terms. But what is best for her career and what's best for us will likely bisect, and I'm not sure what, if anything, she's willing to sacrifice. I'm not worried about our relationship, but I'm aware it will be affected.

"You guys are headed out?" Saylor asks her sister.

Hallie nods. "Matthew is close to crashing."

Saylor stands and walks over to the doorway, taking her nephew and lifting him up in the air. His little arms wave around, and he laughs. The sight makes me smile. I want kids with her— when, if, she's ready for that step. I think I knew that when I heard her talking to Matthew in my favorite coffee shop.

"He seems wide awake to me," Saylor states, grinning at Matthew while he waves at her. "You guys could stay for dinner."

I speak before Hallie can answer. "I made reservations at La Central," I tell Saylor. "Hallie, uh, said it was a nice place."

Hallie smirks a little, like she's suddenly realizing why I asked her for a restaurant recommendation. I hope that's a good sign, but hell if I know.

"We don't have to go," I add, quickly. "It was just a—"

"No. Dinner sounds great. I'll go shower and change." Saylor passes her nephew back to Hallie, says goodbye to her sister's family, and heads upstairs.

More heavy silence lingers in her departure, as we all listen to Saylor's footsteps climb the stairs.

Hallie talks first. "Okay, we're headed out. Bye!" She glances at me. Winks. "Good luck."

I nod, registering the sentiment more than the teasing. That I'll *need* luck.

I know Saylor. But she still manages to surprise me on a regular basis. Honestly, I have no idea how she'll react.

Once the front door closes behind Hallie, Matt, and Matthew Jr., Sandra stands. "I should reorganize the fridge before I lose all motivation. The caterers stuffed all the leftovers in there."

She sends a smile my way, which I return. The fridge might need to be reorganized, but I'm positive this is an attempt to give me and Marcus a moment.

As soon as we're sitting alone, he speaks. "Saylor hasn't asked for my permission about anything in years. You don't need to pretend a word I say will make any difference to her, Adler."

"Just because she doesn't ask doesn't mean she doesn't care," I reply carefully.

I like Marcus. I hate how he raised his daughters. Saylor

still resents him, and I do too, on her behalf. But I know he has regrets, and I don't want her to have any.

"I'm going to ask her regardless of what you say," I continue. "But I'd like to have your blessing."

"You have it, of course," he tells me. The corner of his mouth twists. "Good, uh, luck."

The landline rings, followed by a call from Sandra in the kitchen. Marcus stands, offering me a smile I think he means to be encouraging, then heads for the doorway.

Leaving me alone with my thoughts.

. . .

As soon as we step into the small bistro, someone calls out Saylor's name. It's an echo of her graduation party this afternoon. Every person there wanted to talk to her.

She turns to greet a tall guy with brown hair. "Hey, Andy."

"I haven't seen you since your dad's wedding," the guy—Andy—says. "How have you been?"

"Good." Saylor smiles. "I graduated."

"Yeah, the whole town heard." Andy grins. "Sorry I missed the party earlier."

There's genuine regret on his face. Without asking, I'm positive he has history with her. Running into an ex was not exactly the note I wanted to start this night on.

"You didn't miss much," Saylor responds, then glances at me. "This is my boyfriend, Beck. Andy and I went to high school together."

"And middle school. And elementary school. Plus kindergarten." Andy grins, then shifts his attention to me and holds a hand out. "The famous soccer player. Nice to meet you, man."

I force a smile as I shake his hand, my grip a little tighter than is really necessary. "The rest of the world calls it football."

"Right, right. Logically, it makes sense, I guess." Andy glances at Saylor. "What are you calling it these days?"

"The sport I win at," she replies.

Andy grins. "Should have seen that answer coming."

His tone—not to mention his expression—has turned way too admiring. I'm close to suggesting we find our table when Saylor beats me to it.

"Good to see you, Andy. Enjoy your dinner."

She slips her hand into mine and then pulls me toward the hostess stand. I give my name for the reservation. The woman gawks at me a little before showing us to our table. She fills our drink glasses and passes out menus.

"Are you going to find anything to eat here?" Saylor asks as soon as she opens the menu.

I glance at her. And immediately forget what I was going to say. She's literally glowing in the candlelight, her hair loose in golden waves. She changed into a different dress from the one she wore to her party earlier, this one darker and lower cut.

She's stunning. I feel *stunned*, looking at her.

She looks up, catching me staring. "What? Do I have something on my face?"

"No."

When I don't say anything else, her eyebrows lift. "Oh-kay. Well, did you hear me about the menu? Because I'm not seeing any sauerkraut or bratwurst or—"

I snort. "You have a totally inaccurate impression of German food."

"It can't be *that* inaccurate. I lived there for two months, remember?"

"I remember."

She's offering me the perfect segue into discussing the future—bringing up our future. But before I can decide how to take it, the waitress appears to take our orders. By the time she leaves again, the moment has passed.

The rest of dinner is nice. The food is delicious, and the atmosphere is romantic. But my nerves grow more with each passing minute.

I haven't decided exactly how I'm going to do this. Saylor thrives as the center of attention, but certain kinds of it make her uncomfortable. When she's visited me in Kluvberg and we've gotten photographed together, she's hated it. And I want this to be a moment just for the two of us. Something special, but private. I'm leaving tomorrow, and this trip has been mostly celebratory concerning her college graduation without any serious conversations taking place between us. I don't want to head back home without making it completely clear to her where I stand.

My phone buzzes in my pocket when we leave the restaurant. It's a text from Sophia.

"Say hi to her from me," Saylor says, spotting the name on the screen. "And that we missed her at the party."

"I will," I reply.

But I know Sophia isn't texting to ask about the party. I took her with me to pick out the ring, and she's texted me nonstop ever since asking when I was planning to propose. Hallie will probably message me next.

My steps automatically veer toward the parked car. Saylor pulls me in the opposite direction, toward a large brick building. Behind it, there's a soccer field, the familiar form of a goalpost visible from here.

"This is where I went to high school," she tells me as we walk toward the building. "While you were winning a World Cup, I was playing right here."

"You'll win one too," I reply. "Probably more than one."

Saylor smiles, then tugs me closer to the field. I know where she's headed even before she drops down in the center.

"*Finally*, some stars," I say, staring up at the pinpricks of white light against the black backdrop of the sky.

Her laugh is light and happy, the sound more beautiful than the sight above. "We timed it right, for once."

Every other time we've done this, it's been the middle of the day.

"Speaking of timing…the summer transfer window opens July first," she tells me.

I tense. "I know."

There's a long pause. "Rosenbauch is interested. My agent called yesterday."

FC Rosenbauch is the German women's team closest to Kluvberg. It's the team my mom played for. The team Christina Weber played for. In a perfect world, it's where Saylor would play. In *my* perfect world. But this is *her* career.

"Other teams are interested too, right?" I ask.

"Of course they are."

Despite the heavy moment, I grin at her confidence.

"But if Rosenbauch makes an offer, I'm going to accept it."

"You don't have to do that, Saylor. Not for me, or us." I never want to hold her back in any way. Because she shines brighter than the stars above us and I want everyone to see it. Because I'm terrified it'll end in her resenting me or regretting our relationship.

"Because you don't think we'll make it?"

I reach into my pocket and pull out the velvet box that's been there all night. I set it on her stomach. "Because I'm certain we'll make it no matter where you decide to play. I want you to sign with whatever team you want, and know that I'll support your decision. That it won't change anything between us. That we'll make it work no matter what."

Her eyes dart between me and the box. "Is that…"

"Yes. And I'm not sure if you're ready, and it's okay if you're not. But I want you to know that *I'm* ready. You can answer me in a month. Or a year. A decade. In two years, my contract with Kluvberg will be up. I'll have more options. Whatever you decide on now, it won't be forever."

"You'd leave FC Kluvberg and play for another team?"

"Yes."

"And you'd marry me even if I play in England until I'm too old to pop out any soccer prodigies for you?"

I smile. "Yes."

She stares at me, her teeth sinking into her lower lip. "This wasn't a super romantic proposal."

I exhale, rubbing my face with my palm. "Yeah, I know. I wasn't—"

Her hand finds mine, tugging it off my eyes so I can see her again. "It was perfect."

"I never even asked you."

"So, ask."

I take a deep breath. "Saylor Scott, will you marry me?"

She's smiling, no sign of surprise. That's what I was most worried about seeing, concerned she hadn't even considered this step. And then I realize… "You found the ring, didn't you?"

Her grin grows mischievous, edging into a smirk as she opens the box and takes the ring out, sliding it onto her finger. She raises her left hand above us, the huge diamond glinting brighter than any of the stars in the sky. Blocking most of them.

"I thought it'd be bigger."

I snort.

Saylor rolls so her chin is propped on my shoulder. "I'm kidding. I love it. I love *you*." Her fingers run along my cheek and up to my forehead, brushing some of my hair back. "I was so sure this didn't exist. But you…you made me believe in happy endings again."

I've had an extraordinary life by most measures. Achieved things most people only dream about. I've won championships and I've met important people. Encountered fame and enjoyed wealth. By comparison, falling in love sounds mundane. It's something most people experience, at least once. So is getting engaged. It's a big, common promise.

But I know, kissing Saylor beneath the stars, that no moment in my life will ever matter more than this one.

Exclusive

Bonus

Content

Saylor

L ying awake in the middle of the night is the worst. The rest of the world is quiet and dark and peaceful, while you're stuck with your own oppressive thoughts. If I get up to make tea or watch TV or do anything to distract myself, it'll probably wake Beck. Which will lead to questions about why I'm awake in the middle of the night.

I glance at Beck's still figure beside me in bed. Listen to his deep, even breaths. Look back up at the ceiling.

I should paint it. Or wallpaper it, maybe. Do something to the ceiling, so that tomorrow night when I'm lying here awake— again—it won't be the same boring white stretch of plaster I've spent the past three nights memorizing.

Three. Nights.

Honestly, it's shocking I haven't exhausted myself into a coma yet.

My hand moves to my stomach, under the covers, that familiar swell of anxiety expanding until it feels like I'm drowning, and I reconsider.

It's not shocking.

It's impossible to sleep when you're stuck in a state of perpetual panic.

I glance at Beck again, fast asleep and oblivious.

Well, not entirely oblivious. He's asked me—ten times in the past few days—if everything is okay. And I've made up excuses that have nothing to do with being pregnant, every time. Ten lies.

Because once I tell him, I'll have told him. It will be out there, this massive thing that's much bigger than me and my late period. That's huge and scary and life-altering. That was supposed to happen on purpose, and in five to ten years. After I'd won an Olympic medal and a World Cup and truly proven myself.

Marrying Beck felt big.

Moving to Germany felt big.

But they were choices. Decisions I thought through. And... reversible. People get divorced. People relocate more than once in their lives. I wanted Beck, and I wanted to live here. But I also knew, logically, those parts of life are only as permanent as you make them.

Being a parent is only as permanent as you make it.

My fingers curl into fists as soon as the thought hits. That's my biggest fear, why "mother" has always felt like a title I was uniquely unqualified for. Because I've never been certain I'd be any better at parenthood than my mom was, and no kid deserves to go through that.

I turn my head toward Beck again.

At least this baby will have him. Beck's nothing like my father. If I did abandon my child, he wouldn't fall to pieces the way Marcus Scott did.

I can't picture myself taking off. I love Beck. I love our life here.

And I'm an athlete. Excessive amounts of dedication and determination are necessary to reach the elite level in any sport. Challenges don't usually scare me.

But did my mom know she was going to leave us one day when she found out she was pregnant with Hallie? I doubt it.

I roll onto my stomach, smushing my face in the pillow, and run through passing drills in an attempt to shut off my brain.

At some point, that strategy must succeed, my racing thoughts slowing enough for me to fall asleep, because the next thing I'm aware of is the buzz of Beck's alarm. His practice starts an hour earlier than mine today. He tries to be quiet, quickly shutting the clock off and padding into the bathroom, but the wall isn't thick enough to muffle his morning routine. I can hear the stream of running water, the squeak of the tap turning, the soft snick of a cabinet closing.

When the bathroom door opens, I sit up in bed.

Beck glances toward the motion and smiles.

It's one of those bizarre moments when you see your life through the eyes of a stranger. Or a younger version of yourself. I'm suddenly twenty-one again, sneaking into a world-famous football stadium and spotting the celebrity who'd only existed in my life as a poster on my best friend's wall.

Adler Beck is the sort of person who appears unattainable. A figure you admire but don't get to touch or interact with. I'm married to him, but there are still these flashes when I watch Beck walk onto the field before a match or spot a fan wearing his jersey or see him stroll shirtless out of the bathroom, and I sort of can't believe that this is my real life.

Beck shrugs on a FC Kluvberg shirt and continues toward my side of the bed. He kisses the top of my head. "Sorry I woke you."

"It's fine," I say, covering a yawn with the back of one hand. "I have practice at nine thirty."

"You okay?" Beck asks, frowning when I yawn again.

I'm guessing the dark circles under my eyes have doubled in size since yesterday.

I scrub my palms across my face, muting my reply. "Yeah. Fine."

Make that eleven lies. But he has practice and I have practice and I still haven't decided how to tell Beck about the baby. So... half truths it is.

"Okay. I'll get coffee going."

I muster a smile. "Sounds great."

I've secretly dumped my mug out the past several mornings, because at some point in my life I heard pregnant women aren't supposed to drink coffee. Confirming or rebutting that would require calling my doctor, which I haven't done yet because I feel like I should tell Beck before I tell a random woman I barely know, so I'm caffeine deprived in addition to being sleep deprived.

Beck kisses me once more, then leaves our bedroom.

I exhale a long breath before tossing the covers off and climbing out of bed. By the time I've run through my usual morning routine in the bathroom and gotten dressed and made it into the kitchen, Beck's about to leave.

"Otto's driving me," he says as I approach the island, where he's pouring electrolyte powder into his water bottle. He shakes his head as he twists the cap closed. "Wants to show off the new Audi he got. He's convinced it's some kind of chick magnet—"

"I'm pregnant."

Beck freezes.

I freeze.

Fuck.

I've never been known for subtlety, but that was bad even for me. I didn't consciously decide to say it. It just...came out, like a breath I'd been holding but couldn't contain any longer.

Beck's still not moving. I can't even tell if he's breathing.

His phone starts ringing on the marble counter, Otto's name flashing across the screen.

I swallow hard. "I know you have to go. I'm sorry I—"

"I don't have to go," he says. Aside from his lips, he's completely still.

The screen goes black for a few seconds, then lights up with another incoming call.

"Yeah, you do. We'll...we'll talk later."

His tight grip on the water bottle relaxes, hands grasping the edge of the counter instead. "How long have you known?"

I know he knows the answer. That my recent behavior is suddenly making sense. But we're saying things out loud now, I guess. "Three days."

Beck nods. He looks disappointed, not mad, which is somehow worse.

"I just— I needed some time to... I just needed some time."

His phone starts ringing again. This time, Beck answers, barking German faster than my tired brain can register it. Faster than he normally talks around me, knowing I'm still learning the language.

I ruined this moment, it feels like. For three days, I've agonized over how to tell Beck while processing my own emotions. I'd reached the point where I needed to tell him, but I should have waited longer. I want to be the wife who tosses confetti and blows up balloons and ties a pretty bow around the piece of plastic I peed on. Not the one who glanced between my cleats and the photo of Beck winning a World Cup at sixteen that's displayed in our living room and realized the whole creating-a-child thing is not an equal division of labor.

All parents make sacrifices.

But Beck isn't going to have to temporarily give up his career to have a kid.

I am.

It's November. Frauen-Bundesliga's schedule runs into May. I'll be eight months pregnant then. Unable to finish the regular season, let alone contribute during playoffs. I'll have to consult with the team's doctors as well as my personal one, but it'll become physically impossible for me to play before the spring. I'm already aware of the changes in my body, and they'll only grow more pronounced. Emphasis on grow.

Seconds after he hangs up, Beck's phone begins ringing again.

I grab a quarter-zip I left hanging on one of the kitchen stools and yank it over my head, then scoop my hair up in a ponytail. Maybe Beck will leave for practice once he realizes I'm doing the same.

"Are you keeping it?"

His abrupt question stuns me still, my fingers stuck tangled in a hair elastic. Because of all the thoughts that have bounced around my head during my recent sleepless nights, ending this pregnancy has never been one of them. This wasn't planned. This isn't when I would have chosen to get pregnant. But now that I am...I am. It feels like the choice was already made. Like there was never one to begin with.

I have to clear my throat before I can answer, "Yes."

"Okay." Beck swipes his water bottle off the counter and turns toward the front door.

And I'm no longer unsure or surprised. I'm pissed.

I get that he's shocked. I agree I shouldn't have blurted it out right before he had to leave. But he's going to finish his season. He's not going to have to grow a human and go through childbirth. As far as I'm concerned, *he* should be tossing confetti and blowing up balloons.

"Okay? That's it? Okay is your reaction to finding out you're going to be a dad in eight months?"

His shoulders tense. The small section of Beck's jaw that I can see clenches. "Maybe I'll have a reaction you approve of in three days."

Then he walks out.

$$\cdots$$

Practice is a blur.

Muscle memory is my savior. My body knows exactly what to do even though my brain is distracted.

Carolin, one of the other forwards, tries to talk me into drinks later while we're changing in the locker room. I beg off, using plans with Beck as an excuse, which causes a chorus of teasing from my teammates. I'm the most famous player in Frauen-Bundesliga, and it's only partially attributable to my performance on the field. Game attendance and ticket prices have skyrocketed since Adler Beck started showing up at some of our matches.

The drive home from the practice facility is another blur.

Maybe I'll have a reaction you approve of in three days echoes in my head, the music playing from the car speakers nothing more than white noise.

Beck's hurt I waited to tell him. And I get it. I do. If I found out he waited to tell me something that would change our lives forever, I'd be furious.

But I also thought he'd understand why I waited to tell him this.

Beck beat me home. I can hear his voice in the living room when I walk into the entryway. No others, so he must be on the phone. I take my time hanging up my jacket and keys, eavesdropping on his end of the conversation. It sounds like he's discussing a sponsorship or brand endorsement, probably with his agent.

I kick my sneakers off, tug my socks off, and then crouch to unzip Beck's duffel bag to see if he left any dirty laundry inside.

A flash of blue captures my full attention. I forget about laundry. I stare at the onesie with FC Kluvberg's crest stamped on the front for a good minute before reaching out and holding it up. It's so tiny.

I bite my bottom lip hard, the telltale prickle of tears burning my eyes.

Barefoot, I pad down the hallway and into the main bedroom with the small piece of fabric clutched to my chest.

I take a seat cross-legged on the mattress, smoothing the onesie onto the comforter next to my knee. A few deep breaths later, I pull my phone out of my pocket and tap on Emma's name. She'll sufficiently freak out with me about this.

In some ways, it's scarier now that I've told Beck. It certainly feels more real. I rest a palm on my stomach, like a bump might have magically appeared there in the last couple of minutes. It hasn't. But it will.

Emma answers on the second ring. "Hey."

"I'm pregnant."

Once again, I circumvent the subtle approach.

"What?" my best friend shouts, her voice climbing several decibels from its normal volume.

"I just found out, and I'm freaking out."

"You just found out? Like, you're sitting on the toilet, holding a stick right now?"

"What?" I laugh, and it feels good. A tiny exhale of relief that releases some of the worry swirling inside of me. "No. I found out a few hours ago."

I hate the lie as soon as it comes out.

Emma's one of my closest friends. We've been through a lot together. She would never judge me.

But it seems like I'm already behind. Like something was supposed to kick in as soon as that second line appeared on the stick, and I have to alter the timeline to accommodate that it hasn't. I feel like I just found out seconds ago and that I need to justify that lingering shock.

"Did you tell Beck?" Emma asks.

I exhale. "Yes."

"Did he not take it well?"

"Too well," I reply.

This lie burns worse than the first. But it feels like a betrayal to admit Beck's real reaction, especially since I feel partially responsible for it.

I glance at the tiny outfit on the bed. "He came home with an FC Kluvberg onesie."

"Jesus Christ," Emma mutters. "How did you manage to find a guy who's hot and sweet? They're like unicorns, S!"

I snort. "He's not the one who's going to have to grow a tiny human inside of him and then push it out. Of course he's excited."

I hope he's excited. I think the onesie means he's excited.

"Had you two talked about having kids?" she asks.

"Yes," I reply. "Just in the future. The very distant future." When I'm older and wiser and...older.

"I'm calling dibs on godmother," Emma tells me.

I laugh. It's strange to think that far into the future, past this baby's arrival. But a good strange. "You'll have to fight Hallie for it."

"Have you told her? Or your dad?"

"No," I answer. "I needed to freak out about it more first. Hallie will start mailing me maternity books. My dad will probably cry."

Since meeting and marrying Sandra, my father has gotten a lot more sentimental. He got choked up multiple times during Beck's and my wedding.

"Well, I think it's—" Emma suddenly stops talking. A few seconds later, she adds, "I'm so sorry. I have to call you back."

The line disconnects before I can respond.

I toss my phone on top of the onesie and then lie down, letting the soft mattress mold to the shape of my body. I blow out a long breath when I realize I'm back to staring at the ceiling.

I should try to nap. Maybe now that Beck knows, I'll be able to fall asleep.

There's a soft tap on the door before I can close my eyes. "Saylor?"

"You don't have to knock," I call back. "It's your bedroom, too."

The door opens a second later. All I can see from this angle is the top of Beck's blond head as he approaches the bed.

"Was that Emma?"

He knows me well.

"Yeah." I rest a palm on my stomach, smoothing my shirt down.

"You tell her?"

"Yeah," I repeat. "She wants dibs on godmother."

The mattress dips as Beck takes a seat beside me. He must see the onesie on my other side, but he doesn't mention it. "I guarantee Sophia is going to say the same thing."

"And Hallie's going to be offended if I don't pick her." I groan. Selecting a godmother is a silly thing to fixate on right now, and that's exactly why I'm focusing on it. I'm guessing Beck is thinking similarly. "Can't kids have multiple godparents?"

"Sure," Beck says. "Or we could have multiple kids."

I roll my head to look at him.

"Kidding," he adds.

He's smiling, the corners of his eyes crinkled, but it's tentative. And it fades the longer we stare at each other. A few seconds later, he lies down, tucking one arm behind his head, and then rests his right hand over mine. The warmth of his palm seeps through my shirt and settles on my stomach.

"I'm so sorry."

I've never heard Beck's voice so gentle. So sincere. So concerned.

More tears appear. I swipe at them angrily, because I'm not a crier. Especially not over something as simple as an apology.

"Saylor..."

"I'm fine. Just, you know, hormonal."

"I was an ass for reacting like that. I didn't—fuck—I didn't know what to say. I didn't say a word on the way to practice. Otto thinks I'm having some sort of mental breakdown."

"I shouldn't have told you like that."

His grip on my hand tightens. "It shouldn't have mattered

how you told me. I'm happy, Saylor. I'm so, so happy. But I know it's more complicated for you, in lots of different ways, and I wasn't sure—I wasn't sure what you needed from me. I was scared of saying the wrong thing, so I said nothing, and that was the wrong response."

"I'm sorry for not telling you sooner. I wanted to be happy, too, when I told you, and I needed the shock to wear off first. That took longer than I was expecting." I sigh. "I'm not sure I've gotten there yet, actually."

"We can get there together."

I manage a nod. "Okay."

"How much longer can you play for?"

I smile. It comes easily, like a reflex. Because Beck is the furthest thing from a stranger in this moment. He's the person who knows me best. Who accepts—and encourages—the ambition that others have called me crazy for prioritizing.

"I don't know. I need to talk to my doctor—the team's, too. I wanted you to be the first person I told. Now that you know, I'll set up the appointments."

"Make sure you put them on the fridge calendar so I can clear my schedule."

"I will."

I don't suggest that him showing up at my doctor's appointments is unnecessary. I want Beck there. Lately, I've felt alone, lying on this bed, even when he's been beside me. It feels really good to not be lying on this bed alone anymore.

"I'm sorry it didn't happen differently." Beck exhales. "I know...I know you wanted it to happen differently."

More tears threaten to spill.

I sniff. It's such a spectacular sensation to be seen, to feel like someone else wholly understands you. "I'm not sure I ever would have felt ready, so…"

"This way, he or she will get to watch you win a World Cup and a gold medal."

"And I guess you'll have to win another one, or else look lame."

Beck chuckles. "Yeah. I guess so."

He rolls closer to kiss me, the soft, warm press of his mouth against mine as soothing as the comforting weight of his palm resting against my stomach.

"What if I'm a terrible mother?" I whisper when our lips separate.

"You won't be."

He sounds sure, and I wish I were as confident.

"How do you know? I had a terrible mother."

And this moment, more than any other time in my life, is when I wish I had a relationship with my mom. Wish I had a mom. She's nothing more than a disjointed jumble of painful memories at this point.

I hate her all over again, realizing I'll have to look at my kid one day and explain why he or she will never meet one of his or her grandmothers.

Beck squeezes my hand, anchoring me in the present. "Because I know you, Saylor."

"Exactly! I'm stubborn and selfish and—"

"Stubborn and selfish people can't admit they're stubborn and selfish," Beck tells me. "Stubborn and selfish people don't worry about being stubborn and selfish." He rubs a circle on my stomach. "This baby won the lottery, getting you as their mother."

"Maybe if they want to become a soccer player."

"If our kid wants to play football"—I roll my eyes at his emphasis—"then I pity the players on the opposing team. But that's not what I meant, Saylor, and you know it."

I gnaw on the inside of my cheek. "What if I run?"

"You run all the time."

"I'm being serious, Beck."

"So am I. Everyone gets stressed and overwhelmed at times. That doesn't make you your mother, Saylor. It makes you human."

I open my mouth to respond, and it gets overtaken by a yawn instead. I expect Beck to laugh, but his forehead creases with concern instead.

"Have you been sleeping?"

"Not much," I admit.

"You should rest. I'll shut the blinds and—"

"No. Stay." I fist his shirt, holding Beck in place as I roll so I'm half on top of him. "Stay right here."

"I'd come back," he says, but he doesn't try to move again as I tuck my head under his chin and close my eyes.

"Our bedroom ceiling is boring," Beck comments a minute later. "We should paint some stars up there."

My lips curve upward. I'm drowsy, the elusive oblivion of sleep becoming tangible. "We should. I like the onesie, by the way."

I hear the smile in his voice when he replies, "Me too."

"Ich liebe dich," I murmur drowsily.

The last sound I register before falling asleep is Beck saying, "I love you, too."

Acknowledgments

I often refer to *First Flight, Final Fall* as "Saylor's story" because she was such a brilliant character that she overshadowed everyone else, even the famed Adler Beck. Saylor's bold and resilient, yet flawed and skeptical, and that complexity made her an unforgettable heroine in my mind. She's stuck with me long after I typed "The End," and I hope she inspires you in some way too.

Erica, thank you for your helpful and hilarious feedback. This was my first foray into making writing a career, and I appreciate your kind criticism so very much.

Tiffany, thank you for your dedication and precision. From the blurb to the final stages, you were instrumental in getting this book published. I don't think either of us anticipated where it would lead, and I wouldn't have made it here without you.

Lauren, you turned this dream into a reality. I am so grateful for the way you've fought for my work.

Jessica and the whole team at Entangled, I could not have asked for a more supportive publisher. Thank you for all your hard work to get this book on shelves.

To my parents, who drove me to and from endless sports practices, thank you for being as supportive of my writing as you were of my athletic pursuits.

This was the story that introduced me to so many readers and pushed me to pursue writing. I feel beyond lucky to call writing a career, and that's all thanks to those of you who posted, reviewed, recommended, or shouted your support in any way. Thank you!

*Don't miss the exciting new books
Entangled has to offer.*

Follow us!

f @EntangledPublishing

⃝ @Entangled_Publishing

♪ @EntangledPub

AMARA
an imprint of Entangled Publishing LLC